MISSISSIPPI!

The fifteenth unforgettable volume
in the WAGONS WEST series—
all new rip-roaring adventures of America's
boldest frontiersmen and women who would fight
for their ideals of freedom and justice
against any evil . . . at any odds.

★★★★★★★★★★★★★★★★★★★★★★★★★★★★★★★★★★★★★

WAGONS WEST

MISSISSIPPI!

AMERICA'S MIGHTIEST RIVER SWEPT THEM TO DANGER, DESIRE, AND A NEW CLASH WITH DESTINY.

TOBY HOLT—
A man brave enough to face any peril, strong enough
to fight any enemy, his new mission took him
dangerously far from his cherished family
and lethally close to the West's most
powerful criminal mastermind.

MILLICENT RANDALL—
A prisoner to passions that have carried her to
the limits of shame and into the arms of a
villain she cannot escape.

KARL KELLERMAN—
An ex-lawman with a knave's cunning and no
conscience, he takes whatever and whomever
he wants with violence and death.

WALLACE DUGALD—
A good man horribly wronged by a trusted friend,
he would sell his soul for revenge.

★★★★★★★★★★★★★★★★★★★★★★★★★★★★★★★★★★★★★

EDWARD BLACKSTONE—
A gentleman who hides a fist of steel in his velvet
glove, he must put duty before the woman he loves.

TOMMIE HARDING—
A courageous young woman whose dreams of
happiness are doomed unless she can save
her fiancé from certain death.

KUNG LEE—
Master of a Chinese Tong, absolute power has
made him untouchable; absolute evil makes
him terrifyingly cruel.

DOMINO—
A sinner not a saint in New Orleans, he's a mob
boss who believes in honor among thieves . . . and
in the word of Whip Holt's son.

MARTHA—
A woman so sensually beautiful that even the most
faithful man might risk his marriage to taste the
sweetness of her charms.

Bantam Books by Dana Fuller Ross
Ask your bookseller for the books you have missed

INDEPENDENCE!—Volume I
NEBRASKA!—Volume II
WYOMING!—Volume III
OREGON!—Volume IV
TEXAS!—Volume V
CALIFORNIA!—Volume VI
COLORADO!—Volume VII
NEVADA!—Volume VIII
WASHINGTON!—Volume IX
MONTANA!—Volume X
DAKOTA!—Volume XI
UTAH!—Volume XII
IDAHO!—Volume XIII
MISSOURI!—Volume XIV
MISSISSIPPI!—Volume XV

MISSISSIPPI!

DANA FULLER ROSS

Created by the producers of
White Indian, Children of the
Lion, Stagecoach, and Saga of the
Southwest.

Chairman of the Board: Lyle Kenyon Engel

BANTAM BOOKS
TORONTO · NEW YORK · LONDON · SYDNEY · AUCKLAND

MISSISSIPPI!

A Bantam Book / June 1985

Produced by Book Creations, Inc.
Chairman of the Board: Lyle Kenyon Engel

ISBN 0-553-24976-2

Published simultaneously in the United States and Canada

PRINTED IN THE UNITED STATES OF AMERICA

H   0 9 8 7 6 5 4 3 2 1

This is a work of fiction. While the general outlines of history have been faithfully followed, certain details involving setting, characters, and events may have been simplified.

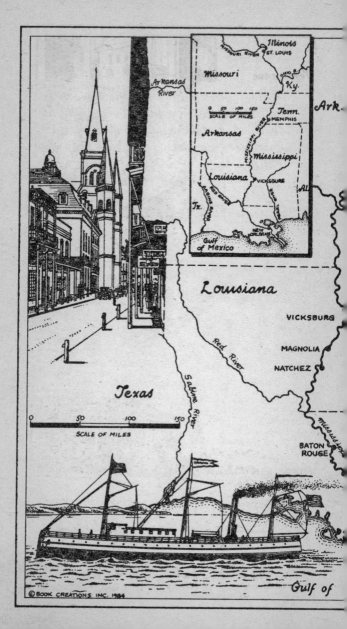

Illinois
Missouri River
St. Louis
Missouri
Arkansas River
Ohio R.
Ky.
SCALE OF MILES
0 50 100 150
Tenn.
Memphis
Ark.
Arkansas
Mississippi
Louisiana
Vicksburg
Al.
Tx.
Red River
New Orleans
Gulf of Mexico

Louisiana

VICKSBURG
MAGNOLIA
NATCHEZ

Red River

Sabine River

Texas

SCALE OF MILES
0 50 100 150

Mississippi

BATON ROUGE

Gulf of

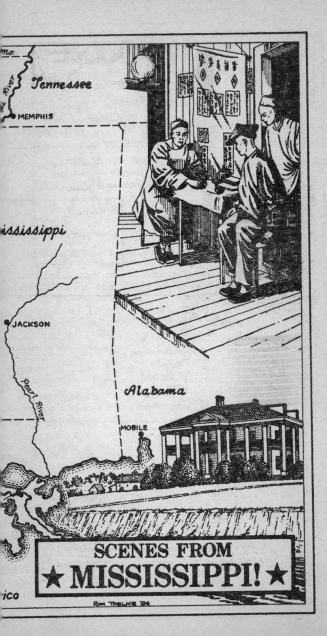

SCENES FROM
★ **MISSISSIPPI!** ★

Ron Toelke '84

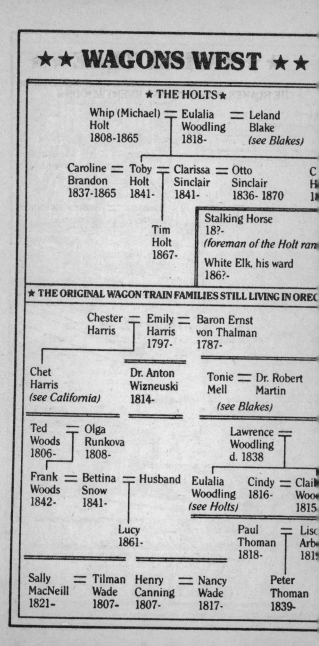

★ ★ WAGONS WEST ★ ★

★ THE HOLTS ★

Whip (Michael) Holt 1808-1865 = Eulalia Woodling 1818- = Leland Blake *(see Blakes)*

Caroline Brandon 1837-1865 = Toby Holt 1841- = Clarissa Sinclair 1841- = Otto Sinclair 1836-1870   C H 1

Tim Holt 1867-

Stalking Horse 18?- *(foreman of the Holt ran*

White Elk, his ward 186?-

★ THE ORIGINAL WAGON TRAIN FAMILIES STILL LIVING IN OREG

Chester Harris = Emily Harris 1797- = Baron Ernst von Thalman 1787-

Chet Harris *(see California)*

Dr. Anton Wizneuski 1814-

Tonie Mell = Dr. Robert Martin *(see Blakes)*

Ted Woods 1806- = Olga Runkova 1808-

Lawrence Woodling d. 1838

Frank Woods 1842- = Bettina Snow 1841- = Husband

Eulalia Woodling *(see Holts)*

Cindy 1816- = Clai Woo 1815

Lucy 1861-

Paul Thoman 1818- = Liso Arb 181

Sally MacNeill 1821- = Tilman Wade 1807-

Henry Canning 1807- = Nancy Wade 1817-

Peter Thoman 1839-

★ ★ FAMILY TREE ★ ★

★ THE BLAKES, MARTINS, AND BRENTWOODS ★

...ualia = Leland = Cathy
...oodling Holt   Blake   van Ayl
...e Holts)   1804-   1814-1865

...nie = Dr. Robert
...ell   Martin
...14-   1798-

                              Sam   Claudia
                              Brentwood   Humphries
                              1797-   1809-

...le = Rob = Beth   Susanna = Andrew Jackson
...ton Martin Blake   Fulton   Brentwood
...46- 1841-   1841-1869 1837-   1839-

...nk Blake   Cathy   Samuel
...dopted)   Martin   Brentwood
...50-   1869-   1866-

★ IN NEW ORLEANS ★

...mie   Edward   Jean-Pierre   Millicent   Jim
...ding   Blackstone   Gautier   Randall   Randall
...0-   1840-   1843-   1845-   *(see below)*
...iah Harding's
...ughter)

★ LIVING IN IDAHO ★

Jim   Pamela
Randall = Drake
1843-   1841-

★ LIVING IN CALIFORNIA ★

...t = Clara Lou   Wong = Wing
...ris Hadley   Ke   Mei Lo
...2-   1823-   1809- 1835-

...ther = Danny   Ginny (Virginia) = Hector
...Gregor Taylor   Dobbs   Mullins
...8-   1823-   1814-   1804-

...Woods   Melissa = Rick = Elisabeta   Child Child
...lor   Austin   Miller Manuel   1849- 1851-
...0-   1824-   1815-   1823-1849

           Child   Child
           1853-   1854-

MISSISSIPPI!

I

The huge stern paddle wheel turned slowly as the great river steamer made its way steadily down the broad, placid waters of the Mississippi. The mighty mile-wide river had long been the principal thoroughfare for moving the produce of the American heartland to market.

Millicent Randall was standing at the prow of the ship. On both sides of the river, she could see enormous amounts of activity as the grain, timber, cotton, and vegetables that were in demand throughout the United States and Europe were loaded on the wharves to be sent to market. The commerce on the Mississippi, she realized, was one of the principal reasons that the United States, with the debilitating Civil War behind her, was becoming a great nation in the 1870s. America truly had been blessed by nature.

The sun was warm. The breeze rippled gently through the soft folds of Millicent's thin, clinging

dress, and even a casual observer would have noted
from the way that the wind pressed the fabric against
the young woman's ripe, full figure that she was
wearing nothing underneath her garment. To a lady
of 1870, Millicent's attire was shocking, but the truth
of the matter was that Millicent, once a prim, proper
young woman from Baltimore, who composed music
and played the flute, no longer qualified as a lady.

Without her knowledge, Millicent had been fed
a Gypsy potion made from mind-altering, central
European mushrooms, and her life had been dramati-
cally changed. Aroused erotically for the first time in
her life by the gambler/businessman Luis de Cordova,
who had used the potion in order to get her to do his
bidding, she had begun to dress and act in a provocative manner. She had gone off with de Cordova to
St. Louis, and on the way he had treated her badly,
using her as bait to engage men in card games—with
Millicent as the prize—and then cheating the card
players so that he amassed a small fortune. Subsequently he had paid for his dishonesty with his life.

Her new companion, Sergeant Karl Kellerman,
who had recently resigned his position with the St.
Louis constabulary, was taking her to New Orleans.
Dazzled by the brown-haired, provocative young
woman—who combined an air of good breeding with
startling sensuality—he had lavished many gifts on
her.

Kellerman had indicated to Millicent that he
liked her unusual attire and heavy use of makeup;
she was so much in love with him that she dressed

and used cosmetics to please him. But whenever she was alone and knew she was not going to be seeing Karl for a number of hours, she became more like her old self, wearing modest clothes and using very little makeup. She had no way of knowing that the recent change in her was due to the fact that the effects of the mind-altering drug de Cordova had used to control her had worn off.

Looking at the cat's-eye sapphire ring she wore on her right hand, Millicent considered herself the most fortunate woman alive. Karl had given her the ring in Memphis on their journey south, and she had no idea that it was tainted with the blood of its previous owner. No, Millicent only knew that her troubles were behind her, that her future was as bright as the river sparkling in the rays of the sun. Everything about Karl and the journey enchanted her, including the fine foods and wines that they were served at every meal, their lavish suite on the ship, and their frequent lovemaking.

When the stern-wheeler put into the old cotton port of Natchez, where a concerted rebuilding campaign was eliminating the scars left by Civil War fighting, Millicent went ashore with Karl and delighted in every moment of the experience. She and Karl made a tour of the city and then went to a fashionable restaurant on the riverfront to dine. Millicent was in her glory. Wearing one of the new gowns he had given her, a low-necked dress of crimson velvet with a matching broad-brimmed hat, she was the object of all eyes. Millicent glowed, aware of the stir she was creating, and the large, well-built, dark-blond-haired Karl, jauntily smoking a long cigar, seemed highly pleased by the fuss that resulted.

Under the circumstances, it was easy and almost inevitable for Millicent to daydream. She had no doubt that she and Karl would marry after they reached New Orleans, their destination, and her mind dwelled lovingly on the details of the luxurious life she would lead as his wife. She was in no way dismayed by the fact that he had not proposed marriage to her: Her daydreams were based on anything but reality.

The riverboat reached the great port city of New Orleans slightly over two days later. In effect the post–Civil War capital of the South, New Orleans was unique among American cities. Tied up along her Mississippi waterfront were the barges that brought the cotton bales of the South, the wheat of Minnesota, Dakota, and Kansas, and the corn of Iowa and Illinois to the city for transfer to the great ships that would carry the produce to the Atlantic seaboard states, to the Caribbean and to Europe, and even to Asia. Manufacturing plants were rising faster than anyone could count them, and a variety of industries was adding to the city's economic strength.

New Orleans was a fascinating cultural mixture of France and Spain, whose colony she once had been, and of the old American West. The restaurants catered to all tastes, with some as rough-and-tumble as frontier saloons and others as sophisticated and unique as any in America. Many of the shops were elegant and expensive, and even the gambling halls and brothels could be almost indescribably lavish.

Millicent was dazzled by New Orleans and its atmosphere. Now, seventy-two hours after her arrival in the Queen City, she was sitting in her dressing room in the suite that Kellerman had rented for them in the Louisiana House, one of the best hotels in town, trying to curb her sense of excitement. She gave in to the ministrations of Effie, the pretty, light-skinned black maid whom Kellerman had hired for her through the hotel. Effie was busy with a comb and brush, arranging Millicent's long brown hair, and the young woman marveled at the efficiency of the maid.

"Every time I go anywhere in this town," Millicent said, "and it doesn't matter if it's a restaurant or a dress shop or where it is, I'm just astonished by the people I see. I've spent the past few years in the mountains and small towns of the West, and I grew up in Baltimore, which is a large city in its own right, but nowhere have I seen women as beautiful as there are on the streets of New Orleans!"

"There ain't none that's prettier than you, Mrs. Kellerman," Effie replied with great sincerity. She had learned that her new mistress was not married to Karl Kellerman but nevertheless did her the honor of referring to her as the wife of her employer.

Millicent smiled and shook her head. "They have a quality that I lack—a kind of sophistication."

"You'd never know it from the way you look and act, ma'am," Effie said flatly. "Now hold still while I pin up your hair." She worked in silence for a moment, then went on, "You know that sad-faced young gent'man we keep seeing all over town? You handle him just right, the way you pretend he don't exist. No New Orleans woman could handle him any better."

Millicent was embarrassed. For the past three days, whenever she had left the Louisiana House, she had been followed at a distance by a well-dressed, clean-cut young man, whom Effie had identified as Jean-Pierre Gautier, a wealthy young New Orleans heir who had lost a sickly wife about a year earlier. He seemed to be much taken by Millicent, and certainly it could not be accidental that he appeared everywhere she went, nodding to her politely and wishing her good morning or good afternoon.

She had handled the situation by ignoring him, for she was afraid Karl would become highly jealous and even violent if she acknowledged the stranger in any way. To her surprise, however, Karl had displayed only indifference to young Gautier's interest in her. She found it hard to understand or appreciate Kellerman's reasoning; apparently, he was confident that he already had possession of her and was strangely willing to let another man seek her company. Furthermore, as he had told her, he had no desire to become involved in unpleasantness with the wealthy, socially prominent Gautier family.

Effie pushed a pair of white egret feathers into Millicent's dark, upswept hair, then examined her own handiwork critically.

"Are you sure you don't want me to come shopping with you this afternoon, ma'am?" Effie asked.

Stepping into the dress that the maid held for her, Millicent replied emphatically, "I'm very positive. After all, this is the day your little boy is coming from his grandmother's house to visit you, and I know how eager you are to see him."

Effie was deeply touched. She worked for a living because of her need to support her young child, who meant everything to her, and she was touched by the consideration of her new employer, who had remembered her casual statement that her son was visiting that day. "Thank you, ma'am, and God bless you," she murmured.

"Nonsense," Millicent replied briskly. "That's the very least I can do for you." She examined herself in the mirror, then picked up her handbag. "How do I look?"

"Just perfect, ma'am! That Mr. Gautier is going to swoon when he sees you today."

Millicent joined in the maid's laugh. "If you happen to see Mr. Kellerman before you leave," she said, "would you tell him for me that I'll meet him back here at five o'clock this afternoon?"

"Yes, ma'am, I'll tell him."

"Be sure you give your son a hug and kiss from me," Millicent said as she left the suite.

Effie began to clean up the dressing table and to hang up clothes that Millicent had not chosen to wear. The maid told herself she was fortunate not only to have found employment that paid sufficient

wages to support her son and herself but also to have
found a mistress as kind as Millicent. In these days
when jobs were not easy to find, necessity had forced
many of her friends to seek work in brothels.

Finishing her chores quickly, Effie was about to
depart when the door to the sitting room opened and
Karl Kellerman's bulk filled the frame.

Six feet three inches tall, with broad shoulders
and a barrellike chest, he stood now with his thumbs
hooked in the belt that held his twin .44 caliber
pistols.

Effie saw him eyeing her attractive face and
figure. She had never been alone with him like this,
and she was distinctly uncomfortable. "You just missed
madam by a few minutes, sir," she said, trying to
conceal her nervousness. "She said she'll meet you
back here about five o'clock. She's gone shopping."

"Thanks, Effie," he drawled, continuing to eye
her speculatively. He was grateful to be free of Millicent that long. The woman's cloying manner and her
ingenuous excitement over being in New Orleans
were beginning to get on his nerves. A scant hour
ago, at the restaurant where he had lunch he had
met a stunning blonde who would be available, he
knew, and he also had his eye on a provocatively
seductive redhead who worked at the establishment
where he had eaten the day before. Right now, he
had a craving for this mulatto, which should be easy
enough to fulfill.

"Well," he said, "both of us have some time to

kill. What do you say we kill it together?" He crooked one long finger and beckoned to her.

Effie's blood ran cold. Not only did Kellerman hold no appeal to her, but far more important, she had no intention of repaying Millicent's loyalty by cheating on her. She made no move.

Kellerman chuckled, reached for her lazily, and pulling her close, began to paw her buttocks with his free hand.

Effie resorted to an old trick and pretended to relax. Then, when he eased his grip, she suddenly wrenched away from him.

Kellerman was surprised for the moment but was in no way disturbed. He could handle any woman.

He reached into a waistcoat pocket, withdrew a twenty-dollar gold piece, and carelessly flipped it to the maid. Effie caught the coin and identified it. Her mind immediately filled with thoughts of the clothing, food, and toys that the magnificent sum of twenty dollars—which represented two weeks' wages—could buy for her little son. She stood indecisively for a long moment as Kellerman's dark eyes seemed to bore into her. It occurred to her that it was even worth jeopardizing her job in order to have so much money all at once. Slowly she began to unbutton the blouse of her uniform, as Kellerman's triumphant chuckle rang in her ears.

Half an hour later, the nervous Effie dressed rapidly. She could hardly wait until she put distance between herself and the brute who had just made love to her with such callousness. "Please tell madam," she said, concealing her hate for him as best she could, "that I'm sorry I won't be seeing her again, but I quit the job here and now."

When Millicent returned to the suite several hours later, laden with packages from her afternoon of shopping, Kellerman, who was drinking a stiff bourbon and water in the parlor as he smoked a long cigar, told her that the maid had resigned and departed. Millicent was taken aback by the news. She had genuinely liked Effie and was surprised by her unexpected resignation. "Why did she leave?" she asked. "What did she say?"

"She said nothing," he lied. "She asked for her wages, which I paid, and she quit. You know the type. She's shiftless and has no sense of responsibility."

Still disappointed, Millicent couldn't help wondering how she could have misjudged the maid's character so badly.

The next morning, Karl left Millicent behind at their hotel suite, telling her he had to go on a little errand involving business. Millicent didn't know what his business was but knew better than to ask. She was content to spend the morning in bed, having been out with Karl until late the night before.

Now the former police sergeant walked slowly down the crowded street toward the New Orleans business district, taking in the sights of the city and enjoying his experience thoroughly. In all of his travels, never had he seen so many chic, stunningly attractive young women as there were in New Orleans. At a rough estimate, he guessed that there were ten beautiful girls in New Orleans for each one in St. Louis, where he had been a detective sergeant.

Certainly he had made the right move when he had resigned from the constabulary and had decided to make his fortune by his wits. And this was the city for him: a place where the pleasures of the flesh were available to men of means.

Karl did not regret having brought Millicent Randall to New Orleans with him, even though her support was costing him a small fortune. Her beauty was exceptional, making her the equal of any woman in New Orleans, and in addition, she was a passionate bed partner. But he was growing tired of her, and he couldn't help thinking how he would enjoy some new diversions, like that blonde and the redhead. He would have to devote himself to meeting these new women after he arranged a few business deals. Also, although he had other plans at the moment, he would would soon look in on his partner, Wallace Dugald, whom he had financed to open a bar near the waterfront the last time he was in New Orleans.

Turning a corner, Kellerman slowed his pace as he approached an inconspicuous, two-story building. On the ground floor was a modest greengrocer's shop with a variety of vegetables displayed in the bins outside on the wooden sidewalk. On the side of the building, a narrow wooden staircase rose to the second floor, and Karl mounted it slowly, halting when he entered a room off the landing. Two men with hard, expressionless faces sat reading the morning newspapers. They looked up at him searchingly, and he was quick to identify himself.

"I'm Kellerman," he said. "Domino sent for me."

One of the pair nodded and grunted. "All right," he said, "we'll relieve you of your pistol. While you're at it, you can leave the knife that you're carrying in the top of your boot out here, too. We'll take good care of your weapons until you leave."

Karl knew better than to argue with the guards and surrendered his weapons to them. One of them disappeared into a back room for a few moments. When he returned to the anteroom, he beckoned abruptly. "The boss will see you."

Karl followed him into a small, drab chamber at the second floor rear. There, seated behind a modest desk, was the gray-haired man who had earned his name because of his love for the game of dominoes. The general public had never heard of him, but he was known in certain circles as the most influential member of the underworld that thrived along the Mississippi River. The police of towns and cities along the great river had reason to believe that he was involved in a variety of activities, from grand larceny to prostitution, but they had absolutely nothing they could pin on him.

Domino's appearance belied his reputation. A pair of metal-rimmed spectacles rested on the bridge of his nose, his gray hair was neatly combed, and he was wearing a worsted, rust-colored suit. Those who did not know him invariably took him for a bookkeeper or some other minor functionary in the city's business world.

Waving a small, neatly manicured hand, Domino did not rise as he pointed his visitor to a chair on the far side of his desk. "Sit down, Kellerman, and I'll tell you why I sent for you," he said in a mild voice. Turning to the guard, Domino ordered him to leave the room so that the two men could speak in private.

Karl felt uneasy under Domino's careful scrutiny.

"I was interested," Domino said, "to learn of your resignation from the St. Louis constabulary. Surely you don't earn enough to live in the style to which you've accustomed yourself on your half interest in the saloon here."

Karl was not surprised to learn of Domino's awareness of his investment in a New Orleans bar. The gang leader made it his business to know everything about anyone engaging in any business in the South.

"I've had no specific plans to augment my income," he said, "but I was intending to look you up and pay you a visit. I can use some extra income these days."

Domino smiled vaguely. "I understand that you're traveling with a real beauty. Women are expensive." He did not pursue the point.

"Yes," Karl replied curtly. "She's expensive."

"I trust," Domino said, "you're not squeamish about assignments that you undertake?"

"Try me," Karl said. He did not intend to boast

that he was directly responsible for two recent deaths, of which Domino was probably well aware.

"I know your background," Domino told him, "and you're just the person to perform a job that has been waiting for the right man. Are you familiar with the Three-Two-One Club?"

Reluctant to reveal his ignorance, Karl shook his head.

"It's in an old Creole mansion on Jefferson Avenue," Domino said. "During the war it was converted into a private gaming club, and it's expanded since that time. Girls are available, of course, and they also serve meals. There is one large room for those who like to do a bit of gambling for high stakes. It's strictly a rich man's club. The security there is lax—surprisingly lax," Domino went on. "I stop in occasionally for an evening of cards myself, and I'm always astonished by the lack of protection. One experienced man who knows what he's doing can collect thousands of dollars in a properly staged holdup."

Karl's face was expressionless. "Sounds interesting," he said. "What's the fee?"

"Twenty percent of the first ten thousand you collect, and twenty-five percent of everything over that amount. Take it or leave it."

"Not so fast," Karl said. "What help will I get from you and from your organization?"

"Absolutely none," Domino told him coolly. "The haul will be so large that I'll automatically be suspected of having had a hand in the robbery. But I intend to turn the tables on the police and on the other gangs of New Orleans. I'm going to be a patron at the Three-Two-One on the night of the robbery, and I expect to be personally robbed and then treated exactly as you treat the other patrons."

"That's very clever of you," Karl said, his mind working quickly. He would be even more clever. Instead of taking all the risks and submitting himself to the dangers of the enterprise in return for a meager twenty or twenty-five percent of the spoils, he decided it would be far simpler and infinitely more satisfying to do away with Domino. Then he could keep the entire proceeds of the robbery for himself. If necessary, he would go into hiding until the repercussions of the affair blew over.

They parted amicably, with Karl retrieving his weapons from the outer office. When he reached the street, he began to walk back toward the Louisiana House, taking his time, going over his whole conversation with Domino. He had been right to come back to New Orleans, he reflected, and so far, he was in luck. He saw no reason his fortunes should change, and as soon as he accumulated enough money, he could have any girl that he wanted.

Pamela Randall sat before the open window of her second-floor bedchamber in the comfortable, spacious farmhouse and looked out at a familiar but beautiful scene. In the background, beyond the ranch that she and her husband owned, stood the impressive, rugged, snowcapped mountains that formed a vigilant, permanent guard over the Idaho Territory. The land stretched as far as the eye could see, and the pastures where the horses and cows grazed were lush and green beneath the warm June sun. The air that blew in from the mountains was crisp and dry. Truly, Pamela thought, she had never been in a region as lovely as this, not even in the rolling, verdant countryside of Sussex, England, where she had grown up.

Beautiful, aristocratic-looking—with her abundant wheat-colored hair piled on top of her head—Pamela was lost in thought as she looked out the window in the direction of the corral and caught a glimpse of her husband's foreman, Randy Savage, dismounting from his horse. Tall, rugged, sandy-haired, and very handsome, Randy had been the reason for Pamela's almost ruining her life. Having had little else to occupy her over the winter months—and intrigued because he was so different from the men she had known in her native England—Pamela had foolishly imagined herself in love with him. And Randy, greatly taken with Pamela's beauty and realizing the way she felt about him, had thought that he was in love with her, too.

Fortunately, their mutual common sense had asserted itself, and they had stepped back from the abyss in time. There was no harm done, and neither was any worse for the experience.

As Pamela continued to watch, another horseman entered the corral and dismounted. It was her husband, Jim Randall, a lean, hard, brown-haired veteran of the Civil War, who had lost an eye in the war and wore an eye patch that gave him an added touch of distinction. Jim had sufficient funds that he could have lived in comfort in his native Baltimore for the rest of his days, but it was typical of him to have come to the West, to have bought a ranch, and to have created a new and useful life for himself. Pamela had met Jim shortly after she arrived in the United States, and feeling it was time to settle down and put a stop to her carefree, coquettish ways, she had married him. Only recently, however, had she learned to appreciate Jim fully, and her heart was filled with love as she watched him.

Jim and Randy began talking. Watching them together, Pamela couldn't imagine how she could have thought herself in love with the foreman. Her husband was extraordinary.

The discussion in the corral was spirited but brief and ended in seeming agreement. Randy hurried off to the bunkhouse, and Jim entered the main dwelling, appearing in a few moments in his wife's bedchamber. "When I picked up the mail in Boise this morning," he said without preamble, "I found another letter from Edward that had just arrived." He handed her the letter, written on hotel stationery.

Edward Blackstone, a dashing, wealthy young Englishman who had been Pamela's next-door neighbor in rural Sussex, had originally traveled with her to America in order to see the country and to attend to business matters here. After Pamela had married Jim, Edward's cousin, Edward decided to travel from Fort Benton, Montana, to St. Louis by boat down the Missouri River because he sought the rich experience. The letter related how he had encountered their mutual relative, Millicent Randall, traveling with Luis de Cordova, who, as it turned out, was a crooked gambler. Edward had killed de Cordova, who had tried to cheat him at cards, and the Englishman had thought that Millicent was safe at last.

But now, Edward said, Millicent had vanished in St. Louis in the company of Sergeant Karl Kellerman, who had left the constabulary there. Edward asked for Jim's help, as well as that of any volunteers he cared to bring with him to St. Louis, where Edward and his fiancée, Tommie Harding, would await reinforcements.

"What a shame to have found Millicent, only to lose her again," Jim said, shaking his head. He and Pamela had been shocked when his staid and reliable cousin had sold her restaurant in Boise the previous winter and had run off with de Cordova, and they had been relieved when Edward wrote that he had found her. But now Millicent's activities were more shocking than ever, and Jim said, "This running away, first with one man and then another, isn't at all like her."

"It's possible there's a simple explanation for her conduct," Pamela replied. "Perhaps the recognition that men find her desirable has altered her personality and caused her to act foolishly."

"Quite possibly you're right," he said. "But whatever may be motivating her, I can't let Edward down. I telegraphed him at his hotel in St. Louis to the effect that I'll be leaving from Boise right away to catch the railroad in Ogden, Utah, and I should be arriving in St. Louis in two weeks' time. I've just spoken to Randy Savage, and he's going with me. Edward doesn't explain why he needs help, but the mere fact that he needs it is good enough for me. He doesn't explain either who this Tommie Harding is."

Pamela put a finger to her lips and pondered for a moment. "Do you remember, dear, just before Edward left Boise for Fort Benton to begin his trip down the Missouri, he told us he was going to sail on a ship of the Harding Line? Could it be that this Tommie Harding is the daughter of the ship's captain, the owner of the line? In any event, it appears that we're going to have a new relative one of these days."

"I hope," Jim said, "that you don't object to my going off to St. Louis to help Edward."

"Of course not!" Pamela told him. "Edward wouldn't ask for help unless he really needed it. We have no choice."

He nodded. "I was pretty sure you'd feel that way," he said, putting his arm around her. "I'll appoint an acting foreman to take charge of operations here at the ranch, and you know I'll come home as soon as I possibly can."

"Don't hurry on my account," Pamela replied. "I'll cope with things here. You stay with Edward for as long as necessary to solve this mystery about Millicent once and for all."

So Jim and Randy left the ranch that afternoon,

traveling by horseback to Ogden. They set an arduous pace for themselves and arrived in the bustling railroad town some ten days later. Leaving their horses at a local stable and wiring ahead to Edward Blackstone, they boarded a Union Pacific train heading east and arrived in St. Louis less than forty-eight hours later.

Edward and Tommie Harding were awaiting the arrival of the train in St. Louis, and they greeted the newcomers warmly. As always, Edward was impeccably and expensively dressed in a tailor-made suit and shirt with lace cuffs. His pencil-thin mustache was neatly trimmed, as was his dark brown hair, and he and the pert, blond-haired Tommie, who was wearing a plain but becoming blue dress, made a good-looking couple. Jim quickly discovered that Tommie was even more attractive, vivacious, and intelligent than he had thought at first glance, and he was very impressed by her.

Because of the presence of the carriage driver, they said nothing about the mission that had brought them all together. Instead, Edward explained how he and Tommie had met and fallen in love and how they had promised Tommie's father, who was indeed the owner of the Harding Line, that they would wait before getting married in order to be sure they were right for each other. In the meantime, they were traveling together, an unconventional arrangement for an unmarried man and woman, but then Tommie was far too independent-minded and free-spirited to be considered conventional. What was more, Edward, always the gentleman, saw to it that they slept in separate rooms when they registered at hotels.

When they reached the hotel, they made themselves comfortable in the living room of Edward's suite. There, Tommie handed Jim a clipping from a recent newspaper. "Read this," Edward said.

Jim read the news story from Memphis that told of the death of a gang leader there. The man, named Jason, had been found in his office, shot to death. It had been a suicide, the article said, but subsequently it had been revealed that one of his bodyguards also had died. No one knew the identity of the perpetrator of the crime or what the link was between the suicide and the murder, but it was speculated that the killer might have been an exceptionally tall and broad-shouldered man with dark blond hair and pale blue eyes. The news story did not reveal how the Memphis police had obtained even that much information about the killer.

Jim finished reading the article and handed the story to Randy.

"Millicent and this fellow, Kellerman, disappeared from St. Louis as though they'd been wiped from the face of the earth," Edward said. "The constabulary here have no definite idea where they've gone, though Commissioner Bowen thought New Orleans would be as likely a place as any, since Kellerman has some business contacts there."

"If they've left St. Louis," Tommie said, "they reserved their steamer or stagecoach tickets under assumed names."

"Why would they do that?" Jim asked, puzzled.

Edward shrugged. "Your guess is as good as mine," he said. "The only reason that has occurred to me is that Millicent knows I'll come searching for her and is deliberately covering her tracks."

"Perhaps we're wrong to search for her," Jim said. "She's of age, after all, and she's free to do whatever she wishes."

"You wouldn't say that if you'd seen her on board ship coming down the Missouri," Tommie told him. "She behaved as though she was a woman possessed, as though she had little control over what she was doing. True, she helped Edward turn the tables on de Cordova, but the minute Sergeant Kellerman came on the scene to investigate, it was as though she lost all control of herself again."

"That means we can't leave her to her own devices," Edward said, picking up the theme from her. "We feel compelled to find Millicent and, if necessary, to protect her—from herself. At first our intentions were to go directly to New Orleans to find her. Then we saw the story from Memphis in the newspaper. So now we propose to stop off at Memphis and talk with the police authorities there."

Randy Savage was puzzled. "I fail to see the connection," he said, "between the missing Millicent Randall and Karl Kellerman and the deaths of the gangsters in Memphis."

"I'm sorry," Edward said. "I should have made it clear from the start that the description of the possible killer, vague though it is, fits Kellerman almost exactly. We want to give the information to the Memphis police. That news story is also why we asked you to meet us here in St. Louis before we started out."

Randy still looked confused.

"Kellerman is a murderer," Tommie explained. "He has Millicent in his possession. If we're going to apprehend him and rescue Millicent, we're going to need all the help we can get!"

Toby Holt was returning to his ranch from a visit to Portland, going down the trail that followed the course of the Columbia River. The sturdy, sandy-haired twenty-nine-year-old, sinewy and lean as whipcord, breathed deeply, enjoying the scent of pines and incredibly fresh mountain air. Like his late father, Whip Holt, he knew utter contentment on the ranch. He had acquired a national reputation as a surveyor for railroad lines, as an Indian fighter, and as a troubleshooter for presidents of the United States, but he was never happier than when he was at home.

His stallion needed no urging either. The great beast increased his speed as he headed toward home.

A surprise awaited Toby as he neared the cleared pasture lands that surrounded the ranch buildings. From a trail in the pine woods off to his left, there emerged a small figure on the back of a rapidly moving pony, a three-year-old boy in complete western attire, even to his boots and broad-brimmed hat.

"Hello, Papa!" the child called cheerfully.

"Well, hello, Timmy," Toby replied with a grin,

and began to search for his wife. He finally caught a glimpse of her, mounted on her mare, partially concealed in the deep woods, and he realized that the wonderful, ever-sensible Clarissa was allowing the boy to ride ahead of her so that he would feel he had been riding all by himself.

Toby was quick to go along with the game. "Where are you going, Tim?" he asked.

The child pointed in the direction of the ranch house. "We race!" he announced.

"That's a fine idea, son," Toby said gravely. "Let's race! One—two—three—go!" Before he was through counting, Tim, crouched low in the saddle, had started off in the direction of the house, his pony's hooves pounding the hard ground of the trail. Toby deliberately reined in his own mount and allowed his son to beat him by several lengths.

Tim was ecstatic. "I won! I won!" he shouted, and hugged his father as Toby lifted him to the ground.

Clarissa approached, and Tim danced around her as she, too, dismounted. "I raced Papa, and I won, Mama. I beat him!"

Sharing his delight, she bent down, picked him up, and kissed him. "I know you won, Timothy," she said. "I saw you. Congratulations."

They made a handsome family: the tall, statuesque Clarissa in her riding dress, her thick red hair piled up under her broad-brimmed hat; the rugged, lean Toby, who more and more bore a resemblance to his legendary father; and the animated little boy, whose youthful features reflected those of both his parents.

Approaching on foot was Stalking Horse, his face bronzed and deeply lined but his bearing erect and sure. The elderly Cherokee had been foreman of the ranch ever since Whip Holt had founded the place.

Tim hurtled toward the Indian, shouting his news. Stalking Horse listened, made an appropriate comment, and then waved Toby and Clarissa toward the house. "Leave your horses," he called. "Timmy will help me get the saddles off and turn the mounts out to pasture."

Satisfied that their son was in good hands, the couple started toward the house together, their shoulders touching. "That boy is a marvel," Toby said. "When I first saw him, I thought for a split second that he was out riding alone."

"There's no way on earth that I'd let him out of my sight," Clarissa replied. "He's too much like his father."

"I'm not sure if that's an insult or a compliment," Toby told her.

She giggled. "It's a fact," she said. "At the age of three he's already a complete Holt. He's too young to realize that he had a famous grandfather and has an equally famous father, but those things don't matter to him. He's already competing like mad with both of you, and someday, he's going to surpass you. I almost feel sorry for his wife."

Toby's face clouded as they entered the kitchen

and Clarissa poured him a mug of coffee from the pot warming on the stove. "I'm not sure how you mean that," Toby said, "but I'm afraid I take it in the worst way. I apologize to you for all the heartache and inconvenience I've caused you."

She looked up at him, her face registering both alarm and compassion. "Don't be silly, darling," she said.

"We've had some rough times," he insisted.

"But we've overcome them, and that's what counts," Clarissa countered. "Of course we've had hard going from time to time. That's the nature of marriage, but it's what people feel for each other that matters. We love each other, so I can't think of anything that could be better." Saying this, she put her arms around her husband.

As they held each other, Clarissa and Toby sensed that this was a moment of perfect communion. They had no need for further words. They were one in spirit, and their love presented an unbreakable barrier between them and the world.

That night after Tim had been put to bed, Toby and Clarissa were joined at dinner by Stalking Horse and White Elk, a nine-year-old Arapaho orphan who had been jointly adopted by the Cherokee foreman and by Pamela Randall. The boy divided his time between them, and it was their hope that he would grow up to represent the best of both the Indians' and the white man's worlds.

The dinner table was laden with platters of delicious, steaming foods, most of which were produced on the Holt ranch. The roast beef came from the cattle that were raised here, the carrots, peas, onions, and potatoes were grown in Clarissa's large vegetable garden, and the apples and peaches that were used in the pies for this evening's dessert came from the ranch's own fruit trees. Only the flour used in the bread and piecrust came from the market in Portland, but even then, Clarissa baked her own bread and pastries, using the fresh butter that was made from the cream of the ranch's dairy cows.

White Elk was very much at home at a dinner table, handling a knife and fork with ease and taking an intelligent part in the conversation. "The weather grows warmer, and snow is gone from the mountains," he said in fluent English, "but the Arapaho will not go on the warpath this year against their white brothers. I am sure of it."

Stalking Horse exchanged a quick look with Toby and decided the flat statement could not be allowed unchallenged. "What makes White Elk so certain of what will be?" he asked.

The boy looked gravely at the old man. "The government has given the Arapaho new hunting grounds that lie in the north of the territory," White Elk said, "far from the new railroad tracks. We went hunting in that region, and my grandfather will remember that game was plentiful and the rivers were filled with plump fish."

Toby decided to test the boy. "Why should good hunting grounds make a difference?"

White Elk instantly rose to the challenge. "Indians

are like their white brothers," he said. "When their bellies are full and they have the promise of more food that is easy to get, they are at peace and will stay at peace."

"Good boy, White Elk," Clarissa said. "Pass me your plate so I can give you another slice of roast beef and some more potatoes. As for you two," she went on to her husband and Stalking Horse, "leave the child alone so he can finish his supper in peace."

Toby had sufficient respect for his wife not to argue the matter. He ate in silence for a time, but his mind was churning. "Stalking Horse," he said at last, "when I was in Portland this afternoon, I called on the chief of police, Peter Thoman, but his office told me that he's attending a meeting in San Francisco and won't be back until the end of the week. I reckon I'll have to wait until the beginning of next week before I have myself deputized."

The elderly Cherokee nodded complacently. "Plenty of time," he said.

Clarissa kept her own counsel. She knew that her husband was getting deputized because he had volunteered to get to the bottom of the vicious attack on Wong Ke, Toby's wealthy Chinese business mentor and friend, who had been mysteriously beaten while on a recent visit to Portland. Ke and his partner, Chet Harris—one of the original members of the first wagon train to Oregon and now a successful businessman in San Francisco—had indicated that members of an illegal Chinese criminal gang—or tong—had been responsible, and Toby was determined to even the score and teach his elderly friend's attackers a lesson they would not forget.

Glancing at her husband, Clarissa knew it was useless to argue with him. He would be impervious to warnings that it might be dangerous for him to investigate the incident and that it would be best to forget the matter and leave well enough alone. When a Holt's sense of justice was disturbed, he moved heaven and earth until he felt a wrong had been righted, and Clarissa knew it would be a waste of time to speak to Toby about the matter until he had obtained vengeance for Wong Ke.

Toby saw the worry in his wife's eyes and wanted to reassure her, to tell her that everything would work out fine, but in all honesty, he could not. He had a strange premonition that he was in danger. A new incident, in some way connected with the attack on Wong Ke, would take place in the near future, and his life would be threatened by it. But he could not allow that knowledge to deter him from doing what he regarded as his duty, however, just as he could not bring himself to mention the potential danger to Clarissa, worried as she was already.

II

Karl Kellerman was tiptoeing out of the hotel suite when Millicent Randall half sat up in the bed and called to him softly.

"Go back to sleep," he said, turning to her. "I've got an important business appointment this morning, so you may as well sleep until noon. I'll come back and pick you up in time for dinner."

Falling back on the pillows, with her thick brown hair framing her face, she raised her arms to him. He came to the bed and bent down to kiss her dutifully, and she threw her arms around his neck and tried to pull him into the bed with her. Lifting her face, she kissed him passionately.

Karl returned her kiss briefly, then managed to extricate himself from her grasp. "Lovemaking will have to wait until later," he told her, speaking softly. "I have a business appointment that I simply must keep."

Millicent sighed petulantly, then dropped her

arms and watched him as he silently let himself out of the suite.

Stopping first for a light breakfast in the hotel's restaurant, Karl then started out on foot across the city. As he drew nearer to the docks on the Mississippi River waterfront, the neighborhood changed from one of wealth to one of penury. The buildings grew shabbier, the clothing and food shops here were inexpensive, and there were a number of cheap brothels. The men and women on the streets were wearing rough, working-class attire, and Karl was conspicuous in his expensive clothes.

When he was about two blocks from the river, he came to a little building on which a small sign was hanging, identifying it as Dugald's Bar. As he entered, Karl saw that the place was crowded with merchant seamen, presumably from a recently arrived freighter, even though the hour was early. Waiting on the customers was a mild-mannered little Scotsman with gray hair, Wallace Dugald, Karl's partner and co-owner of the bar. In spite of his gentleness, Dugald was sufficiently authoritative to keep the unruly customers in line.

Dugald nodded to Karl as he carried a tray of drinks to a table in a far corner. Karl sauntered behind the bar and poured himself a glass of beer. While he was sipping it, Wallace Dugald returned to his post as bartender.

"I read in the papers that you retired from the St. Louis constabulary, Karl. I've been expecting you to show up here any day now. Welcome to New Orleans."

"Thanks, partner," Karl replied jocularly. "It's good to be here. I never spent much time in this place since the day that I provided you with the financing in return for fifty percent, but still it feels like home."

"Just say the word," Dugald told him, "and it'll *be* home. I'm not complaining about our business arrangement, but I'd be delighted to have you working here side by side with me."

"Thanks very much, Wallace," Karl said, "but I'm not sure yet what I'm going to do to earn my living. I spent a lot of years on the police force, so I want to take my time deciding what I'm going to do from here on in. It's a decision that I can't make too quickly."

Wallace looked owlish when he grinned. "As soon as the customers clear out of here," he said, "I've got a surprise for you. Maybe it'll help you make up your mind."

Not understanding the significance of the remark, Karl shrugged and said, "In the meantime, let me give you a hand behind the bar. That'll speed things up a bit." He hung up his jacket, rolled up his shirt-sleeves, and began to pour drinks swiftly and efficiently.

The merchant seamen left the bar late in the morning to search for girls, and Wallace turned to Karl. "We have just enough time for you to see the surprise," he said, "before the noon crowd begins to arrive." He led the way behind the bar to the far end, and there raised a trapdoor in the floor, which revealed a narrow flight of stairs that led to a cellar.

Following him through the trapdoor, Karl descended to the cellar. The only light was provided by a stubby candle that Dugald had lit and now carried in a battered brass holder.

Wallace crossed the room and went to an old-fashioned iron safe, which, after he put down the candle, he opened with a key. Inside were two identical cloth bags that made a clinking sound when he moved them.

"Here," he said, "are the profits from one full year of operations. I had the money changed into gold coins at the bank because they take up less space, and I divided them equally. One of these is yours, and the other is mine. If you like you can go over my accounts for the year, and I'm sure you'll find they'll tally to the penny."

"That won't be necessary," Karl said, and picking up one of the bags, he weighed it experimentally in his hands. His legitimate share of the profits amounted to a good deal of money, but he knew there were still not sufficient funds to pay for keeping up his hotel suite, meals at good eating places, and other expensive habits.

"I don't have to look at the ledgers or count the money, Wallace," he said. "I trust you. After all, we're partners!"

Wallace was pleased. "I'm glad you feel that

way, Karl," he replied. "I've never trusted banks, which is why I've kept the profits right here in the safe. Go on, take your share now."

"I'm in no hurry," Kellerman said. "The gold won't rust in your safe, so I'll leave it right where it is until I decide how to use it."

His mind racing, he already was making cold-blooded plans. Somehow—in a manner yet to be determined—he would dispose of Wallace Dugald permanently. Then he would take both bags of gold. The combined profits would provide him with a nest egg sufficient to live in the manner to which he was growing accustomed. Adding to this the money he would earn doing the job involving the crime boss Domino, he would have a small fortune. He would be able to afford the company of the blonde on whom he had an eye, and Millicent Randall be damned!

Suddenly the whole future looked bright. "It sure was a lucky day," he said, "when you and I became partners."

Millicent, wearing an expensive, revealing gown, dined with Karl at one of New Orleans's fanciest restaurants. She was supremely happy. The food and wines were perfect, every patron in the place took notice of her, and her lover was strong, handsome, and impressively virile. She was prepared for a wonderful evening and was stunned when Karl said to her, "I'll drop you off at the hotel after dinner. I have some business that requires my attention this evening."

"You left me to go on business this morning, too," she said indignantly.

"I've got to work," he said.

She couldn't help pouting. "At this time of night?"

"Night, day, any time at all," he replied, his manner brutal. "The money doesn't grow on trees to pay for supper at a place like this, and I don't find the cash in the streets to buy you dresses like you're wearing tonight."

"I—I'm sorry, Karl," she murmured. "I don't mean to be a burden on you."

"You're no burden," he told her, "but I've got to have the freedom to do what I must to earn a living for us."

"I'm ready to go back to the hotel," she said meekly. "Try not to be too late tonight."

He replied coldly, "I have no idea what time I'll be coming back tonight. Don't wait up for me."

Karl walked Millicent back to their hotel and then continued on his way, going rapidly to Dugald's Bar. There he changed into the inconspicuous attire of a working man: flannel shirt and woolen trousers. Dugald, meanwhile, was busy serving customers.

Karl stood for a time at the rear of the establishment inspecting the patrons; finally he settled on a grizzled man who sat alone at a table. The tarnished gold braid on his cap and on his cuffs revealed that he was a merchant marine captain. The officer interested Karl, and he decided this might be the kind of man he was looking for.

After pouring himself a tankard of ale and picking up a bottle of whiskey, Karl took the empty seat across from the captain. They soon fell into conversation, and Karl encouraged the relationship by pouring the officer a fresh drink from time to time.

The man, seemingly mild-mannered and quiet, was Captain Robin Kayross, a Greek sea captain. He was the master of a large steam-propelled freighter, the *Diana*, which plied the seas between New Orleans and Hong Kong. It developed that he was not self-employed but was hired by the ship's owners, who lived in San Francisco.

After several of the strong drinks that Karl quietly poured for him, Captain Kayross began to discuss his lot in life more freely. "There are some," he said, "who envy me. They think that being master of my own ship must be paradise. Well, it isn't. I don't mind telling you that except for a few fellow Greeks—some of my officers and about half a dozen members of my crew—I have hell's own time keeping a full crew. Every chance they get—and in almost every port I visit—officers and crew jump ship, and I've got to begin again the whole process of recruiting. It gets harder and harder."

"Is there any particular reason they jump ship?" Karl asked with pretended innocence.

Robin Kayross snorted. "They have fifty reasons," he said stridently. "For one thing, they complain day and night about the quality of the food I serve. I'll admit the diet is monotonous because I save money by buying foods in large quantities, but nobody ever gets sick and dies from what he eats on board the *Diana*. If I can tolerate the meals, so can my crew!"

Karl wore his most interested-looking expression as he poured out another drink for the captain.

Kayross continued, "No matter how many men I sign on, they always claim that the crew is short-handed. It doesn't matter if I put to sea with twenty men or with thirty, I hear the same thing. Well, sir, I don't mind telling you that I don't believe in coddling sailors. When a man goes to work for me, he can expect to work long, hard hours for his money. Putting to sea on the *Diana* is no vacation, and every last man who works for me finds that out in a hurry. Either he works or he feels the bite of a rope's end on his bare back, and there's no two ways about it. So I'm less than popular with my crew, particularly as I hold back pay as an incentive for working hard. They claim that often I withhold their wages completely, but I'm damned if they can ever prove it."

The man was totally lacking in scruples, Karl thought, and that was all to the good.

"I'm not saying I'm all that unhappy," the captain went on, chuckling quietly. "One way or another I manage to fill my purse, and that's what really counts. What my crews don't know won't hurt them, and the same thing goes for the ship's owners. All the same, hiring conditions are so bad that I swear to you in the name of Beelzebub that I'd give

almost anything to have a crew made up of shanghaied seamen. That way there'd be no problem.
They'd work their tails off or get whipped for their
pains. They'd get fed whatever slops we wanted to
give them and would be damn glad to get them.
They'd get a few hours of rest at night, just enough
to keep them going all the next day, and I wouldn't
hear a peep out of them. There's only one way to run
a ship! With whips and chains!"

Karl sipped his own drink and stared thoughtfully into the contents of his glass. "I wish I knew
whether you were serious or joking," he said softly.
"I could make suggestions about how to go about
shanghaiing some men if you were really serious."

Kayross was suddenly cautious. "How do I know
you're not a member of the New Orleans constabulary?"
he demanded. "How do I know you aren't assigned
to a squad that's trying to break up the gangs that are
impressing ordinary citizens as seamen?"

"I tell you plain, and I tell you true, that I don't
represent any constabulary," Karl said emphatically.
"I have no power to arrest anyone. You can believe
me or not, as you choose, and if you get it into your
head that I'm trying to trick you, then be damned to
you!"

"It does no harm," Kayross said, "to be careful."

"No harm at all," Karl replied. "To show you *I*
meant no harm, have another bottle—on me."

"I'll have another if you'll drink with me." Kayross
had no intention of getting drunk while this burly
stranger remained sober.

Karl went behind the bar and took a bottle. "You and your Greeks," he said, returning to the table and pouring out two whiskeys, "could try to kidnap yourselves a crew off the streets of New Orleans, though to be sure, gathering a full complement of men by impressment can be a very dangerous pastime."

"Especially in a foreign country where you have no friends on the bench," the Greek said. "That's why I'd much rather pay cash for merchandise. It's safer and neater."

Karl sipped his drink, then stared at the sea captain over the rim of his glass. "Let me get this straight," he said. "You're willing to put up a certain amount of money in cash for every shanghaied seaman who's handed over to you. Is that correct?"

Kayross examined the contents of his drink and then raised his glass to his lips. "You have the general idea," he said.

Kellerman had grown tired of fencing. "How much?" he demanded brusquely.

The captain was reluctant to name a figure, but his hand was being forced. "I'll pay five hundred dollars," he said, "for every man who's handed over to me, free and clear, to work on board the *Diana*."

The former St. Louis detective laughed as though really enjoying himself. "Suppose I made a deal with you," he said. "I'd be taking all the risks, and I sure wouldn't lift a finger for a rotten five hundred dollars a head. It just wouldn't be worth my neck."

"How much would you want?" Kayross demanded.

"One thousand dollars per man."

"A thousand dollars!" Kayross acted as though he had been stabbed. "I don't operate a freighter in the rich Atlantic service, you know. I'm forced to take the long route around South America to the Orient, where I'm subject to the bargaining wiles of the Chinese. All I can afford to pay is seven hundred dollars per man and not one cent more."

Kellerman shook his head sadly. "All you have to do," he said, "is rustle up cash for your payments, but I've got to take chances with every man I impress. I can't go any lower than a rock-bottom fee of eight hundred dollars per shanghaied man. Take it or leave it."

Seemingly lost in thought, Kayross stared at the contents of his glass. Then he helped himself to a small sip, smiled bleakly, and said, "You have a deal."

They shook hands, and at Kellerman's suggestion they adjourned to the waterfront in order to inspect the *Diana*. They walked together to the docks and soon came to the steam-powered ship. She was about fifteen years old and had been subjected to careless treatment. Litter was scattered on her decks, and she was badly in need of paint.

As Kellerman accompanied the captain on board, however, he noted with approval that the Greek seamen on duty were carrying loaded rifles.

Captain Kayross led his visitor below to the

hold, the boiler room, and the coal storage quarters, where the shanghaied seamen would be chained until the *Diana* was far out at sea. Cockroaches were everywhere underfoot, and an insistent series of scratching sounds indicated that numerous rats were scurrying out of the path of the approaching humans. None of that mattered to Karl. All he could think of was the money he would make providing a crew for this disreputable ship.

Cindy Holt, the pretty, vivacious twenty-year-old daughter of the famous Whip Holt and stepdaughter of Major General Leland Blake, commander of the U.S. Army in the West, was home at Fort Vancouver, Washington, from Oregon State College for the summer holidays. Her mother and stepfather had been called away on a military inspection trip, so she eagerly accepted the written invitation awaiting her from her sister-in-law, Clarissa. It was always a treat to eat supper and stay overnight at the ranch house, visiting with her brother Toby and with Clarissa and little Tim. She needed only the presence of her fiancé, Cadet Henry Blake of the U.S. Military Academy, the adopted son of her mother and General Blake, to complete her joy. She and Hank, a high honors student at West Point, had a private understanding, and she comforted herself with the thought that in two more years, after he won his commission as an army officer, they would be able to marry. Until then, she was learning to exercise patience.

General Blake's boat carried Cindy and her mare across the Columbia River to Oregon, and avoiding the town of Portland, where she intended to visit friends later during her stay, Cindy struck out at once for the Holt ranch.

The summer air was warm and fragrant, and a long, lovely twilight softened the mountains in the background. Cindy's mare, thoroughly enjoying the occasion, too, began to canter of her own volition.

All at once, Cindy saw a sight that made her blood run cold. Stretched out stiff-legged in the underbrush off to the left ahead of her was a gelding that had been shot and killed. On the opposite side of the trail, a man lay stretched on the ground, and his shirt, soaked and caked with blood, indicated that he, too, had been shot.

The man opened his eyes with a great effort and managed to focus on the young woman as she approached him and dismounted.

Slowly and with great deliberation, he began to fumble with his belt. "He searched me," he muttered hoarsely, "after he shot me, but I had the papers hidden in . . . secret compartment. Please see that they reach . . . General Blake. Tell him that government courier did his best." With a hand that trembled, he gave the girl several sheets of very thin paper that were folded into a small square.

Cindy took the folded papers from him, not bothering to explain that she was General Blake's stepdaughter. She knew the man had been wounded too badly for her to help him unaided, and she bent over him, intending to ask him what she could do for him before she went to her brother's ranch for help. But she realized with dismay that the man had stopped breathing and had already died.

As Cindy, now deeply upset, rose to her feet, dropping the papers she had been given into the pocket of the buckskin jacket she wore, she sensed rather than saw that someone was lurking nearby.

Suddenly a shot rang out, and a bullet whistled near her.

Truly the daughter of Whip Holt, Cindy reacted coolly. She snatched her own rifle from the saddle sling, raised it to her shoulder as she wheeled, and fired in the direction from which the bullet had come. Thrashing sounds in the underbrush told her she might not have missed her mark by much.

Taking advantage of the brief respite, she leaped into the saddle, dug her heels into the mare's flanks, and was off to a flying start in the direction of the Holt ranch. She bent low in the saddle as two shots rang out and a pair of bullets passed overhead. One of them was too close for comfort, so she squirmed around in her saddle as her mare continued to plunge forward and sent another shot from her rifle in the direction of her pursuer. When she saw Toby's ranch house and the outbuildings directly ahead, she knew that she was out of the range of her enemy.

Toby had heard the sounds of gunfire and had come into the open carrying his own rifle. Now he saw his sister riding toward him at breakneck speed, crouching low in her saddle. As she dismounted she breathlessly told him about the dead messenger and the person who had fired at her.

Stalking Horse and a half-dozen ranch hands now arrived at the scene, and Toby instantly waved them into action. They plunged into the woods, but when Stalking Horse reappeared after about a quarter of an hour, he shook his head. "Nobody is in the woods," he said. "Whoever followed Miss Cindy ran away. That's good for him, because if I find him, I put a bullet into his heart."

Meanwhile, the ranch hands had brought back the body of the messenger, and Toby told two of the hands to take the dead man to the Portland city morgue. Then he led his sister into the house. There, Clarissa awaited them and produced a pot of tea that helped to soothe Cindy, who then repeated her story more calmly.

Toby unfolded the sheets of paper and began to read them. "These are very interesting," he said. "They've been sent by General Layton at the Presidio in San Francisco, who received them from an anonymous source. They implicate a number of Chinese in San Francisco and several others in Portland in a Chinese smuggling ring."

"What are they smuggling?" Clarissa asked.

"Chinese immigrants principally, in defiance of United States immigration laws, and also opium."

"There are no laws to prevent the importation of opium into the country, are there?" Cindy asked.

Her brother shook his head. "No, but there's a strong ground swell of public opinion against the importation of opium. A large number of upstanding citizens claim that when it's used for nonmedical purposes, it's extremely harmful. It seems that members of a San Francisco tong have been making a vast sum of money on opium and immigration."

"Do you suppose," Clarissa asked thoughtfully, "that there's any connection between the tong that's involved in this smuggling operation and the attack on Wong Ke?"

"Perhaps," he replied, "though since the source is anonymous, there's no way to press any charges. General Layton was sending the papers to General Blake for his opinion. In any event, I promised Ke and Chet that I'd look into the involvements of the tong carefully, and this is the first lead of any kind that we've been given."

"One thing is for certain," Cindy said. "Someone is going to great lengths to prevent the authorities from learning too much. The courier carrying this information was murdered, and whoever killed him sure did try to stop me from leaving the scene of the killing with the papers."

Toby nodded thoughtfully, then said, "With the general out of town, I'll do the next best thing and take these documents to Peter Thoman, the Portland police chief, and to Tilman Wade, the director of security for the state. They're back in town now and may know something more."

They dropped the subject and devoted the rest of the evening to family matters. Little Tim had not yet retired, so his aunt sat with him while he ate his supper and then she told him a bedtime story. Later, at the dinner table, the talk centered on Cindy's recent activities and the news that she heard from Hank Blake in her correspondence with him.

After breakfast the following morning, Toby saddled his stallion and started into Portland carrying the courier's documents. He was satisfied that, in the absence of General Blake, the interests of the public were well served. Chief Peter Thoman was the son of Paul Thoman, one of the original settlers, and ably represented the younger generation. Tough old Tilman Wade, the state director of security, had also traveled to Oregon on the first wagon train to cross the continent, and he was unyielding in his fight against criminals. Together the combination of youth and age formed a team that had enjoyed remarkable success in its fight against crime. Oregon ranked high among the states in its record of protecting its citizens from criminal elements.

As Toby rode quietly through the pine woods, banks of clouds appeared overhead. Glancing up at the sky, he knew that rain would fall later in the day.

Suddenly the explosive crash of a rifle shot shattered the morning silence, and a bullet whined past Toby's head.

Reacting immediately, he urged his stallion to a full gallop in the direction of where the shot had

come from and grabbed one of his pistols. Crouching
low in the saddle, he was prepared to shoot as soon
as he caught a glimpse of the man who had fired at
him.

No more than a half minute elapsed before Toby
caught a glimpse of another rider far ahead in the
woods, beating a hasty retreat from the scene. Still
riding hard, Toby aimed his pistol and fired a shot at
the fleeing figure. The distance was too great,
however, and the rider disappeared from sight into
the thick pine woods that extended for a considerable distance in all directions before finally giving
way to cleared land on the approach to Portland. The
rider could enter the city at any one of a score of
places, and his tracks would be lost among those of
the hundreds of other horses and vehicles in the
area. Further pursuit would be a waste of time, and
Toby reholstered his pistol regretfully, realizing that
his would-be killer was free to renew his assault at
some later date.

Toby continued on his way toward the city.
Obviously he had been shot at because he was suspected of carrying the papers that had resulted in the
death of the courier. Someone was very anxious that
these documents be intercepted and not passed on to
the authorities.

The courthouse on Fourth Street was a large,
imposing building, like the other public structures
located on one of two adjacent parklike public squares.
Here were the offices of federal, state, and local

officials. The second-floor office of Tilman Wade overlooked bustling Fourth Street, and Toby stood with
the balding Wade while they awaited the arrival of
Chief Thoman.

"If your pa was still alive," the older man said,
"he'd be every bit as amazed as I am. There was
nothing but trees and bare land here when we finally
called a halt to our wagon train, and today the population of Portland is about eight thousand people. What
really astonishes me is the prediction that we'll have
double that number by the time 1880 comes. The
faster the town grows, the more complicated the job
of maintaining public order becomes."

"I don't envy you, Tilman. It was a lot simpler
in my father's day when he and a half-dozen others
kept the peace by keeping their rifles oiled."

They were interrupted by the arrival of Peter
Thoman, who was exceptionally tall, extremely thin,
and was acknowledged to be a very efficient police
chief.

Toby told the officials his sister's experience the
previous evening, then showed them the documents
she had been given by the dying courier. He also
told them of the attempt on his own life less than an
hour earlier.

Both men read the papers with interest. "You
will note," the police chief said, "that the tong is
never mentioned by name. That's because no out-
sider ever learns its name. That is one of the secrets
the Chinese guard zealously. However, there is no

doubt in my mind who the head of this tong now is. Kung Lee is his name, and he has effectively eliminated the former leaders and has seized complete control, showing no mercy to them or to anyone else. If my memory serves correctly, Wong Ke told you that Kung was responsible for the attack on him."

Tilman Wade fingered the butts of the Colt repeating pistols that he carried in his belt. "Even without these papers," he said, "I'd be inclined to suspect a tong headed by Kung. They've demonstrated repeatedly that they have no respect for American laws. They're a vicious group."

"Well, we agreed that I was going to be deputized as a federal marshal so that I could go after the tong," Toby said matter-of-factly. "I guess now is as good a time as any."

Tilman looked very much concerned. "The circuit judge is sitting in the federal court, all ready to swear you in, Toby," he said, "but are you really sure you want to take on the responsibility for chasing after Kung Lee's gang? I mean, here you've finally gained the chance to settle with your family on your ranch and to live like an ordinary citizen."

"I promised Wong Ke and Chet Harris that I'd do all I could to track down the ruffians who attacked Ke," Toby said solemnly, "and I'm going to keep my word to them. They're not only business associates; they're like family to me, and I'm very much in their debt. In addition to which, I don't like the idea of the tong defrauding the American public by illegally importing Chinese laborers and bringing large amounts of opium into this country. It's my duty as a citizen to help put a stop to such practices."

"You've more than earned your share of good citizenship, Toby," Peter Thoman said. "This country would be in great shape if everybody's contribution equaled yours."

Karl Kellerman claimed that business affairs would keep him occupied all day, so Millicent was once again thrown on her own resources. Dressing modestly and with just a trace of makeup, she spent a couple of hours shopping and then returned to the Louisiana House for a noon dinner, sitting alone on the far side of the dining room as the orchestra played classical selections.

Before she had a chance to study the menu, the hotel manager appeared at her elbow. "Madame Kellerman," he said, using the name under which she was registered, "may I have the honor of presenting to you Mr. Jean-Pierre Gautier, a member of a prominent New Orleans family, who also happens to be a majority stockholder in this hotel."

Millicent looked up at the thin, extremely well-dressed, dark-haired young man who was bowing to the waist before her. He was the one who had shadowed her whenever she had been alone, following her into shops and restaurants and keeping watch over her on the streets. She pretended, however, never to have seen him before and simply extended her hand and murmured, "How do you do."

He handled her fingers as though they were made of the most fragile glass. "I am overwhelmed, Madame Kellerman," he said. "If you are not expecting anyone for dinner, may I join you?"

His sincerity was so obvious that she was amused as well as flattered, despite her earlier resolve to avoid him at all costs. What was more, Karl seemed not to care what she did, and so she told him, "Sit down, by all means."

He promptly took the chair opposite her and asked for the privilege of buying her an aperitif. She consented graciously, and he immediately ordered from the hotel manager, who went off to get a waiter to serve them.

"I hope," he said, "that you don't mind the presence of the orchestra. They're one of the additions to the hotel for which I'm responsible."

She laughed aloud. "How could I not like the music of Brahms," she said, "especially the waltzes?"

He was impressed. "You are a musician, Madame Kellerman?"

"My name isn't Kellerman," she said. "I'm Millicent Randall, the name I had when I was born, and I am indeed a musician. I play the flute, and I studied for many years at the Baltimore Conservatory, where I also composed for the flute."

"I'd love to hear your compositions," he said. "I'm afraid I have no musical talents myself, although

I much appreciate music. The most I can claim is that I do my part in sponsoring the symphony orchestra here." They had quickly discovered a mutual interest in music and discussed nothing else as they each drank two glasses of wine. Millicent had not had the opportunity to talk about music with anyone since she had left Baltimore, and she chatted happily, feeling as though floodgates had been unexpectedly opened in her.

In time, Jean-Pierre revealed his own background. He was the heir to one of the larger French fortunes in New Orleans and had been married to a woman whom he had loved dearly and who had died after a long and painful illness the year before. He made no secret of the fact that he had been captured by the very sight of Millicent, and ever since she had come to town some days earlier, he had spent most of his waking hours trying to arrange an introduction to her.

She was somewhat less than frank in her response to him. She spoke freely of her life in Baltimore and subsequently of her travels in the West and the establishment of her cousin's ranch in Idaho, but she offered no explanation whatever of how she happened to come to New Orleans, and she blithely ignored the existence of Karl Kellerman.

When Jean-Pierre asked for the privilege of seeing her again, she became equally elusive, telling him she would be happy to meet him for a noon or evening dinner but that it was impossible for her to set up engagements far in advance. What she did not tell him was that her day-to-day existence was still ruled by Kellerman's whims. When he had business that took him elsewhere, she was forgotten. But when he wanted her company, he expected her to be immediately available to him.

Jean-Pierre, however, seemed more than satisfied with any arrangements she cared to make, even though her planning was tenuous at best.

By the time they finished dinner, parting company when they left the table, it was obvious that Jean-Pierre Gautier was infatuated with her. Millicent was relieved, even though she knew it was selfish to feel as she did. The fear had been growing within her for several days that Karl might desert her, and she wondered what she would do if she found herself alone in a strange city. Jean-Pierre offered her a measure of security, however, and she was grateful that she had met him. In spite of her outward sophistication, she was afraid to face the world alone, and she felt better able to cope knowing that Jean-Pierre was ready and able to assist her in every way possible.

Occupying the ground floor of the dilapidated wooden building in San Francisco's Chinatown was a curio shop that sold trinkets and souvenirs of China. On the second floor, at the far end of a rickety wooden staircase, were quarters that casual visitors to the shop assumed to be the home of the proprietors of the modest little establishment. But beyond a door of heavy oak, a surprise awaited the few persons ever to gain admission to the place. Here, the floors were covered with magnificent, handwoven Oriental rugs. On them stood superbly wrought vases and statuettes of porcelain, and on the walls hung precious Chinese paintings. At a glance, the place represented the Orient at its most sumptuous. A room on one side of the suite was furnished like an American office, however. Here stood a large, mahogany desk, a reclining chair, and a number of visitors' chairs of carved oak. The walls were graced with expensive portraits by American artists.

Behind the huge desk sat Kung Lee, the tong leader who was said to be the most powerful Chinese man in North America. In his mandarin robes of black he did not look like a man of power, however. His build was frail, his hair was gray, and he wore horn-rimmed glasses. He could have been anywhere from fifty to seventy-five years old. His right hand moving delicately, swiftly, he was writing a letter, his brush strokes firm as he made the Chinese characters.

His efforts were interrupted when a nondescript-looking serving man in black jacket and trousers came into the room and bowed. "Forgive the intrusion, Celestial Leader," he said, speaking in the educated Mandarin tongue, "but Chung Ai has just returned to San Francisco from Portland and craves an audience with you."

Kung Lee sighed, slightly annoyed by the interruption. "Send Ho Tai to me," he said, "and after he has entered this room, wait for a few moments, then show in Chung Ai."

Ho Tai, a burly native of the north of China, ambled into the room. His appearance was unlike that of the scholarly Kung Lee in every way. The newcomer was short and squat, a man with a knife-scarred face. He carried a double-edged blade of exceptional sharpness in the belt of his all-black attire.

Ho Tai bowed to Kung Lee, but there was no conversation between them. The older man's gaze rested on his henchman for a moment, and Ho Tai seemed to know what was expected of him. He moved silently to a corner of the room, his step surprisingly graceful for someone of his build, and there he folded his arms and stared impassively straight ahead.

The door opened again, and Chung Ai advanced noiselessly into the room. He bowed low before Kung Lee, who offered him a chair, which he sank into gracefully, ignoring the presence of Ho Tai. Chung Ai was dressed like a ranch hand in an open-throated flannel shirt and worn work pants stuffed into calf-high boots. He wore a brace of pistols in his belt, and in one hand he carried a broad-brimmed hat.

Chung Ai reported diligently and at length on his most recent activities. He related how he had shot the horse of the official U.S. courier and, after bringing down the animal, had proceeded to put another bullet into the man. Before the courier had died, Chung Ai had searched him in vain for the precious documents that he was taking to General Blake at U.S. Army headquarters. He had been diverted from his task by the arrival of Cindy Holt on the scene and had seen the dying man take the papers from a secret compartment in his belt and give them to her.

Carrying the telltale documents, the girl had escaped and gone to the house of her brother, the famous Toby Holt. The following morning, Holt had started in the direction of Portland when Chung Ai had intercepted him in the forest and had fired at him.

"Ah." Kung Lee pressed his fingertips together and sighed gently.

"With deep regret," Chung Ai said, "I must inform Your Excellency that my attempt to kill Toby Holt failed, and I only just got away with my life. I did not dare to linger and exchange gunfire with Toby Holt. All who have attempted to exchange fire with him in this way have paid for their foolishness with their lives. I would have gained nothing had I engaged in such an exercise."

The older man pursed his lips. "What became of Holt after you shot at him and missed?" he asked.

"He went into Portland, where he met with the authorities. This article appeared in the Portland newspaper." He took a frayed clipping from his shirt pocket and passed it across the desk.

Kung Lee's face remained expressionless as he

read that Toby Holt had been sworn in as a United States deputy marshal.

"I am sure that—at the very least—we can expect interference at some future date from Mr. Holt," Kung Lee said with regret. "I do not look forward to the prospect of such a man as that one meddling in my affairs."

"I offer you a thousand apologies," Chung Ai said. "I did the best I could."

Kung Lee pressed his fingertips together and pronounced sentence. "Failure," he said, "is intolerable to me. I recognize only success. And there has been none. First, you failed to do away with the meddler Wong Ke. Then you failed to stop the courier with the telltale documents. Last, and most grievous, you failed to do away with Toby Holt, who now will become our greatest enemy."

Chung Ai began to explain his position further, but he was so terrified he could only babble.

Kung Lee glanced at Ho Tai, who had remained immobile throughout the conversation. The tong leader inclined his head almost imperceptibly.

Ho Tai moved forward swiftly, his wicked knife glistening in his hand. He struck with lightning speed and cut Chung Ai's throat from ear to ear. Then, just as swiftly, he lifted the dead man's body into his arms before too much blood spilled onto the fine Persian carpet, and took the body out the back door and down the outside stairway. There, in the concealed backyard of the little building, Ho Tai placed the body in a crate labeled *Imported Porcelain* and covered the remains with sawdust. The crate would be sent to a curio shop owned by a rival tong, and the surprised owners would see how Kung Lee dealt with people who failed him.

Meanwhile, Kung Lee sat behind his desk, his eyes rooted to the spot where blood had stained his priceless antique rug. At last he pressed the bell to summon his manservant, and when the man entered and bowed, the tong leader instructed him, "Remove the carpet at once. I'm afraid it has suffered irreparable harm. Fortunately, I have several others that I like equally as well. Put a new carpet in its place, and be sure your hands are clean so you do not soil it!"

III

The police commissioner of Memphis, Charles O'Shea, leaned back in his swivel chair and looked at each of his guests in turn. Edward Blackstone, his handsome face reflecting the seriousness of his intent, anxiously regarded the commissioner, awaiting his statement. Pretty and vivacious Tommie Harding regarded her fiancé—she was far more concerned about his reaction than anything that the head of the Memphis police force might have to say.

"I'm glad," O'Shea said, "that my department isn't alone in showing an interest in the activities of Karl Kellerman. He was a good enough detective during the years that he was on the St. Louis force, but in all my dealings with him, I never trusted him completely. Although I can't put my finger on what was wrong with him, I'm willing to swear that he was less than honest."

"You have no hard evidence, then, that proves

61

his connection with the criminal world?" Edward asked.

The commissioner shook his head. "We don't have a shred of it," he replied. "Some of my men go along with what you think and are prepared to swear that Kellerman had a hand—quite possibly the major hand—in the death of the Memphis gang leader and one of his bodyguards recently. But they can't prove it, and neither can you. I'd love to get my hands on him and have a little heart-to-heart chat with him, but he's too clever, and I'm sure he has his alibis already worked out."

"Nevertheless, you have no objection if I attempt to speak with him about a certain lady who was last seen in his company and who happens to be my cousin?" Edward persisted.

"Not at all," Commissioner O'Shea replied, "and I have a little information that will be of help to you." He opened a desk drawer and took out a file. "I heard from New Orleans just the day before yesterday. According to the New Orleans police, Kellerman has indeed turned up there, as you and Commissioner Bowen in St. Louis surmised. Kellerman is a part owner of a saloon known as Dugald's Bar in a working-class district, and he's been spending a great deal of time there ever since he got into town."

"Did the report confirm," Edward asked anxiously, "whether he was traveling with a lady?"

The commissioner studied the report for a few seconds more and then closed it decisively. "Kellerman's weakness," he said, "has always been women. He appears to be incapable of leaving them alone. To answer your question more directly, several members of my department saw him when he stayed overnight here, and they said he was traveling with a brown-haired strumpet, if you'll pardon my language, ma'am," he added to Tommie. "Apparently she had the manners of a lady, more so than most of the other women who've associated with him, but in her dress and in the way she made up, she was nothing but a strumpet, plain and simple."

"Unfortunately, Edward," Tommie said softly, "that sounds like an accurate description of Millicent."

"However," the Memphis police commissioner went on, "the report from the New Orleans police doesn't indicate whether this same brunette is still with Kellerman."

Edward did his best to conceal his disappointment. "At the very least," he said, "once we catch up with Kellerman, he'll have to tell us what's become of Millicent. If she isn't with him, at least he should know where she's gone."

"I wish you good luck in tracking down Kellerman," the commissioner said, "and if you don't mind, I'll give you a word of advice: When he wants, Kellerman literally breathes charm, but in his natural state, he's inclined to be ruthless, rough, and very tough."

"We're prepared for all contingencies," Edward said. "I have two strong men in my party who will come to my assistance if there is any trouble. But I also believe that the more informal our get-together, the better it will be, and so I intend first to visit him alone. In the event that Millicent isn't with him, he'll be far more inclined to talk and reveal her whereabouts if he feels that I'm just paying him a quiet, friendly visit."

He and Tommie took their leave of the commissioner soon thereafter, and when they returned to their hotel, they reported on their meeting to Jim Randall and Randy Savage.

"Obviously," Jim said, "we have no real choice in the matter. We'll have to go on to New Orleans, find Kellerman, and ask him for Millicent's whereabouts. At least the end appears to be in sight."

Edward was less certain, after suffering many disappointments, that they would find Millicent soon, but he said nothing about it to the others.

A howling gale blew in from the Gulf of Mexico, and New Orleans was inundated with heavy, steady rains. The weather was perfect for Karl Kellerman's purposes. At his own suggestion, he relieved Wallace Dugald behind the bar of their establishment so that the Scotsman could take a nap. During the next two hours, three solitary drinkers managed to brave the elements and to patronize the bar. Karl accorded each of them the same treatment, putting a drug into their drinks that rendered them unconscious. Then he carried them, one by one, down to the cellar, where he bound them hand and foot and gagged them. He told himself that in return for this minor effort, he had earned twenty-four hundred dollars.

He congratulated himself, reflecting that his timing was perfect. Captain Robin Kayross had promised to come by later that night with several members of his loyal cadre. Karl would be awaiting them, as arranged, with the first of his shanghaied seamen.

Wallace returned from his house after an absence of a little more than two hours, and now Karl intended to put into effect the second part of his plan.

By including Dugald in the ranks of the unfortunates who would be compelled to work their way across the Pacific and back on board the *Diana*, Karl would be able to take complete possession of both bags of gold that reposed in the cellar safe, and any future profits that the bar earned would be exclusively his. In addition, before this night ended, he would perform the gaming house robbery that Domino had set up for him. He would earn large sums before dawn.

As Wallace stood in the entrance, removing his outer clothing, rainwater dripped from him and formed a puddle on the floor of the saloon. "It's pretty fierce out there tonight," he said. "This is the worst weather I've seen in a long time."

"It strikes me this is a good night for us to celebrate," Karl told him.

The very idea struck Wallace as absurd. "What is there to celebrate?"

"We're celebrating the fact that I've joined you here and intend to take an active part in the business."

Wallace became more enthusiastic. "That's great, if you mean it, Karl," he said. "I've been working seven days and seven nights a week, and I can stand some relief now and again."

Karl nodded. "You've been spending far too much time at the bar. It's only common sense that you take it easy, maybe even go on a little trip." His smile broadened as he thought that Wallace would indeed go on a trip very soon.

Sending Wallace to sea as a shanghai victim was by far the best solution to the problem of what to do with him. As a matter of principle, Karl disliked the idea of killing the man responsible for his acquisition of two bags of gold; in addition, if he murdered Wallace, he would have the problem of disposing of his body. Shanghaiing him and sending him to work on board the *Diana* would get rid of him without a trace, and yet Karl's own hands would be clean.

Walking behind the bar he asked, "What will you have?"

Wallace hesitated. "I've always made it a rule never to drink on a night when I'm going to be serving customers."

Karl laughed jovially. "As you can see, there isn't a customer in sight, and judging from the downpour out there, we're going to have the whole evening to ourselves. If I remember correctly, you like rye whiskey and water."

"Right," Wallace replied, beginning to relax. "Make it a mild drink, if you will."

"You bet," Karl told him, busying himself behind the bar. Turning his back to his partner for a few moments in order to conceal what he was doing, he poured into Dugald's drink several drops of the powerful drug that he had purchased at an apothecary shop earlier in the day, the same medicine that had already proved itself with the men who were sleeping in the cellar, bound hand and foot. Satisfied that the medication had no taste and no smell, he handed Wallace the glass, then poured himself a somewhat stronger drink.

"Here's to our partnership," he said. "Long may it continue to flourish." He raised his glass to his lips.

Dugald also drank. "Amen to that," he said, then sipped again. "This tastes pretty good," he went on. "I was colder than I realized. This is really one hell of a rotten night."

For the next quarter of an hour, Karl kept up a light stream of conversation. Afraid that the drug was having no effect, he considered feeding Wallace another dose, but at last his patience was rewarded, and he saw Dugald's eyelids beginning to droop.

"This is very strange," Wallace said thickly. "My drink must be more potent than I realize. I can hardly hold up my head."

Karl thought it best not to reply and waited for the Scotsman to lose consciousness.

Wallace peered at him, eyelids drooping. "This

is strange," he muttered. "You look like you're gloating, Karl. Why are you gloating?"

Karl still thought it best to make no reply.

"You're up to something!" Wallace cried, his voice thickening as the drug continued to take effect. "One mild rye and water wouldn't make me feel like this. You doped me. You put something in my drink!"

Karl continued to say nothing.

With a last burst of energy, Wallace shook a fist under the younger man's nose. "I don't know why you did it, but you've tricked me, Kellerman!" he cried. "Why have you done this to me? Damn your soul to hell!"

All at once, he lost consciousness and sagged to the floor.

Karl's leering grin broadened. He opened the trapdoor, and throwing his partner over one shoulder, he descended to the cellar. There he made Dugald's wrists and ankles secure with lengths of rope, and as he had done with the other victims, he tied a gag around his partner's mouth. If he awakened prematurely, he would be unable to make a fuss or call for help.

Placing the unconscious body next to that of his other victims, Karl allowed himself a sigh of relief. For all practical purposes, Wallace Dugald was already confined to the hold of the merchant ship. Now glancing at his pocket watch, Karl noted that it was time to leave for the gaming establishment. If he could keep to his schedule, he would return to the bar in time to turn over the unconscious men to Captain Kayross.

He left the cellar and felt supremely confident as he slipped a six-shooter into one pocket and a blackjack, a length of lead pipe covered with leather, into another. Donning his hat and coat, he locked up the bar and ignored the elements as he walked briskly to 321 Jefferson.

"I'm here for some action!" he told the guard on duty at the entrance, and pushed his way into the old mansion.

Pausing at a landing on the way to the second floor, Karl tied a bandanna around his face, knotting it at the back of his neck. Then, one hand on the butt of his pistol, he entered the principal game room, shutting the door behind him. There were two card games in progress, and several people were sitting at a bar over which a bartender presided. There were twenty-five to thirty well-dressed patrons in the room, including one man in plain civilian clothes sitting at the bar, whom Karl recognized from meetings he had attended as a lieutenant of New Orleans police. It was obvious that the official was working as a security officer in the place, probably earning a large sum for his after-hours work. But having spotted him in advance, Karl was way ahead of the game; he knew the man could be disarmed before he posed any threat.

Scanning the patrons quickly, Karl was relieved when he saw that Domino was very much engrossed in a game with one of the card dealers. So far, the former detective-sergeant from St. Louis thought, everything was going his way.

"Ladies and gentlemen, give me your attention," Karl called as he took his pistol from his pocket. "First off, I'll ask those of you who are armed to surrender your weapons at once. We'll start with you, lieutenant."

The police officer, embarrassed by the public recognition, took a pistol from an inner coat pocket and slid it across the floor to a place at Karl's feet.

"Thank you, sir," Karl said crisply. "Your turn, Domino."

The middle-aged gang leader feigned indignation, his eyes boring into his hireling as if to say, "No nonsense from you. Do your job the way I told you." But he at last produced his pistol and got rid of it in the same way as the police lieutenant.

"I'll appreciate the contributions of any other firearms or knives that any of you may be carrying," Karl went on jovially. "Believe me, my friends, it will be to your advantage to get rid of your weapons now. I'm inclined to become nasty—in fact, I develop a terrible itch in my trigger finger—when I discover that someone is still armed. So no funny business. I've got my eye on everyone in the room. One false move and I shoot the first person who doesn't do as I say."

The two card dealers relieved themselves of knives, and several of the other patrons got rid of pistols.

Karl circled the chamber slowly, relieving each

individual of cash. He refused to take any jewelry from either the ladies or the men, reasoning that he would need to call on an accomplice in order to rid himself of the gems. He well could be identified and brought to justice if he began to deal in stolen jewels.

Karl deliberately waited until he had robbed all of the other patrons before he approached Domino again. It had galled him to think that he had been asked to surrender the better part of his booty to the gang leader. His plan, however, would ensure that he was beholden to no one, and he was so confident of his luck and his ability that he had no fear of reprisals from any of Domino's men. Indeed, Kellerman even believed it was also possible that he might be able to take over many of the lucrative functions of the gang leader's organization.

For a few seconds his resolve faltered as Domino's steely eyes bored into him. But at last he said, "All right, it's your turn now."

The gang leader dug into his trousers pocket and dug out a thick roll of money. "Here," he said gruffly, dropping the money into Karl's hand.

As Karl stashed the money away in his own pocket, Domino began to search elsewhere. "I've got some more that I can give you," he said.

This was just the opportunity Karl needed. "I warned you what would happen if anybody tried to reach for a hidden gun," he said stridently, and was about to shoot when a woman standing nearby screamed. Karl was momentarily unnerved, but he still squeezed the trigger.

Domino staggered and crumpled to the floor, then lay still in a pool of blood.

His mission brilliantly accomplished, Karl lost no time in taking himself elsewhere. Flinging open the door, he raced down the steps two and three at a time, knocking the guard at the entrance to one side and tearing the bandanna from his face as he dashed out into the street. He ran to the curb, where several carriage drivers awaited possible fares. Leaping into the carriage at the head of the line, he promised the driver a double fee if the man would shake all pursuers.

They started at once for the center of town, and the driver was so adept that no one succeeded in following him. Karl kept his word and paid the man a double fare, then darted around the corner and caught another carriage for hire, which took him close to the waterfront. Discharging his second driver, he walked rapidly by a circuitous route to Dugald's Bar, where he unlocked the door and let himself in. He was much relieved when a quick glance in the cellar revealed that Wallace and the other victims were precisely where he had left them, still unconscious.

He had barely reemerged on the main floor when Robin Kayross arrived, accompanied by several of his loyal crew members, one of whom was driving a cart. The four unconscious men, Wallace Dugald among them, were taken from the cellar and piled into the cart, and an oilcloth cover was used to conceal them.

This was no time for conversation. Kayross handed

the former sergeant thirty-two hundred dollars in cash, then disappeared with his shanghaied cargo. Now at last Karl had the time to count his gains from the night's spoils. He was astonished to discover that his haul from the gaming establishment was far larger than he had anticipated: He had taken in thousands of dollars in return for one night's efforts. Now he could start living the life he craved, buying expensive clothes, eating only in the town's finest restaurants, and continuing to lead Millicent Randall on while making a play for both the luscious blonde and the expensive redhead who had interested him. By displaying courage and presence of mind, in one night he had assured his future.

Wallace Dugald's head ached, and he felt a tremendous thirst as he awakened. Little by little he became aware of his surroundings. He was lying on a filthy, foul-smelling mattress, and near the upper end was a container. The odor told him it was a chamber pot. The floor was made of metal and was filthy with a thick coating of coal dust. Nearby, something glowed inside an open door, and he finally realized it was a huge boiler of some kind. The heat was almost unbearable, and there was no daylight, no fresh air.

More to the point, he became conscious of his own predicament. A thick iron band encircled his right ankle, and he was chained to a stanchion from which he could move only a few feet in any direction.

As he watched, a small group of short, brown-skinned men appeared and began to shovel coal into the furnace. As the proprietor of a bar frequented by seamen, Wallace had become accustomed to judging men from all over the world, and he took it from their coloration and facial features that these men were Malays and Lascars.

The men—who were wearing loose-fitting, Western-style trousers but no shirts because of the heat—were not chained, and he called out to them eagerly, "You there! Where am I, and what's the meaning of these chains?"

There was no reply as the brown-skinned men went about their work.

Captain Robin Kayross approached, wearing the cap and jacket whose faded, tarnished gold braid symbolized his authority. In one hand he carried a short, ugly cat-o'-nine-tails. "You're awake, I see," he said.

"That I am," Wallace replied, "and I demand to know the meaning of this outrage. Why am I chained in this awful place?"

Kayross lashed out and struck him full across the face with the whip. "You'll address me as 'sir,'" he said, "and you'll speak to me respectfully because that's due my rank. Do I make myself clear?"

Wallace was infuriated, but the blood oozing from a cut the whip had inflicted on his upper lip served as a reminder that he had no choice. "Yes, sir," he said.

"That's more like it," Kayross said. "Just keep in mind that you'll be whipped into obedience any time you start acting up. You're lucky you weren't killed, you know. But you look smart enough to do what you're told to stay alive."

The man looked familiar, and all at once, Wallace placed him. He was a sea captain who had spent long hours in the Dugald Bar drinking and talking in low tones with Karl Kellerman. Suddenly he remembered that Karl had drugged him, and he put the whole picture together. Karl had rendered him helpless and then delivered him into the hands of this equally unscrupulous fellow.

"I intend taking no chances and being forced to shoot you because you were trying to escape. You're staying right where you are until we put out to sea, and if you behave yourself, your chains will then be removed, and you can move to the fo'c'sle with the rest of the crew. In the meantime, you'll keep the engine stoked like it is now; that way, we're ready to take off and put out to sea any time we want. You'll obey my officers, or you'll get the hide ripped off you. I find that when common sense fails, one language my indentured seamen always understand is the langugae of the whip." He swished the cat-o'-nine-tails back and forth. "Do what you're told when you're told to do it, and you'll be fed two meals a day," Kayross said. "I hope I make myself clear."

"Very clear, sir," Wallace replied, digging his fingernails into the palms of his hands. No one would ever know the great effort that his docility cost him.

Kayross grunted and then called out to the Lascars and Malays who were lurking in the shadows.

"Let the fate of this miserable one be a lesson to you," he said to them. "Do that which is expected of you, and you will be well treated. Disobey me and my officers, and you will be reduced to the level of this poor slave. For your own good, remember my words!" Not bothering to glance again in the direction of Wallace, he stamped off and left the furnace room.

For a long moment, no one stirred or spoke. Then one of the Malays obtained a cup of cool water from somewhere and handed it to Wallace. The gesture was so unexpected that Wallace's voice was husky as he thanked the man. Taking the cup, he drained it in order to relieve his burning thirst. Turning away, he picked up a shovel lying on the floor next to his dirty pallet, and thrusting it into the nearest pile of coal, he began to feed the furnace.

His mind racing as he thought about the dilemma in which he found himself, he worked until his torn shirt was wet with sweat and clung to his body. Rivulets of perspiration descended from his forehead and burned his eyes, but he merely blinked them away. He was lost in thought, and as he and the brown-skinned men kept the furnace burning up to the point that Captain Kayross had specified, he was seething with anger at his partner, who had no doubt sold him for a handsome sum. Now he faced a miserable existence as a common seaman, and unless he behaved in an exemplary manner, he would be severely punished.

Gazing into the fire with eyes that blazed like

the coal flames burning there, he spoke in a voice that throbbed with emotion. "If I could," he said aloud, "I'd break these chains and smash them over the head of my double-crossing partner. I've lost the gold that I accumulated through long hours of work, and with it, my half-interest in the saloon that was my whole life. I'm condemned to an existence that will be the death of me if I don't watch my step.

"But I intend to live! No matter what may happen, I'll stay alive and protect myself. Above all else on earth, I crave revenge against Karl Kellerman." Ordinarily shy and mild-mannered, he spoke now with a soul-shattering intensity that seemed to shake the metal floor of the furnace room.

"So help me God," he declared, "I will obtain vengeance against Karl Kellerman if it's the last thing on earth that I ever do!" He shook his fist in the light of the furnace, and his shadow leaped high against the bulkhead. "I'll do anything that's needed," he swore. "If I must, I'll even sell my soul to the devil, but I will obtain vengeance!"

The changes in Karl Kellerman were so pronounced that Millicent Randall was deeply concerned. He was no longer the devoted suitor, the loving companion with whom she had left St. Louis and, compromising her whole future, had accompanied to New Orleans. More often than not, he behaved like a total stranger. He had been transformed into a man who spent increasingly vast sums of money on a stunning wardrobe with which no other man in New

Orleans could compete. Instead of accompanying her on her shopping expeditions and escorting her to dinner and supper at the finer restaurants of the town, he now left her to her own devices. He seemed to think that as long as he provided her with money for her shopping excursions and meals, nothing further was required of him.

On several occasions, her confusion and loneliness had impelled her to accept dinner invitations from Jean-Pierre, but she preferred to avoid the young French heir. It was plain that Jean-Pierre was infatuated with her, but she didn't feel free to accept his attentions. True, Karl was indifferent to her, but she still loved him and even still hoped that someday they might marry. What was more, she was afraid Karl would take it quite amiss if she were to spend her time with another man, let alone one as handsome and gallant as Jean-Pierre.

Karl, however, felt no similar inhibitions, telling Millicent daily that his work was responsible for his absences. Several evenings each week his work kept him busy all night, and he did not return to the hotel suite until midmorning the following day. Then he only appeared long enough to bathe and change his clothes, have breakfast with Millicent, then leave again. Meanwhile, he paid court to the lovely blonde with whom he had become acquainted at the restaurant. When she resisted his advances, however, he began to lay siege to the red-haired beauty he had also seen, and here he was far more successful. Within a short period of time, thanks to the many gifts that he lavished upon her, he was engaged in a violent affair with her.

Millicent had no way of knowing where he went or who accompanied him, but she began to grow suspicious. On several occasions she thought she smelled perfume on the clothes he left for the laundress.

This particular morning began like so many others that had preceded it. After having eaten breakfast in the dining room of the Louisiana House, Millicent and Karl returned to their suite, where he meticulously adjusted his expensive new cravat in the mirror and took a flower from a fresh bunch in a vase to put in his lapel buttonhole.

"You'll have to keep yourself occupied today," he said. "I'm afraid I'm going to be tied up at work."

Something within Millicent rebelled, but she made no reply.

He reached into a pocket and peeled off a one-hundred-dollar bill from a wad of notes. "This is in case you find something that strikes your fancy while you're shopping. I suggest you eat your noon dinner here and charge the meal to the suite."

"What will you be doing?" she demanded, unable to control her fury. "Eating dinner in a private room somewhere with your romance of the moment?"

Karl retreated at once into a hard shell. "I beg your pardon," he said distinctly. "I prefer to ignore that comment, and I would rather pretend that you never said it."

She had gone too far to stop now; her suspicions

were getting the better of her. "You aren't nearly as clever as you like to believe," she said hotly. "You've succeeded in convincing yourself that you've had me badly fooled, but you haven't. I think I could name the exact date that you started cheating on me."

Karl feigned great indignation. "I've told you many times that I have business to conduct," he shouted angrily. "If you don't want to believe me, that's your prerogative, and you're free to walk out on me whenever you wish. But what will you do then? You'll have no money and nowhere to go. That means you'll wind up in the only place that's open to you—one of the many brothels for which New Orleans is noted."

Millicent, suddenly frightened at the picture he painted, began to weep.

Karl reached out and slapped her hard across the face. "Your tears won't win you any sympathy from me," he said harshly. "Stop that crying!"

Not knowing that the sight of feminine tears drove him into a frenzy, she wept still harder. Suddenly he reached out, caught hold of one of her wrists, and twisted her arm behind her back. "Damn you!" he shouted. "I told you to stop crying!"

She thought he intended to wrench her arm from its socket. The pain was excruciating, but she managed, somehow, to stem the flow of tears.

Having resorted to physical abuse, Karl was incapable of stopping. He twisted her arm still harder, and moaning because of the intense pain, she collapsed onto the bed.

"I go when and where I please," he told her roughly. "Hereafter, you'll keep your thoughts on the subject to yourself, and if you don't like what I'm doing, you'll still smile and keep up a front as though you're enjoying life with me. I have no intention of supporting you if you're going to complain all the time, make life miserable for me, and get yourself all red-eyed in the process."

Grinding her teeth together until her jaw ached, Millicent continued to stifle her sobs.

"Be glad I don't throw you out into the street," he said. "From now on, be grateful for any attention that I may pay you, and act accordingly. I expect you to be ingenious in the ways that you display your gratitude to me." He gave her arm a final, excruciating wrench. Then, after examining himself in the mirror, he left the suite, slamming the door behind him.

Burying her face in her pillow, Millicent gave in to her feelings and wept at length, sobbing hard. Ultimately, she cried herself out, then, rising dully, went to her dressing table, where she removed all her cosmetics. In her misery, she had forgotten all about Jean-Pierre's offers of kindness, and she believed she had no one to advise her, nowhere to go for help. She felt totally trapped. She would be forced to do as Karl had demanded and go along with whatever he did, pretending that she liked it. Never had her future seemed so bleak.

*   *   *

The house was located in an old, middle-class, Creole section of New Orleans and had a wrought-iron balcony on the second floor overlooking a small, informal garden. The balcony opened onto a large, simply furnished chamber, and into it, carrying a tray of food, came a hard-faced young man who was unaccustomed to the role of nurse that he was being obliged to play.

"Here's your noon dinner, Domino," he said. "It ain't much with all that mush in it, but we're fixing exactly what the doctor said you could have."

Domino, his face pale, his head swathed in bandages, struggled to a sitting position in the four-poster bed. "I'm grateful for every bite of food the doctors allow me to eat," he said. "I'm gathering strength day by day, and that's all that matters."

"I'm sure you're right, boss," the young man replied, placing the tray in his superior's lap.

"I get chills," Domino said as he began to eat, "every time I think of that woman's scream deflecting Kellerman's aim. Another quarter of an inch and the bullet would have gone into my brain and finished me. That was as close a call as I'll ever have." He shuddered and ate more rapidly.

The younger man shifted his weight uncomfortably from foot to foot. He was under instructions to discuss whatever Domino wished to talk about, with one exception. Under no circumstances was he to refer to the incident in which the gang leader had almost lost his life. He had no idea what he was to do when Domino insisted on raising the subject himself.

The older man grimaced as he downed a glass of fruit juice. "I wonder how soon the doctors will let me have some whiskey to drink again," he said, and his sigh hung in the air.

His young associate knew the question required no answer and was relieved.

The gang leader quickly finished his meal, devouring every bite of the food. He was behaving like a model patient because he knew that the more closely he followed the orders of his physician, the sooner he would enjoy a complete recovery.

As the young man took the lunch tray and left the room, Domino sat back and reflected how he would repay Karl Kellerman for his treachery. The gang leader had begun by instructing his associates to keep completely mum in regard to the state of their employer's health following the shocking incident in the gambling hall; that way no one would know if Domino was alive or dead. He wanted Karl Kellerman to spend his days in a fool's paradise, thinking he had disposed of the crime leader, when in the meantime Domino would be planning ways to dispose of Kellerman that would cause him the most prolonged agony possible. Domino didn't yet know exactly what he would do to the man, but when the time was right, Karl Kellerman would suffer the tortures of the damned.

IV

Edward Blackstone had booked passage for his party on board the *Mississippi Lady*, an elegant paddle-wheeler that was a combined passenger and cargo ship. Ordinarily the voyage from Memphis to New Orleans on such a vessel would have been a delight from beginning to end, but Edward was too preoccupied and too anxious to find Karl Kellerman. Consequently, he was in no mood to enjoy the serene beauty of the journey down the Mississippi, nor could he appreciate the delights of such river towns as Natchez and Baton Rouge.

Tommie made no attempts to persuade Edward to relax. She was aware of his single-minded devotion to duty, and she recognized his need to find Millicent and to persuade her to give up the abandoned life that she was leading. Until he achieved that goal, everything else was secondary to him.

Even Edward's constant companion, Robin Hood, the little monkey dressed to resemble the hero of the

British legend of the Middle Ages, failed to amuse Edward these days. So Tommie paid more attention to the animal than she usually did, took care of his feeding, and kept him with her for long periods.

At last, the party arrived in New Orleans and went straight to their hotel. While they were settling into their rooms, Edward went down to the lobby and consulted with a hotel employee as to the whereabouts of Dugald's Bar, which he proposed to visit that same night. He got directions on how to get to the place, and then he returned to the suite that he and his companions occupied. Jim and Randy awaited him in the parlor.

"I think," Edward said to them, "that we should eat an early supper tonight."

"Good," Jim replied.

"Then we can set out immediately for the saloon that Karl Kellerman owns," Randy proposed.

Edward shook his head. "I'm sorry to disappoint you, gentlemen, especially after you've traveled such a great distance in order to help recover Millicent, but as I mentioned, I believe I should face Kellerman alone at this first meeting. Since I've met him previously, I think I know a little something about him. I don't want this initial meeting to get his back up. I'm sure I'll accomplish a great deal more if I go to him calmly, and quietly inquire about Millicent's whereabouts. If it should prove necessary, then you shall certainly come with me to a second meeting, but I hope that it won't be necessary."

Jim Randall smiled ruefully and fingered the

butt of the Colt repeating pistol that he carried in a holster on his belt. "I've got to admit that I'm disappointed, Edward, and that I've been spoiling for a fight with the no-good rotter who ran off with Millicent without marrying her. But I agree that it's better if he cooperates with us voluntarily rather than by our using fists and firearms, so I suppose that means that I've got to back off and give you the benefit of a first meeting with the devil alone."

"I'll be on my guard, never fear," Edward told them, "and thank you for your confidence, gentlemen. I can assure you that I won't let you down."

The door that led to Tommie Harding's bedchamber opened, and the young woman, who had already changed into a simple but attractive black dress for supper, came into the parlor. Jim and Randy, reasoning that she and Edward might want to spend some time alone, discreetly retired to the room that they shared.

"You look lovely this evening," Edward told her when they were by themselves.

She inclined her head demurely. "Thank you, sir." Then she hastened to add, "I think this dress will be quite appropriate for our meeting tonight with Kellerman."

"Whether or not the dress is appropriate is a moot point," he said. "As I mentioned earlier, I don't want anyone coming with me."

Tommie looked as though he had slapped her across the face. "I don't understand," she said. "I know Kellerman every bit as well as you do. After the death of de Cordova, when he was still a police officer, Kellerman spent a long time interrogating me on my father's boat. I also spoke to him at length at supper that same night."

"I can't deny anything you've said," Edward told her, "but all the same, this isn't a social occasion. I'm calling on Kellerman to settle a serious matter, and he's got to be made to recognize the validity of my demand. If you come with me, the whole tenor of the meeting will be different. I want you to stay right here in the hotel and not budge from this suite until I get back. From all I've heard, New Orleans can be a very tough town for a woman alone, and if I'm forced to leave your side tonight for any reason, you'd be totally unprotected."

"You sound," she said indignantly, "as though I've spent my whole life in cotton batting. I'll have you know that I've traveled up and down the Missouri River with my father, visiting every town on the water, and by that I mean every rough frontier community. I can assure you they're all a darn sight tougher and nastier than New Orleans. Relatively speaking, this is a community for ladies and gentlemen, and I can promise you, I get along here just fine!"

Edward had enough problems on his mind without being forced to worry about Tommie's welfare, too. "You may be perfectly right," he said. "The streets of New Orleans may be as safe as those in London, but all the same, I want you to stay indoors tonight and not to leave the hotel, and I expect you to abide by my word."

Tommie became infuriated. "What gives you the right to give me orders?" she demanded.

Edward controlled his own temper with a great effort. "My concern for your safety and well-being gives me every right to look after you," he said, "and to ask you in the name of common sense to behave yourself. It was only with the gravest reservations that I allowed you to accompany me even this far in the first place." His tone softened, and he took her hands in his. "I'm not regretting for a moment that you're here; I love you, and I want you with me all the time. If I thought it was to our advantage to take you with me, I'd certainly take you with me tonight. Under the circumstances, however, I find nothing to be gained. Be good enough to reconcile yourself to the need to stay here in the hotel, safe and sound, and to keep Robin Hood company during the few hours that I'll be gone!"

Tommie said nothing, but inside she was still seething about Edward's command to remain in the hotel suite all evening. Having acted as chief of her father's crew on countless Missouri River voyages, she had enjoyed a measure of independence rare to most women in the age in which she lived. She had learned to take care of herself when danger threatened, and consequently, she vowed that nothing would stop her from following Edward when he went out to see Karl Kellerman.

They ate their dinner in the hotel dining room, and as soon as Edward left them—with Jim and Randy heading for the card room to enjoy a game of

poker while they waited for Edward's return—Tommie
went up to their suite and quickly threw a long, dark
gray cape over her shoulders. Before she could get
out the door, however, Robin Hood leaped onto one
shoulder and clung to her. It was impossible for her
to disengage the animal quickly, so she had to make
the best of things by allowing the monkey to accompany her. If she took time to pry him loose and leave
him in the suite, Edward would be out of sight by
the time she reached the street.

So with the little monkey—clad in a green dou-
blet and a matching hat with a jaunty feather in
it—clinging to her shoulder, Tommie followed Edward and, staying in the shadows, made her way
behind him toward the waterfront district. Neither
Tommie nor Edward knew it, of course, but Millicent Randall had every intention of following Karl
Kellerman that same night and determining to her
own satisfaction whether he was being unfaithful to
her or whether he was really engaging in business.
After his abusive treatment of her that morning, she
had spent a long, introspective day and had ultimately concluded that she needed specific information if she was to take action of any kind. She had to
admit that most of the evidence she had accumulated
to prove Karl's infidelity was circumstantial. She
merely assumed—but did not know for certain—that
he was seeing another woman.

In the back of Millicent's mind, a loose plan was
taking shape. If Karl indeed proved unfaithful to her,
she would slip away and would join Jean-Pierre

Gautier, who, she now saw clearly, would be delighted to help her in every possible way. Jean-Pierre had indicated that he believed Karl was unworthy of her, although he had never said anything specific against him, but his own interest in her was sufficiently great that she knew he would take her in, give her shelter, and provide her with whatever funds she needed. At the very least, she reflected, she had an alternative and was not reduced to sitting in her bedchamber at the Louisiana House wringing her hands helplessly while Karl cavorted with some other woman.

Early that evening, Karl had returned briefly to their hotel suite to wash up and put on some expensive cologne. Millicent was not surprised when he said he was required to go elsewhere on business and that she was to eat supper alone in the hotel dining room. She agreed so quickly and meekly that he was convinced he had taught her a lesson that morning when he had abused her.

Instead of doing as he had bidden, however, she gave him a head start of only a few seconds and then silently followed him into the corridor and down the stairs. She had dressed with special care in a dark, unadorned dress, which she wore with black shoes and stockings. Over her gown she threw a short, dark cloak.

Fortunately Karl was in no hurry and took his time as he sauntered down the street and headed toward the wharves. Millicent followed him at a safe distance and had no difficulty in keeping pace with him. She raised an eyebrow when she saw the neighborhood becoming shabbier, for she had assumed that he was so fastidious that any woman with whom he chose to associate would have a background of wealth, breeding, and culture.

Various male passersby who saw Millicent heading down the street immediately assumed that she was a prostitute and made verbal advances to her. Terrified, she ignored them.

At last Karl came to Dugald's Bar, which he had been keeping closed during the day, ever since Wallace had been shanghaied. He unlocked the door, entered, and lighted the gas lamps. Taking off his expensive suit jacket and rolling up his sleeves, he went behind the bar and began wiping down the counter with a rag.

Two men now entered the bar and greeted Karl boisterously. Millicent, surreptitiously watching the exchange through the window, had no way of knowing that the pair were Karl's henchmen, both of whom were addicted to opium and depended on him for the money to buy the drug. As a result, they did whatever he wished.

Millicent caught her breath as two other patrons who had been awaiting the opening of the establishment for the night made their appearance and Karl served them. Watching him as he prepared their drinks, the woman felt faint. Karl's regular, frequent absences from her company were not caused by his attentions to another woman. They were due exclu-

sively to the fact that he was working in a saloon
called Dugald's Bar.

Now Millicent was convinced she knew why he
had become so angry when she had accused him of
being unfaithful to her. He had been badly hurt, and
she could not blame him for feeling as he had. She
felt certain she had accused him falsely.

Karl had concealed his vocation from her because he had not wanted her to know that he was
earning a living doing menial work. Obviously he
wanted her to believe that he was plentifully sup-
plied with funds through his various business connec-
tions and had no need to do a common laborer's
work in order to support them in style. Her heart
overflowed with gratitude to him, and at that moment,
she loved him more than ever before. Closing her
eyes and leaning against the building for support,
Millicent was almost overcome by feelings of tender-
ness for Karl. Not only had she misjudged him, she
thought, but he had been motivated in all he had
done only by his love for her.

The two patrons who had entered earlier left the
premises, and a husky, young cargo handler came in,
sat down at the bar, and ordered himself an ale. As
Karl turned away to fill his glass, he exchanged swift
glances with his two henchmen, who were seated
nearby. The newcomer was a splendid specimen and
would be a perfect recruit for Robin Kayross, who
would be paying Dugald's Bar another visit that same
evening.

Karl promptly slipped some knockout drops into

the new arrival's mug and then pushed it across the bar to him. The young man took a few swallows and soon became woozy. Immediately thereafter, he lost consciousness.

As he slumped forward on his stool, sprawling across the bar, Karl signaled to his two confederates. Knowing what was to be done, they were on their feet instantly. They opened the trapdoor to the cellar, carried the unconcious cargo handler down the rickety staircase, then bound him securely hand and foot.

At that moment Millicent entered Dugald's Bar, unaware of what had just taken place, thinking only how wonderful Karl was.

Karl caught his breath and gaped at her. Talking rapidly, she apologized to him profusely for her suspicions, which she admitted were groundless, and she thanked him at length for working to support her while concealing his vocation from her. Relieved by her ignorance, Karl eagerly accepted her interpretation of events and played his part to the hilt. "I'm glad you understand at last," he said. "I'm sorry that I had to get rough with you this morning—"

"Oh, I understand!" Millicent cried, "and I don't blame you in the least."

Karl allowed her to hug him briefly before he led her to a table situated in a far corner at the rear of the room. "I'll get you a cup of coffee. Just be sure you stay out of the way while you're drinking it. I don't want any customers who come in here to think that you're available to them for purposes of their own, so pay no attention to anyone and mind your own business."

"Oh, I will," she said.

"It well may be several hours before I'll have the opportunity to escort you back to the hotel," he said. "As you can imagine, I'm more or less stuck here. Until then, I want you well out of the way."

"Don't worry about me," Millicent told him. "I've already caused you enough troubles, and I'll be very good until you're ready to leave."

He seated her at the corner table, half facing the wall, where she would be unaware if any other customers encountered the same fate as the cargo handler. The thought occurred to Karl that if the need arose, Millicent, in her innocence, could provide him with the perfect alibi for his own evening's activities; he could turn her unexpected appearance to his own advantage.

Millicent sat meekly at the rear corner table, quietly accepting the cup of coffee that Karl brought her and, her eyes downcast, paid no attention to his two henchmen when they returned from the cellar where they had deposited the cargo handler.

Watching Millicent as she sipped her coffee, Karl reflected that his luck was good. He was leading a charmed life; it appeared that he could do no wrong.

Edward Blackstone had no idea that he was being followed, so it didn't occur to him to turn and look back. He was not in a hurry, and as he went out into the busy streets of New Orleans, Tommie had no difficulty in following a short distance behind.

As the neighborhood changed block by block, she became uneasy and was annoyed with herself because she had failed to take any weapons. She discovered that she was strangely comforted by the presence on her shoulder of Robin Hood. The little monkey could offer her scant protection if some stranger assaulted her, but at least the animal was company of some kind.

Eventually Edward reached his destination. Pausing to peer in through the window, he saw Karl Kellerman very much alive and in command of himself and his surroundings, standing behind the bar. Millicent was nowhere in view because the table at which she sat was just out of sight from the window.

Edward now went into the saloon. Tommie immediately moved forward and replaced him at the window.

When he saw Edward, Kellerman instantly realized that the Englishman was searching for his cousin, and that once he found her, he would try to learn about Kellerman's affairs. His mind racing, Kellerman knew he could not tolerate an investigation, which might unmask him and send him to prison.

Instantly alert, Kellerman called out softly to his two henchmen, who were sitting at the far end of the bar. "See that tall, fancy dude standing in the entrance?" he demanded. "He's dangerous! Knock him out and dispose of him, but be careful. He's likely to do you some real damage if he suspects you're after him."

Millicent turned and was electrified when she saw Edward standing in the doorway. She heard the instructions that Karl gave the pair at the bar, and though she had no idea what Karl was up to, she now realized that her original instinct had been right: Whatever it was, Karl was up to no good. Clearly Edward had made this surprise appearance at Dugald's Bar in order to find her, and Karl was determined to prevent him from achieving his goal.

Jumping to her feet and moving forward, Millicent began to signal frantically to Edward, warning him to beware of the two men at the bar. Her gestures were plain to Tommie, who was watching the developing scene outside the window. Edward, however, misinterpreted her signals. He was not suffering from any lack of alertness, but he was so delighted to see Millicent that he thought she actually appeared to be welcoming him, and he started to go toward her.

Tommie wanted to cry out as the pair at the bar separated and began to rush Edward from behind.

Millicent's signals became frantic, and she called out, "Edward! Edward, look . . ." Ignoring Kellerman at the bar, Edward continued heading toward her.

Tommie was paralyzed by fright, her heart rising to her mouth as she watched one of the pair, armed with a length of leather-covered lead pipe, strike Edward sharply across the back of the head. He became unconscious and sagged to the floor.

The pair caught hold of him, and producing lengths of rope, they expertly began to bind his ankles and wrists. They relieved him of his pistol and found under his coat jacket the little derringer he kept concealed there. As a final touch, they tied a gag around his mouth. Then, still moving swiftly, one of them opened the trapdoor to the cellar. Then rejoining his companion, he and the other man picked up Edward, carried his unconscious body down to the foot of the rickety staircase, then came up again and carefully closed the trapdoor behind them.

Millicent was so stunned that she was incapable of moving. When she looked at Karl, she saw an unfathomable expression in his eyes, and something in his smile made her blood run cold.

"If you'd stayed at the Louisiana Hotel, as I told you to do," he said, "you wouldn't be in any trouble right now. But you were curious, and now you've found out far more than is good for you. You may find it hard to believe this, but I have nothing personal against you. Unfortunately for you, however, you know enough to create one hell of a lot of trouble for me in the wrong places, so I've got to protect myself. I hope you'll understand." He turned to his two henchmen. "Tie her up, gag her, and put her downstairs, boys," he said. "But there's no need for any rough games with her. She won't put up any fight. Treat her gently while I figure out what's to be done with her."

The men turned to her immediately, and she offered them no resistance as they tied her hands and feet and tied a gag around her mouth. Then they opened the trapdoor again and, between them, carried her down the precariously wobbly staircase to the cellar below. There the horrified Millicent saw Edward and a stranger trussed and gagged, both of them lying unconscious on the floor. The henchmen exchanged a look, and instead of stretching her out on the cement floor beside their other victims, they propped her against the nearest wall and left her in a standing position.

Then the trapdoor above closed again, and Millicent was plunged into darkness.

Tommie Harding, still peering in surreptitiously through the window, faced a terrible dilemma. Seeing Kellerman's hirelings return to the main floor of the bar after depositing Millicent below, she realized that the same fate quite possibly awaited her if she revealed her presence. What could a lone, unarmed woman and a small monkey possibly do against two armed thugs and Kellerman?

Equally to the point, she was in a part of New Orleans that was totally alien to her, and she could wander aimlessly for a long time before she stumbled onto the nearest police headquarters. Common sense told her that neither Edward nor Millicent would be held indefinitely in the cellar of Dugald's Bar; eventually they would be moved elsewhere. Therefore, if she left now and sought help from the police, there well might be no sign of either her fiancé or his cousin in the bar by the time she returned. Knowing Kellerman, she realized that he could swear to the

authorities that he had seen neither Edward nor
Millicent, and there would be no way on earth that
she could prove she was telling the truth.

Consequently, she had to stay and keep watch,
no matter what happened. It was the only way that
she could try to protect Edward and his cousin.
Wherever they were taken, she would follow them
there, and perhaps then she would have a better
chance to summon the help of the police.

Tommie suddenly realized that a passerby had
halted, and she tried to shrink against the wall adjacent to the saloon's window. However, the man sauntered closer, studying her carefully. She didn't want
to look directly at him but was able to make out that
he was wearing seamen's garb.

"How are you tonight?" he asked, his English
slightly accented.

Tommie made no reply.

"You look very lonely," he said, coming still
closer.

"You've made a mistake, sir," Tommie said, ad-
dressing a point in space above and behind him. "I'm
not the type of woman you appear to think me."

The sailor laughed easily. "All I'm thinking," he
replied, "is that you're very pretty and very lonely."
He reached out tentatively for her.

Conquering the feeling of panic that welled up
within her, Tommie drew back. "I must beg you to
be careful," she said desperately. "My monkey has
been trained, and he will scratch your eyes out."

The sailor laughed derisively. Robin Hood heard

the man's derogatory tone, felt the tension in the air, and began to grimace and chatter angrily.

"There, you see?" Tommie demanded. "There's nothing I can do to stop him." The monkey continued to chatter even more rapidly.

The sailor looked dubious. He had no desire to test the animal, however, and so he reluctantly drew back, stared at Tommie for another instant or two, then turned on his heel and made his way down the street. Tommie stroked the animal's head softly. "That was wonderful, Robin," she whispered, "just wonderful."

Pressing close to the outside wall of the saloon, Tommie peered through a corner of the dusty window and saw Kellerman and his henchmen laughing boisterously. She found herself praying that they would move Edward and Millicent soon. Since she alone knew of their plight, she alone was in a position to save them. No matter how dangerous, she had to stick out her mission to the finish.

Toby Holt planned to pay a visit to San Francisco in order to confer with Chet Harris and Wong Ke, the enormously successful businessmen who controlled so many enterprises on the Pacific coast. They knew more about the existence and activities of the tongs than did anyone else, and he wanted to learn whatever he could from them.

On the eve of his departure from the Portland area, his wife Clarissa gave a small dinner party. The guests included his sister Cindy and his closest friend and business associate, Rob Martin. With Rob came his second wife, Kale, a reformed courtesan who was a stunning beauty, with violet eyes and long blue-black hair gathered in a bun at the nape of her neck.

They drank glasses of sherry before supper, and Kale dominated the conversation. "You don't know," she said, "how fortunate we are to be living in the American West, where people are taking advantage of the trend toward women's suffrage."

"You're right, Kale. State universities are opening their doors to women now," Cindy said. "Eventually the movement may spread all over the country."

"The success of women's suffrage is so great it can't be reversed," Kale said. "People like Susan B. Anthony, Elizabeth Cady Stanton, and Lucy Stone—who has flatly refused to take her husband's name of Blackwell—are leading what has become a positive crusade."

"How far do you expect women to carry their crusade?" Toby asked.

"The frontiers are unlimited," Kale replied. "Once women start being educated on an equal basis with men, they'll enter the professions. There'll be lady doctors and lady lawyers, as well as teachers. In various states here in the West, women can already vote on such matters as local bond issues and local taxation. Laugh if you want to, but I predict that the day isn't that far distant when we'll have universal female suffrage."

"I'm in favor of it," Toby said. "The way I see this thing is that any woman who wants to can learn as much about national and international issues as any man."

"Hear, hear!" his wife said.

"You're being awfully quiet, Rob," Kale said. "Do you disagree with us?"

Tall, red-haired Rob Martin swirled his glass of sherry, seemingly lost in thought. At last he replied, "It's not that I disagree with what you're all saying. It's just that you, Kale, have come a long way. You have traveled a hard road in order to win acceptance from the people of Portland, and I hate to see you setting yourself back. Some men have no use for women's suffrage, and I hate to see them taking out their anger on you."

"If they do," Kale said with spirit, "it's because they're shortsighted and ignorant of what's at stake. It isn't accidental, you know, that I've become a champion of women's suffrage. When I was a girl I was terribly ambitious, and my family had nothing—no money and no influence. I knew of only one path I could follow to become relatively well off financially and attain a measure of power, if not prestige. I became a prostitute. Oh, I hated myself whenever I stopped to think about it, but my goal remained steady and unvarying. Obviously, I didn't obtain real peace of mind until I left my profession and married, but I'm damned if I want my stepdaughter—or anyone else's daughter—to suffer because she's a female. If we're really living in the land of the free—and I believe we are—let's prove it by giving our daughters every opportunity that we offer to our sons!"

"You put it so well, Kale," Cindy said in admiration, "that you leave nothing for Clarissa or me to add. I'm glad I'm a woman, and I'm glad I am living in a time when we'll see the results of our fight for suffrage bear fruit."

"All I ask," Rob told her, "is that you do nothing to jeopardize the acceptance that you've struggled so hard to win."

"I agree to that," Kale said, "provided I do nothing to injure my self-respect. That comes first."

Her husband agreed, and everyone present thought the issue was resolved. No one had any idea of the problems that would face Kale in the months that stretched out ahead.

The following day, Toby left for San Francisco. The stagecoach ride from Portland was long and tiresome. Finally arriving he checked into his hotel and for once got a night's sleep after days on the road. Early the following day, he sat in the wood-paneled, richly furnished office of the millionaire Chet Harris, explaining all about the documents that incriminated Kung Lee's tong and that had been sent on to General Blake. Also present at the meeting was Chet's partner, Wong Ke. The big, somewhat over-weight Chet and the slight, ascetic-looking, elderly Chinese man made a strange pair. They had met years earlier during the California gold rush, had made a fortune together, and had become close friends as well as business partners.

Their offices were located on the heights overlooking San Francisco Bay, and as Toby listened to Ke, he looked at the magnificent panorama spread out below him.

"American society," Ke was saying, "is becoming increasingly industrialized and therefore more complex, so it stands to reason that as immigrants from other lands come here, they cling to old ways, many of them bad, as forms of self-protection. This is certainly true of the Chinese, who have transferred their powerful tongs, or secret protective societies, from Canton and Shanghai to the shores of North America."

"Have they always been as vicious as they are here?" Toby asked.

Wong Ke shook his head. "No," he said. "They began as secret patriotic societies during the Opium Wars with European powers. As our Chinese cities were occupied, the patriots went underground and opposed the rule of the foreign devils in private. Unfortunately, by the time the tongs spread across the Pacific, they were already involved in illegal activities and were using terrorist tactics to control people. The vicious beating they recently administered to me in Portland is typical of their methods. They have no place in America and serve no useful function in American society. I'm opposed to them and to their methods."

"Do they specialize in any types of illegal activity?" Toby asked.

The elderly Chinese man shook his head. "The

modern tong reaches out its tentacles into every phase of Chinese society in the United States. Nothing is immune to them, nothing escapes their interest. They earn large sums of money from the importation of opium and from illegal immigration. They collect extortion money from local merchants, and they have a stranglehold on prostitution and gambling in every Chinatown in America. They hound restaurant owners, and they try to intimidate businessmen like me. Unfortunately for them, I have a tough old hide, and I don't scare easily."

"What can you tell me," Toby asked, "about individual tongs?"

"There are several with headquarters in Canton and branches in such cities as Shanghai and Hong Kong, the British colony. Several have successfully managed the leap across the Pacific Ocean so far, but there is one that has most of the power, wealth, and influence in the United States. Its name is a closely guarded secret, and I don't think that the name matters much to outsiders. However, what matters is that the authorities now have in their possession the documents that were being delivered to General Blake, documents that could help implicate the tong in illegal activities. As you've learned, the head of the organization is a man named Kung Lee. We can tell you where to locate him—we have our own sources of information—but let me say that if and when you meet him for the first time, you'll be impressed by him as a cultured, witty, and sophisticated gentleman. But don't let his surface manner fool you. He has his delicate fingers in crimes of every sort, from illegal immigration to gambling and prostitution. He rules his empire with an iron hand. It's said that he's as powerful in his way as the dowager empress is in China, and to call the organization that he rules an empire is no exaggeration."

"He must indeed control a great fortune," Toby said.

Wong Ke nodded emphatically as he pressed his fingertips together. "That which Kung Lee rules," he said, "is truly an empire and worth many millions of dollars. No one knows exactly what its real worth is, just as no one really knows how extensive its roots extend beneath the surface of American society. All I know for certain is that Kung Lee's tong cannot be eradicated overnight. That's an impossible achievement."

Chet entered the conversation for the first time. "In order to better understand the makeup of the tong hierarchy," he said, "you've got to know that Kung Lee, like any absolute ruler, is surrounded by advisers, aides, bodyguards, and hatchet men. His person is regarded as almost sacred, and he has layers of helpers who shield him not only from the general public but from his enemies."

"Let me tell you, Toby, about Ho Tai, who is just one of Kung Lee's bodyguards," Ke said. "He's a burly, short, squat man, hideously ugly, and is the most dangerous of foes. I happen to know that he underwent long training as an assassin in Canton and in Hong Kong. He is responsible to no one but Kung Lee, and his one aim in life is do the bidding of his employer."

"I don't know whether Ho Tai has earned his notorious reputation," Chet interjected, "but he is said to be the most dangerous of hatchet men and the deadliest of knife throwers. He's allegedly killed many opponents. No one knows the exact number, and the stories are undoubtedly exaggerated. Nevertheless, he's a killer with a long list of victims."

"If his misdeeds are so well known," Toby said, "I'm surprised the authorities don't have him picked up and sent to prison."

"It has been impossible," Wong Ke said, "to gather any substantial evidence against the man. Witnesses are afraid to testify, and no one will speak up against him. He is known to enjoy the complete confidence and protection of Kung Lee, and that is all that he needs in order to do as he pleases."

"I can see where Mr. Kung Lee and I are headed on a collision course," Toby said, smiling grimly. "First, you were attacked, then my sister was attacked, and so was I. I think the time has come for me to meet Mr. Kung Lee face to face and exchange a few words with him."

Chet sighed. "I could close my eyes," he said, "and swear that I hear Whip Holt speaking. I thought he was the only man on earth who didn't know the meaning of fear and was prepared to step into a lion's den at a moment's notice, but he *wasn't* the only one. He has a son who is exactly like him, who also doesn't know the meaning of fear. I hate violence, and I shudder to think of what may happen when you and Kung Lee come face to face."

"I don't know if anyone has ever had the courage to tell him what people think of him," Toby said, "but we'll find out soon enough what happens when he's forced to listen to the truth!"

It was a typical morning in the Chinatown curio shop. Earlier, several tourists from the East Coast had visited the establishment and made predictable purchases of carved chopsticks and of pseudo–temple bells.

Quiet had reigned for an hour or two, and now a lone visitor wandered into the shop. Certainly he did not look like a tourist. In his late twenties and heavily bronzed as a result of spending the better part of his life outdoors, he was tall and sinewy. His broad-brimmed western hat rode on the back of his head, and his attire, from open-throated shirt to trousers stuffed into leather boots, indicated that he was a working westerner who probably lived on a ranch.

The handles of two knives protruded from his belt, which was filled with bullets. Two Colt .44 repeating pistols were hanging in their holsters. The weapons were not new, and it was apparent from a glance at the handles that they had seen much use.

Instead of examining the many objects for sale

piled up on the shelves in the shop, the stranger glanced around the place and then approached the old man who was ostensibly the proprietor. The Chinese man found himself looking into the palest blue eyes he had ever seen. They had a mesmeric quality and seemed to bore into him.

"I am here," Toby Holt announced, "to see Kung Lee."

The old man was stunned, and while he gestured feebly, his young companion raced out and hurried off up the stairs.

Toby, guessing the young man's destination, appeared in no hurry. He strolled around the shop, seeming completely at ease.

After a few minutes' wait, a short, squat Chinese man, his ugly face covered with scars, appeared in the door. "What you want?" he demanded.

Toby's expression did not change. "You must be Ho Tai," he said mildly.

The Chinese bodyguard's eyes gleamed malevolently, but he made no reply.

"I didn't come here to see you," Toby said, his tone still civil. "I made it very clear that the purpose of my visit is to see Kung Lee. Will you be good enough to tell him I'm here, please?"

Still saying nothing, Ho Tai flexed his fingers.

Toby remained pleasant, but a firm note crept into his voice. "I know that Kung Lee makes his headquarters in this building," he said. "I've also gone to the trouble of finding out that he's in town, so the chances are good that he's under this roof at this moment. I have no quarrel with you, nor with anyone, but I intend to see him. Be good enough to tell him that Toby Holt is here." His hands dropped to the butts of his pistols. "Tell him now," he suggested, a hint of urgency in his voice.

The old man backed away nervously and put a table laden with curios between himself and the other two men. He was ready to duck down to the floor in the event that a shooting match developed.

Ho Tai was in no way intimidated by Toby, but he was under standing instructions to preserve the facade of peace, if not peace itself. "I find out if Kung Lee see you," he announced, his tone surly, and without further ado he whirled and made his way up the stairs.

Watching him, Toby noted that the bodyguard was exceptionally light on his feet.

After a very brief wait, Ho Tai reappeared at the landing on the second floor. "You come now," he said.

Toby mounted the stairs under the bodyguard's watchful, alert gaze.

"You give me guns and knife," Ho Tai commanded, extending a hand.

Toby looked at him and laughed. "There is no way that I'll surrender my weapons," he said. "Wherever I go, they go."

Ho Tai backed down and continued to practice peace. Shrugging, he led the way down a narrow corridor on creaking floorboards and then stood aside when they came to a closed door at the end of the hallway. He knocked and, opening the door, rested one hand on the hilt of a light but deadly throwing knife that he carried in his belt.

Toby knew the bodyguard was ready to intervene instantly if it should prove necessary, but he paid no further attention to the man. Instead he concentrated on the Chinese man, apparently about sixty years of age, who sat behind a large desk. Attired in black mandarin robes, Kung Lee was smiling, his expression revealing none of his hatred for this unwanted visitor. He waved Toby to a chair opposite where he himself sat.

Keeping one hand on the hilt of his knife, Ho Tai moved to a convenient corner and stood within full view of the visitor's chair.

"Thank you for receiving me on such short notice, Mr. Kung," Toby said politely.

"Not at all," the tong leader said, maintaining an air of great civility. "I am honored that a man of your reputation should visit my humble office."

Toby discounted the compliment but nevertheless was gratified that Kung Lee had heard of him. Perhaps his reputation would make his present task somewhat easier.

"I've been looking forward to this meeting with you, Mr. Kung," he said. "I believe that a meeting of the minds will solve a number of potential problems."

"I am aware of no problems, Mr. Holt," Kung replied, and folded his hands.

"I try to take the long view," Toby said blandly.

"My father was partly responsible for the settlement of the West, and I've followed in his footsteps by taking a hand in its development. Therefore, anything that happens in this part of America—for better or for worse—is of interest to me. You might say I make it my business."

"So?" Kung commented politely, and waited for his visitor to continue.

"I'm very fond of the team of financiers, Chet Harris and Wong Ke," he said. "Not only are they old family friends, but it so happens they manage some property that I own. I was naturally quite distressed when Mr. Wong was severely injured in a brutal attack during a recent visit to Portland."

"I heard of the incident," Kung replied blandly. "It was very distressing."

"I wonder," Toby said pleasantly, "if perhaps your distress was caused by the fact that Mr. Wong was merely beaten half to death rather than killed. If he'd been killed outright, there would have been no way to track his attacker. As it happened, the blame for the assault on him is laid completely at your doorstep, Mr. Kung."

The tong leader showed no animosity. "I am sure you realize, Mr. Holt," he said, "that you'd have an exceptionally difficult time proving your allegation in a court of law. Evidence to convict me or my tong is totally lacking."

"You're speaking of evidence presented in the law courts, Mr. Kung, but as you know every bit as well as I do, the West has found it impossible to wait for the long arm of justice to catch up with the development of the country. Again and again we of the West have been forced to take the law into our own hands rather than wait for the courts to act."

"To be sure," Kung Lee replied. "And it is for precisely such reasons that we of the West have found it necessary to defend ourselves. Vigilante justice is all well and good, but those who are falsely accused must be able to stand up in their own defense and drive off their persecutors."

"One of the most fascinating pastimes in this part of the country," Toby replied, "is that of determining who is the persecutor in any given situation. I'm sure that Wong Ke, who almost lost his life as the result of a completely unjustified beating, would insist that he had been the victim, and I must say I agree wholeheartedly."

Kung remained silent.

"There's a more recent case that I find equally fascinating," Toby continued, carefully regarding Kung. "A courier employed by the United States government was shot to death near my Oregon ranch while in the process of delivering some documents intended for my stepfather, General Blake, the commander of the Army of the West. The killer—or someone closely associated with him—subsequently tried to attack my sister and then me in vain attempts to gain control of those documents, which implicate the tong headed by you with the smuggling of opium as well as human beings. For your information, Mr. Kung, those papers have been read by various officials and are now safely in General Blake's headquarters at Fort Vancouver."

Kung Lee stared hard at Toby. "You accuse my subordinates and me of murder and of attempted murder, Mr. Holt. These are exceptionally grave charges. Can you substantiate them?"

Toby smiled lazily. "As I've already told you, Mr. Kung, I have no interest in substantiating them in a law court. I'm not an attorney, and I don't know the legalities involved. Let me just say that I'm satisfied in my own mind that you and your tong are guilty, and that's good enough for me. You started this war. I didn't, but I intend to finish it. Either you'll back off and leave well enough alone, or you're in this for a fight to the finish. I wanted to give you fair warning and to find out for my own satisfaction exactly where you stand. As for your toady yonder," he continued, nodding in the direction of Ho Tai, "I urge you to call him off, or he'll find that he's taken a larger bite than he's capable of digesting."

"You go too far, Holt, and you try my patience." For the first time, a semblance of stridency crept into Kung Lee's voice. "I have tried hard to deal civilly and politely with you. I have tried to warn you to stay within the law, to confine your interests to matters that are truly of concern to you, and to steer clear of affairs that are none of your concern. But you have persisted. You have believed the glowing publicity you've acquired as a result of your fights with savage Indians and with stupid criminals on the frontier. You are prying into serious matters that are none of your business. Very well, if you insist on playing with fire, you'll be burned. You have been warned, Holt, so be on your guard from this time forward." He rose to his feet.

Toby stood at the same moment, and they bowed to each other formally.

Ho Tai's hand closed over the hilt of the knife he carried in his hand. Before he had time to draw it, however, Toby struck with lightning speed. He pulled his knife from his belt, and in the same instant, he threw it with dazzling accuracy. It landed in the wooden paneling of the wall no more than a quarter of an inch from Ho Tai's head.

In the same split second, another knife appeared in his hand, and he threw it with equal speed and force. It cut into the arm of Kung Lee's chair and quivered there.

"There's no need to return those knives, gentlemen," Toby said mildly. "I have plenty of others where they came from. Keep them as souvenirs, and whenever you look at them, think of me." He smiled slightly.

The two Chinese men stared at him in amazement.

Bowing again, Toby deliberately turned his back on the pair and took his leave, walking slowly out of the room. He knew he was taking a terrible risk, and the hair on the back of his head bristled when he realized that a knife well might land in his back at any moment. At the same time, however, he knew of no better way to show his contempt for men who relied on terror and threats to operate their empire.

His gamble paid off. Both Kung Lee and Ho Tai were so stunned that they were incapable of taking advantage of the opportunity that Toby contemptuously handed them as he left the room, descended the stairs, and walked into the street.

But the battle lines had been drawn, the unequal feud had been moved into the open, and the next time the principals met, they would fight to the finish.

V

Tommie Harding was weary as she maintained her lonely, dangerous vigil in the street outside Dugald's Bar. But she grew alert when Captain Kayross and several of his loyal crew members appeared in a dilapidated cart pulled by a workhorse, and she drew farther back into the shadows. Robin Hood still sat on her shoulder, not understanding what was happening and clinging to her as someone who was familiar to him in a strange world.

Meanwhile, both Edward Blackstone and the other male victim lay unconscious, bound and gagged on the cellar floor. Millicent Randall, still propped against the wall, was terrified as she heard Kellerman and Kayross come down the rickety stairs and begin discussing her.

"Here's a fine kettle of fish," Kellerman said. "Yonder is a wench with whom I was having an affair. She got nosy, and her curiosity led her to find out too damned much about me and my business, so

I had to immobilize her several hours ago. I wonder if you have any use for her."

"We'll soon find out," the sea captain said. Approaching her, he held up a lighted candle to get a better look. Millicent would have pulled away from him but was incapable of movement.

Tearing her blouse open with his free hand, Kayross looked at her breasts intently, prodding them as though she were cattle. Then he reached out and gropingly felt her buttocks.

"She's rather dirty and smudged at the moment," he said, "but she looks as though when she's cleaned and properly made up, she can be quite handsome."

"That's right," Kellerman said. "She's a real beauty."

"Her figure is good, and that's important," the captain declared.

"What do you have in mind?" Kellerman asked.

"The imperial viceroy in Canton," Captain Kayross said, "keeps a large harem in his palace there. He's especially partial to white-skinned girls, but they're much more difficult for him to obtain than are Orientals, as you can imagine. Once he hears that this wench is available, he'll pay any price for her. You and I can share a fortune."

"That solves the problem very nicely," Kellerman said.

The captain was lost in thought for a moment or two. "We'll also have to make certain," he finally said, "that she will be cooperative when I present her to the viceroy. She'll have to learn some Eastern customs, like how and when to kowtow."

"She's very bright," Kellerman said sarcastically. "I'm sure she has the ability to learn whatever will be required of her."

"She'll have the entire Pacific crossing to learn," Kayross replied, "and I have just the right instructor for her. If it's all right with you, we'll transfer her to the *Diana* along with the new indentured seamen, and she can begin taking lessons immediately."

"The sooner the better," Kellerman said indifferently. He and the captain mounted the steps, and when they closed the trapdoor behind them, blackness once again enveloped the interior of the cellar.

Mortification, fear, and violent anger suffused Millicent. She had been stupid beyond belief. First she had become involved with Luis de Cordova, and as if she had not suffered enough in that relationship, she had taken up with Karl Kellerman, who was even more brutal and callous in his treatment of her. The prospect of becoming part of a harem filled her with horror and loathing, but she was helpless, unable to escape what appeared to be her certain destiny. Only the remnants of her shredded pride prevented her from weeping, and as she leaned against the cold, damp stones of the cellar wall, she wished that she would awaken and discover that she had merely dreamed the dreadful situation in which she found herself.

Before long, Kayross and Kellerman returned with the Greek members of the ship's crew. Aided

by Kellerman's two henchmen, they carried the unconscious bodies of the men, along with Millicent
Randall, up the stairs and piled them into the horse-
drawn cart. A tarpaulin concealed the captives from
the gaze of any stray passersby who might be abroad
at this very early hour.

The cart, driven by one of Captain Kayross's
crew members, creaked as it moved off through the
silent city. The captain and his remaining men followed on foot close behind it and kept a wary watch
that proved unnecessary. The streets remained silent
and deserted.

Only Tommie Harding was aware of what was
happening. Following the cart at a distance, she was
careful to stay in the shadows at all times. As she
walked, she kept looking for a constable, but no
policemen appeared, nor did anyone else.

The cart rumbled down the cobblestones, and
the thumping of the workhorse's hooves seemed to
obliterate the pounding of Tommie's heart. After
walking for what seemed like a considerable distance,
Tommie marveled at what she had done so far. She
felt certain that her luck would run out at any time
and that her presence would be discovered.

A huge shape loomed up ahead in the murky
night, and although Tommie was thoroughly familiar
with waterfront districts, she was so tired that it
took her several seconds to realize that they had
arrived at the docks and that the bulk was that of a
steam-propelled freighter.

The workhorse halted beside a gangway that was

lowered from the main deck of the vessel to the wharf, and crew members immediately transferred the captives to the ship.

If Tommie had been thinking clearly, she would have marked the name and the exact location of the ship and would have gone off in search of the police. But her long night's vigil had dulled her mind, and she could think only that she had to follow Edward at all costs and know where he was being concealed. Awaiting her opportunity, she sneaked on board and crept behind a mound of cargo lashed to the deck. Looking out from this vantage point, she searched in vain for Edward.

She had no way of knowing that Millicent had been taken to one of the cabins on the upper deck that was reserved for passengers while Edward and the other male prisoner had been taken below to the hold, where they would remain until they regained consciousness. But Tommie knew enough about ships to realize that she could not wander where she pleased in search of Edward. At any moment she could unexpectedly come face to face with one of the officers or seamen.

All at once, a terrible sense of panic assailed her. She had been concentrating so hard on her problem of finding Edward that everything else had been obliterated from her mind, and only now did it occur to her that Robin Hood was no longer perched on her shoulder. The little monkey had vanished since coming on board the freighter.

*   *   *

When Edward Blackstone finally awakened, he was instantly alert. Smelling the stale air and feeling the hard deck beneath his prone body, he knew at once that he was in grave danger. He confirmed this impression when he discovered that his wrists and ankles were bound. An ache at the back of his skull told him that he had probably succumbed to a sharp blow. It was dark in the hold, but the smell of the sea and the slight motion told Edward that he was on board a vessel. He knew also that Karl Kellerman was responsible for his predicament.

Edward found that he had limited mobility but could move his hands up and down several inches. Thus he was able to reach into the hip pocket of his trousers and was infinitely relieved to discover that he still had possession of the small knife that he always kept hidden.

Wedging the open-bladed knife into a crack between two floorboards in the deck, Edward began to press and rub his wrist bonds against the sharp blade.

Suddenly he was startled when something soft landed on his legs, and he looked down to see a small monkey dressed in green perching there. Robin Hood began to chatter delightedly.

Edward had no time to wonder how Robin Hood had gotten there. Moving his wrists up and down against the knife, he continued to saw frantically. Soon the strands of rope began to part, and ultimately they fell away and Edward's arms came free. Quickly removing his gag and untying his legs, Edward picked up the knife and cautioned the monkey to remain silent. Then he looked around. Seeing the other man now awake and cursing as he found himself in the same predicament as Edward's, he cut away his bonds. The man thanked him profusely and said his name was Sam. Edward introduced himself. Meanwhile, Robin Hood leaped up to his accustomed perch on Edward's shoulder.

Neither Edward nor the man he liberated knew why they had been brought to this place, but they were determined to find out. With Edward in the lead, they opened a heavy metal door and found themselves in front of a mammoth furnace, where Wallace Dugald and three other unfortunate wretches were shoveling coal into the open maw of a blazing boiler. All four were chained.

Experimenting swiftly, Edward managed to strike a link on each man's chain with the sharp blade of a heavy metal coal shovel, using such force that the link parted. Thereafter, it was relatively easy to pry the two ends apart and set the imprisoned men free.

Rivers of perspiration cut through the grime of coal dust on Wallace's face and torso as he said in a voice so choked with emotion that it was barely audible, "Thanks be to the Almighty for this deliverance. I thank you, Lord, for hearing my prayer and giving me the chance to even the score with Karl Kellerman. You may hold me to my bargain, Lord: I don't care what becomes of me once I've had the chance to kill him in a way that will repay him for the terrible misery he has caused me. I swear to you, Lord, I won't rest. I'll work day and night until I've obtained vengeance against this evil Kellerman, who is a blot on all that is good, for your sake and in your name. Amen."

Even though it was blazing hot in front of the big furnace, a cold chill crept up Edward's spine as he heard the words of the enraged Scotsman.

Millicent had been shoved into a cabin that at first glance was both spacious and comfortable. It had two portholes that overlooked the Mississippi River and was furnished with a large, bare-mattressed bed, a dressing table amply stocked with cosmetics and perfumes, a table, several chairs, and a chest of drawers.

A Greek crew member had escorted her into the cabin. On his heels was a short Malay woman, slender but wiry, whose age was almost impossible to guess. She was brown-skinned, with dark eyes, and she was dressed in a simple, knee-length garment that stressed her scrawniness. She wore no shoes but seemed to enjoy oversized jewelry, for she had on large hoop earrings, and several massive bracelets. Her head was wrapped in a turban. In her belt she carried a long kris, a sword with a razor-sharp, weighty blade, and in one hand she carried a wooden rod that was about a yard long.

Captain Kayross now appeared and spoke to the woman at length, glancing frequently at Millicent and gesturing toward her as he explained her identity and what he had in mind for her teacher. Listening intently, the Malay woman nodded from time to time. Her eyes gleamed, and a hint of a smile appeared at the corners of her thin lips.

When the captain left, the woman moved swiftly. She took the gag from Millicent's mouth and cut the bonds that tied her ankles together, but left her hands still bound. "You sit!" she commanded, and pointed to the dressing-table stool.

Millicent moved to the seat and sank onto it gratefully. She was extremely weary after her long night of tension and captivity.

The woman went to a cabinet, took a jug from it, and removed the stopper. She lifted the container to her mouth and, after taking a large swallow of the contents, wiped her mouth with the back of her free hand. Then she held the jug up to the prisoner's mouth. "You drink now!" she said. The contents had a nauseating odor, and Millicent's stomach turned over. Unable to use her hands to get rid of the offending jug, she averted her face.

The woman lost patience. Grabbing Millicent's hair, she tugged fiercely, forcing her mouth open, and poured the liquid into her.

Millicent's mouth felt bruised, and the liquid soaked the front of her clothes, but she had to admit that the beverage, whatever it was, gave her a measure of renewed strength.

The Malay woman jerked the prisoner around to face her and began applying makeup. She paused briefly when she was almost finished, and Millicent was stunned when she caught a glimpse of herself in the mirror. Her lips were painted dark red, her eyes were almond-shaped, and her high cheekbones were emphasized with rouge. The overall effect was to give her a distinctly Oriental appearance.

Chuckling to herself, the woman removed her kris from her belt and, slashing with it, cut Millicent's clothes from her body from head to toe. Her attire fell away, leaving her completely naked, and the woman even took her shoes and threw them out the nearest porthole into the Mississippi River.

Then, after deliberately cutting the bonds at Millicent's wrists, the woman stood, went to the cabin door, and unlocked it. "I no keep you tied and locked up here," she said. "You go any time you want go. Many men on board. They catch you and fix plenty good." She exploded in laughter.

Millicent knew that the woman spoke the truth. If she appeared on deck, naked or otherwise, the sailors would be certain to catch and rape her. She was confined to the cabin as surely as she would have been had she still been bound hand and foot and had the door been secured.

The woman stood in front of her with arms folded, the wooden rod in one hand. "You be slave to viceroy," she said. "Now we practice. You be slave, I be viceroy. You kowtow!" She indicated that Millicent was to make physical obeisance before her. Startled and uncertain as to what was expected of her, Millicent started to move slowly.

The Malay woman prodded her viciously with the rod, then began to beat her unmercifully across the buttocks with it. The pain was excruciating. Millicent had no choice but to stretch herself out on the floor and press her face and body close to the dirty, foul-smelling rug.

The woman hit her again and again with the rod. "You kowtow more!" she cried. "More!"

Writhing in pain, Millicent tried to press herself still deeper into the rug. At last the beating stopped, and the woman motioned for her to rise.

Her backside throbbing, her whole body aching, Millicent got to her feet. To her dismay, the Malay woman again directed her to sit at the dressing table and submit to having additional makeup put on to repair the damage where perspiration and contact with the rug on the floor had smudged and wiped away some of the cosmetics.

Suddenly the woman jarred her by slapping her hard across the face. "No move!" she commanded.

Somehow Millicent was able to force herself to sit very quietly while she submitted to the crude ministrations. Finally satisfied with what she had done to the captive's face, the woman chuckled coarsely as she daubed rouge on Millicent's nipples. Standing back to study the effect, she pinched the nipples and then prodded her victim with the rod. "Now," she said, "you practice kowtow."

Millicent seethed in impotent rage. As she stretched out on the dirty rug, making her obeisances and once again being forced to submit to a beating, she was filled with a desire to attack and kill her tormentress. But she knew that her physical strength was far inferior to that of the Malay woman, and there was nothing she could do but to keep herself prostrate and accept the punishment.

After a time, the woman grew tired of her sport and pointed her rod to the foot of the bed. "Now you sleep," she ordered.

Millicent was so exhausted that she obeyed and soon fell into a troubled sleep.

The woman moved to the head of the bed, rearranged the pillows there to her satisfaction, and, leaning against them, sat cross-legged as she kept a close watch on her charge.

Robin Kayross paced up and down the bridge of the *Diana* and stared out toward the warehouses of the New Orleans waterfront district, which were barely visible in the early morning darkness. Soon dawn would be breaking, and he had a major decision to make.

He was playing a dangerous game, but he was ahead, and he intended to stay ahead. Realizing there was only one way he could ensure his own safety and that of his ship, he summoned his first mate to the bridge.

"We face a potentially dangerous situation," the captain said. "We have a number of shanghaied American citizens on board, and now we also have an American woman, whom we're going to sell to the viceroy in Canton. The American authorities are inclined to be ruthless in the protection of their citizens, and if they should come on board and inspect the ship, we could be in terrible trouble."

"I've been thinking about the problem, too, and I agree with you, sir," the mate replied. "You and I could be held responsible and spend long terms in jail."

"It seems to me," Captain Kayross said, "that the *Diana* is in too prominent a place for our good. If any one of our captives should manage to get loose on the deck and make a scene, dozens of people on shore might become aware of the commotion and notify the police. We need privacy between now and the time that we set sail for Canton and Hong Kong."

The mate nodded vigorously. "That's my thinking exactly, sir," he said.

"Very well." The captain became crisp. "I've got to go ashore on some urgent personal matters. I want you to move the *Diana* immediately. We have made enough money on the aliens, opium, and cargo we brought here to make a profitable trip back to the Orient, so we can leave this dock permanently. And we have plenty of coal on board. Sail the ship to the delta country of the Mississippi River south of New Orleans. I'm sure you remember the place in the bayous where we anchored last year after we had that trouble with the authorities."

The mate nodded eagerly. "Of course, sir! I'll never forget it. That'll be a perfect spot for us now. The prisoners can shout their heads off there, and the only ones who will hear them will be the alligators and snakes."

"Take no unnecessary risks," Captain Kayross told him. "You'll find the charts for the bayous in the

chart room, and I want you to follow them without
deviation. I'll join you later in the day, after you've
anchored."

"Very good, sir," the mate replied.

"Fortunately," the captain said, "we've kept up
the fire in the furnace so we have a head of steam
worked up. There's no reason to delay."

"I'll weigh anchor and cast off at once, sir," the
mate told him. "Don't you worry, we'll be anchored
in the bayou waiting for you whenever you show
up."

Deep in the hold of the *Diana*, Edward Blackstone heard the stories of Wallace Dugald and the
other men who had been kidnapped and spirited
aboard the Greek freighter. At last, the whole picture was clear. Karl Kellerman had abducted the
unfortunate men after putting knockout drops in their
drinks at Dugald's Bar and then had turned them
over to the ship's personnel. The captain of the vessel was intending to utilize the services of these
unfortunates as slave labor.

Now that Edward had freed himself as well as
the others, however, the picture had changed dras-
tically. There were six desperate men in the hold,
including Edward, and all of them were determined
to regain their freedom, no matter what the cost.

"We can't just lash out indiscriminately," Edward told the group, having completely forgotten the
presence of Robin Hood. "We've got to plan our
moves carefully and act accordingly. Our worst handi-

cap is our lack of weapons. All we have among us are a number of metal shovels, various lengths of chain, and my one small knife."

"The Greeks carry pistols," one of the men replied, "and their officers have swords, too."

"How many of them are there in all?" Edward asked crisply.

The others conferred among themselves and finally decided that they had about a dozen active enemies including the captain. They had no way of knowing that Kayross was not on board at the present time.

"Most of the remaining crew," one burly man said, "are either Malays or Lascars. I suspect that they came on board the same way we did and were shanghaied from their homes. They've not only been sympathetic to us, but I have me a hunch they'll desert ship without hesitation. One thing is sure— they won't join in any fight against us."

His comrades agreed heartily.

Edward accepted their word. "That reduces the odds against us appreciably, but we're still handicapped by a lack of weapons. What we'll have to do is lay ambushes for our enemies, one by one, until we gain control of enough weapons to fight on equal terms. What we've got to do right now is to plot the best way to get our hands on some pistols and swords."

They conferred quietly, several of them making impractical suggestions that Edward vetoed. All at once, they became aware of the throbbing of the engine and of tremors in the deck beneath their feet.

"The ship is moving!" Wallace said bitterly. "We must be putting out to sea!"

"Maybe, but maybe not," a thin, tall man declared. "I know every inch of the waters around New Orleans. Come with me, Dugald, and we'll see for ourselves." He and Wallace crept away while the rest remained in the hold.

After a wait that seemed interminable, the party heard soft footsteps approaching the hold. Firm grips were taken on shovels and chains.

"Who's there?" Edward called softly.

"We're back!" said one of the returning pair, and the others breathed more easily as the two men came into the room.

"The freighter," the man who knew the Mississippi said, "sure isn't following the main channel that empties into the Gulf of Mexico, so wherever we're headed, we aren't going very far. Most of the other channels end in swamps or feed into lakes in the bayou country."

The rest of the group felt vastly relieved that the freighter was moving into a sparsely settled region of the Mississippi delta rather than out to sea.

All the same, Edward reasoned, it would be wrong to delay. The group's greatest natural advantage, that of surprise, would be lost if they waited too long. His comrades agreed to initiate action as soon as possible.

Although Edward was unfamiliar with the particulars of this vessel's layout, he knew enough about ships in general to make a rough plan, and the others agreed to it without discussion. Only Wallace commented.

"If Karl Kellerman is on board," he said, "he's mine. I don't want anybody else killing or injuring him by accident. I reserve the right to end his life myself!"

One of the first party to have been shanghaied led the group to a passageway that extended from the hatch to the entrance of the furnace room. "Sooner or later," he said, "they're sure to send a couple of men down to make certain that we're feeding the furnace."

Edward silently stationed his comrades on both sides of the narrow passageway, cautioning each of them to maintain absolute quiet until the signal was given that they could talk. Tensely they settled down to await the arrival of foes. Their inability to see clearly in the dark passageway, combined with the vibration of the moving ship, contributed to the mounting tension.

The vigil seemed unending. For what felt like a very long time, the freighter kept up a somewhat better than moderate speed. Then the engine slowed down, and the vibrations eased up. Shortly thereafter, a lighted lantern moved down the passageway, and voices were heard in the distance.

"The coal stokers," one voice said in disgust, "are the laziest swine who have ever sailed the seven seas."

"If they've allowed the fire in the furnace to die down," the other said, "they'll deserve a beating. And they shall have it. I'll personally whip every last mother's son of them."

The footsteps came closer, and the light in the passageway edged steadily nearer.

The victims of abduction scarcely dared to breathe for fear that the slightest sound or motion would reveal their presence prematurely.

Crouching between two large crates of cargo on the main deck of the *Diana*, Tommie was stiff, sore, hungry, and weary. She realized she had made a major mistake in blindly following Edward when he had been carried, unconscious, aboard the freighter, and now she was trapped. She assumed that at least one guard was on duty to keep watch on the cargo, and if she stood upright or moved, she would be seen and would meet Edward's fate. Somehow their futures were bound together.

All of a sudden, something landed on Tommie's shoulder, startling her, and she looked up quickly to see Robin Hood perched there. Delighted that he had returned safely to her, she patted him, and he began to chatter quickly.

At the same time, the ship's engine was turned on, and the whole freighter vibrated. The sound, fortunately, was loud enough that it obliterated the soft noises made by the little monkey.

Suddenly Tommie noted that there was a smudge

of coal dust on the animal's little coat and another on his feathered hat.

Carefully brushing off the garments, she murmured, "Where on earth have you been, Robin? Oh, if you could only talk!" The monkey appeared to be shaking, and the thought occurred to the young woman that he might be frightened.

Now, to Tommie's horror, the ship had moved from the dock into the open Mississippi River and headed slowly downstream. The first thought that occurred to her was that the vessel had started a voyage to some distant port. In consternation, she knew that her presence on board surely would be discovered after a day or two at sea. She had done nothing to help Edward, who was still a prisoner of the ship's crew. All she had succeeded in doing was to ensure that she, too, would be captured.

Ultimately, Tommie's familiarity with riverboats restored her common sense, and she grew calmer. Peering through a narrow space between the crates, she could see that the freighter was no longer navigating on the principal route of the Mississippi River but had turned into a small channel. Dwellings and other signs of human habitation disappeared from the banks of the river, and the countryside became increasingly desolate. From what she knew of the geography of the region, Tommie reasoned that the ship was moving into the remote and uninhabitable swampy country known as the bayous.

It was a relief to realize that the ship's master was not putting out to sea. At the same time, Tommie knew that the freighter was leaving civilization behind and that wherever it might be going, she would have to rely on herself to come to Edward's aid.

The insistent prodding of the wooden rod awakened Millicent, and she instantly became aware, too, of the ship's motion, but she had no chance to think about the fact that the ship was under way. The Malay woman, sitting cross-legged at the opposite end of the bed, was reclining against pillows and grinning evilly at her.

"You practice kowtow! Now!" the woman commanded.

Half-asleep, Millicent dragged herself off the bed and made an obeisance. She had anticipated a blow with the rod, but nevertheless it was a shock when the woman struck her hard. Her rage mounting with each blow she received, Millicent was nevertheless compelled to endure the torment until the Malay woman stopped because her arm was growing tired.

"Now you sleep!" she commanded.

Tired, battered, and bruised, Millicent painfully climbed back into bed and soon fell asleep again.

Too late, a length of chain clanked its dismal warning as Edward brought it down full force onto the head of the unsuspecting ship's officer. The man staggered forward a step or two and crumpled to the deck, dying without making a sound.

Wallace accorded the same treatment to the other mate, and he, too, died silently. There was no need for any assistance from the other shanghaied men.

The refugees obtained a rich harvest of weapons. The two officers had been carrying three pistols and two swords, which the shanghaied men eagerly appropriated. In addition, they took the lantern, which would prove useful to them in the critical time ahead.

Edward was the only member of the group who knew how to use a sword, so he helped himself to one of the blades. The other he gave to Wallace, who took it but insisted on keeping his chain, also. "I'll be able to do double damage," he muttered, his anger unassuaged by the action he had already seen.

Believing that the arms they had acquired helped to equalize the odds that had been so much against them, the group surged upward. They came to a closed hatch directly overhead, accessible by means of a ladder attached to a bulkhead. Edward halted beneath the hatch and beckoned his comrades to gather closely around him. "When we move into the open, lads," he said, "don't bunch together. You'll make too tempting and too good a target. Spread out and take cover wherever you find it. We'll move quickly, with the men who've acquired arms leading the way. Wherever you see an opponent, cut him down quickly and without mercy. Then, make certain you help yourselves to any weapons he may be carrying and share them with your companions. I'll do my best to keep all of you within sight, and as our fight develops, I'll try to issue any additional instructions that might be needed." Without further ado, he climbed the ladder and cautiously pushed the hatch open. None of the ship's personnel appeared to be within sight, and the entire group scrambled into the open behind him without being detected.

Edward discovered that they were far aft on a deck that contained boxes and cases of cargo. He waved his companions to port and starboard. As they started to advance cautiously toward the prow of the freighter, two Greek seamen and a pair of Malay sailors—who were about to prove themselves loyal to Captain Kayross—appeared in the open.

It was unnecessary for Edward to order an attack. He and his men surged forward, making the quartet the objects of their hatred and frustration. Wielding chains and shovels with abandon, they assaulted the startled seamen. The pistols were ready for instant use when circumstances made their use feasible.

No force could have contained Wallace, who was endowed with a maniacal strength as he hacked wildly with his sword and wielded his chain with equal abandon. His rage was so great it shook him to the core, almost consuming him. He was determined to even the score with every last one of his tormentors.

Edward was equally outraged, but he relied on his skills developed over a period of years rather than on brute strength. The sword he had acquired became an extension of his right arm as he slashed and cut with it, wielding it with such grace and rapidity that it was almost impossible for the men at whom its aim was directed to halt it.

A thrust aimed at an opponent's throat found its target, and another blow almost decapitated one of the Malays. In all, Edward accounted for three of the enemy in a matter of seconds, while Wallace clumsily but effectively disposed of the fourth.

Edward took another pair of pistols from the dead men, which he gave to two of his comrades. Then, leaving the bodies of the dead where they had fallen, he waved his group forward. The brief encounter had created more of a commotion than Edward and his men realized, and other seamen and officers began to gather amidships. Somewhat to Edward's surprise, there were a number of Malays and Lascars in this group as well, along with the Greeks. He had been wrong to believe that the Malays and Lascars would automatically fall in with his own group; obviously their loyalty was with Captain Kayross because he paid their wages.

In almost no time, a battle was raging. The shanghaied men ducked behind crates and boxes in order to protect themselves from the pistols of their foes, and the crew members did the same.

Edward knew it was imperative that his men maintain the momentum they had achieved. "Keep moving, lads. Keep moving forward!"

The shanghaied men, inspired by his example and thirsting for revenge, continued to press, step by step, toward the prow of the ship. The air was filled with bullets now as shots were freely exchanged.

Edward's colleagues were strangers from different walks of life. They were united only by the fact that they had suffered a common personal catastrophe, but their anger at their treatment had given them the courage of lions. They responded like military veterans to Edward's orders to keep their heads down in order to avoid enemy sniper fire, and they carefully conserved their ammunition, firing their pistols only when they had clear targets.

There was a brief lull in the exchange of gunfire, and to Edward's astonished dismay, a blond head appeared above the tops of the crates that separated the two forces. Tommie Harding stood upright with Robin Hood clinging to one shoulder.

Edward had no idea how she happened to be on board the freighter, and although now he knew why the little monkey had appeared out of nowhere, this was not the time to ask for explanations. "Tommie!" he called. "Get down and stay down! Don't expose yourself to crossfire!"

She obeyed at once, smiling broadly when she heard his voice. She remained hidden between two crates, rejoicing because she knew Edward was safe.

Edward's voice reached her again. "We're moving past your position," he called. "Make no attempt to follow us—stay in concealment. I'll let you know when it's safe for you to come out into the open."

Again, pistol shots were exchanged by the two forces, and the little monkey on Tommie's shoulder began to tremble violently. She stroked him reassuringly. "Don't worry, Robin," she whispered. "Edward has taken charge, so everything is going to be all right."

Raving and cursing as he advanced, Wallace continued to press forward, waving his sword and seemingly impervious to enemy bullets. His ferocity and anger served to goad the other shanghaied men, and they pressed forward, too. At Edward's insistence, their advance was cautious. He was taking no chances.

As he dashed from one row of crates to the next, Edward unexpectedly came upon two men, a Malay and a Lascar, who were crouching behind the nearest box. With his sword he quickly disposed of them.

He found that the pair had been carrying clumsy, British-made weapons that were copies of Colt repeating pistols. Nevertheless, he was grateful for the acquisition of still more firearms, and he kept the pistols for his own use. By this time, every member of the little band carried arms, and Edward was convinced that they could look after themselves.

A bullet plowed up a furrow in the planking of the deck only inches from the spot where Edward was crouching. The enemy's aim was far too accurate for comfort, and he searched for his foe.

All at once, he saw that the Greek first mate of the *Diana* was standing on the bridge of the ship and taking aim at him again. Sighting the officer down the barrel of the cumbersome pistol, Edward pulled the trigger.

Ordinarily he was a superb shot, but the weapon was faulty, and his bullet lodged in the mate's shoulder. However, the officer dropped his pistol to the deck and grasped his shoulder. He shouted out something to the crew that Edward could not make out.

Just then, the young Englishman realized that a retreat was under way. The mate and the other Greeks who formed the nucleus of the crew raced to the starboard side of the vessel, where they lowered the ship's gig into the water and hastily climbed down a rope ladder hanging over the side of the vessel into the boat.

As Edward and his companions ran to the railing on the starboard side of the freighter, the Malays and Lascars, including both those who had been loyal to Captain Kayross and those who wanted no part in the combat, leaped to the rail and plunged into the swampy waters of the cove, where the vessel was now riding at anchor.

The ship's gig made steady progress toward the shore, as the Greek crew members bent over the oars. While Edward and Wallace stood side by side at the rail, watching in fascinated horror, alligators materialized from several parts of the cove and began to bear down on the men who were swimming with all their strength toward the shore. The huge creatures resembled half-submerged logs as they drew nearer to the fleeing seamen.

The alligators opened their huge jaws, and the waters became bloody as they went after arms and legs. The air was filled with the screams of the helpless, dying men. As the churning, foaming waters turned red, a slow chill ascended Edward's spine, and he rubbed his arms vigorously. "May God have mercy on their souls," he muttered.

At his direction, Wallace led their comrades in search of another ship's boat, which they found near the stern. They lowered it with difficulty into the waters of the bayou, and when that task was completed, Edward called to Tommie that it was safe for her now to reappear. She stood and moved toward him slowly, her gait unsteady.

As Edward reached for her and took her into his arms, Robin Hood jumped from her shoulder to his, chattering wildly. As the monkey continued to express his opinion of all that had happened, Edward and Tommie, oblivious to the presence of the remaining men, embraced and kissed.

Millicent Randall was prodded awake frequently and ordered by the Malay woman, "Now you kowtow!" Regardless of whether she moved rapidly or slowly, she was beaten for her pains and was forced to suffer still another beating as she kowtowed. The cruelty of the woman was unbearable.

One time when Millicent was awakened, she distinctly heard the sounds of pistol fire and shouts on the deck. She looked across at the Malay woman, but her captor seemed to be paying no attention to the commotion. Suddenly Millicent froze.

The woman was dozing on the pillows at the head of the bed. She had slumped on them, and her kris had fallen out of her belt and was lying beside her.

Scarcely aware of what she was doing, yet at the same time realizing that she was being given an unexpected opportunity to escape, Millicent reached out and grasped the handle of the sword.

At that instant the Malay woman opened her eyes. Instantly wide awake, she reached with both hands for the length of steel, unmindful of the fact that the double-edged blade was razor sharp.

The kris sliced into the palms of her hands and the insides of her fingers, causing her to bleed profusely, but she tightened her hold.

Seeing the pain and the hatred in the woman's glittering eyes, Millicent instinctively tightened her hold and pulled harder. The woman responded by tightening her own grip, causing her hands to bleed still more heavily as she tried to wrest the deadly blade from her captive. The pain that the woman suffered was excruciating, but she withstood it in silence, and her grip firm, she exerted all her strength as she continued to pull the deadly sword toward her. Beads of sweat appeared on her forehead, and rivulets ran down her face, but she ignored them, just as she ignored the blood spurting from her hands.

Struggling with all of her inferior might, Millicent noted that the point of the kris's blade was aimed directly at the body of her tormentor and was on her left side in the middle of her chest. It was about a half-inch from her body. Suddenly a horrible idea occurred to Millicent, and she knew she had to utilize it. She, who had never committed any deed that had caused physical injury to another human being, no longer had a choice. If she failed to act immediately, she would be made to pay dearly.

The rage that had been building within her decided the issue, and without giving the matter further consideration, she released her grip on the handle.

The Malay woman had been tugging at the blade with all of her might, and she could not lighten her efforts in that split second after Millicent released her hold. The woman's force behind her deadly grip plunged the blade deep within her own body. Collapsing over the kris, she fell dead onto the bed.

Millicent gasped. Never had she seen death so close. As for the Malay woman herself, Millicent felt neither compassion nor pity. The woman had chosen to live violently, and now she had died violently.

Of more immediate concern was Millicent's need to escape. She went over to the Malay woman and hastily began to unwind the turban, which was made of soft silk. She was gratified to discover that there was yard after yard of it, long enough, she knew, to be wrapped in some way around her body. First, however, she had to get out of the cabin. Hastening to the door, Millicent listened carefully and could hear the sounds of the battle raging on deck. Not knowing what was taking place but fearful she would get into more difficulty if she exposed herself, she opened the door cautiously and crept to a pile of crates. Finding that one was partially empty, she hid herself in it, prepared to bide her time until it was safe to come out.

* * *

It was the urgent desire of the entire company
to put as much distance between themselves and the
Diana as possible, but there was one thing they still
had to do: find Millient Randall, since Tommie was
sure she had also been brought onto the ship. But
after splitting up and searching the entire vessel,
Edward and his men found no trace of her, only the
cut-up body of the Malay woman, whose death was a
total mystery. There was nothing more they could do
and so two of the men descended into the ship's
boat, which they held steady while Tommie slowly
went down to it, going hand over hand down the
rope ladder. Edward Blackstone was the last member of the group to reach the boat, and as he picked
up a pair of oars, his comrades did the same. Tommie sat in the prow with her back to it, the monkey
perched on her shoulder as the men rowed toward
the shore. The vessel cut through the water, and to
the relief of everyone present, the alligators kept
their distance.

At last the shore loomed directly ahead, and
several of the men leaped from the boat onto dry
land, then pulled the craft after them. The boat the
Greek crew members had used to make their escape
was beached nearby on the shore, but there was no
sign of the men. No doubt they had fled in the
direction of New Orleans.

Edward stepped ashore, then picked up Tommie and deposited her on the ground. "If my sense
of direction hasn't failed me," he said to the assem-

bled group, "New Orleans is due north of here. But I'm afraid we have a walk of a considerable distance before we get back into the city."

"That's all right," Tommie replied. "We're safe and we're together, and nothing else matters."

With one accord, the group headed toward New Orleans. They reached the waterfront district shortly after noon and went directly to Dugald's Bar, which, as Edward had anticipated, was closed and locked for the day. There was no sign of Captain Kayross or Kellerman or, more importantly, Millicent.

"I suggest that all of us go home," Wallace said, "and that we plan to meet back here later this evening, say around midnight. We have a score to settle with Kellerman, and I'm not abdicating my right to be the first to put a bullet into him!"

"Not until he tells us what has become of my cousin," Edward put in.

They went their separate ways, with Edward and Tommie heading for their hotel. When they reached it, they found no sign of Jim Randall or Randy Savage, and they went to their rooms and changed their clothes, then had a meal in the dining room, the first food they had eaten in almost twenty-four hours. Then they went upstairs again. By this time, the couple had exchanged information fully, with Tommie explaining how she had happened to be on board the freighter when the fight erupted.

"Didn't you realize the risks involved?" Edward demanded. "Didn't you know you were taking a terrible chance with your own life?"

"You were in danger," she replied, "and I didn't stop to think of anything else."

When they reached their rooms, they found that Jim and Randy were still out. Robin Hood, whom they had left in the parlor of the suite while they dined, was exhausted and sound asleep on the sofa. They left some fruit that they had obtained from the dining room on a small table next to the sofa. Then they stood for a moment or two, looking at each other. "I'll have quite a story," Edward said, "to pass on to our children and grandchildren."

"I was so concerned about you," Tommie replied, "that I didn't stop to think of myself or of the danger I might be in until bullets started flying. But I guess I acted stupidly," she went on. "I wanted to help, and I tried to help, but I succeeded only in getting in the way and then making your job more difficult. I should have had faith in you and known that you'd be able to escape."

"The fact was," Edward began slowly, "that you cared about my welfare more than your own." He put his hands on her shoulders and looked deeply into her eyes. "We've been betrothed long enough. It's time we get married."

"I agree," Tommie said, "but we can't marry unless my father gives us his blessing. I have no doubt he will, but unless we can intercept him by telegram, we would have to wait until he reached the headwaters of the Missouri River, turned the *Big Muddy* around, and sailed back to St. Louis. So, tomorrow, we'll start trying to reach him at one of the regular stops."

"You get into such trouble when you're left to your own devices," he said, "that it's very difficult to wait. Unfortunately, I agree with you, however, and we won't be married until your father comes back to St. Louis and then, I hope, to New Orleans. The moment he gets here, you're going to become my wife."

There was no need for words, and Tommie just nodded. They continued to look at each other, and suddenly their patience snapped. They were wrapped in each other's arms, and their kiss became increasingly passionate, increasingly demanding.

They wanted each other badly, and that aphrodisiac overcame the exhaustion and the uncertainties that they had suffered the last twenty-four hours. Out of consideration for Tommie's father, they could not be married until he formally gave them his blessing and was present for the ceremony, but they had succeeded in winning their gamble with death and felt there was only one way they could celebrate their victory.

They moved to Tommie's bedchamber, where they quickly undressed and embraced again on the bed. Now they felt only an overwhelming desire that swept all else to one side, and their lovemaking became increasingly frenzied. With the absolute honesty of two people in love, they cast aside all pretense and freely gave of themselves.

When Edward took Tommie, she clung to him,

and they soared to a mutual climax that seemed to last forever and that left both of them utterly limp, totally exhausted and spent. The events of the previous night had taken a heavier toll than they knew, and they fell sound asleep in each other's arms.

When Jim and Randy returned to the suite that day, having gone out looking for the missing Edward and Tommie, they were greeted by an excited Robin Hood. The monkey chattered at the two men long and rapidly. They soon discovered that Tommie and Edward had returned safely from their adventure, and they curbed their curiosity until the following morning, when the couple awakened in time for breakfast and a conference, at which Jim and Randy were told the entire story.

After what seemed like an eternity of waiting, Millicent realized that all sounds of the battle had ceased. She opened the lid of the crate, and seeing no one, she crept out, carrying the long turban cloth in her hand.

The ship seemed deserted, but suddenly she halted and gasped. The body of a dead Malay seaman was crumpled a short distance from her down the deck. In the next few minutes, Millicent discovered two more bodies on the decks, and her brain reeling, she decided that the freighter was a death ship. She searched in vain for a boat that would take her ashore, and it finally dawned on her that the boats had disappeared when the living had fled.

She was not particularly superstitious, but the

stench of death was in her nostrils and contributed to her feeling of hysteria. Looking across the expanse of water toward the trees that lined the shore, she knew only that she had to leave the *Diana* or lose her mind.

She was an excellent swimmer, thanks to the childhood summers she had spent on the shores of Chesapeake Bay. Quickly wrapping the turban around her head, to keep the material from getting wet, she climbed down the rope ladder and dived into the bayou, striking out for the shore, her strokes long and powerful.

Only when she was able to stand in knee-deep water and was making her way ashore did she glance over her shoulder, and not until she saw two half-submerged "logs" drifting rapidly toward her did she realize the danger she was in. Those logs were mammoth alligators, and in her panic, she fled up to the shore and retreated a considerable distance into the woods before she paused for breath. To her infinite relief, the alligators had not followed her, and she knew she was safe.

At last she was able to devote her attention to her appearance. She removed the turban from her head and then wound it loosely around her body, beginning at the calves of her legs and working upward. After winding it several times around her breasts, she brought it up over her shoulders and was relieved to find that it even covered the upper portion of her arms. Millicent's feet were still bare, but she had no way of obtaining shoes.

Now a much greater problem faced her. She had no idea where she was or how she would get back to New Orleans. She would just have to trudge through the jungles of the bayou country until she found someone or something that would show her the way.

Still, her luck had been good so far: She was free of the Malay woman's torture, and she had escaped a fate as a concubine in the harem of an Oriental potentate. She would find the strength to walk barefooted all the way back to New Orleans, even if it took her many days.

VI

A cool breeze blew through the open sides of the stone gazebo in the spacious rear yard behind the sedate New Orleans home. In the gazebo was a large reclining chair with a small table set up on either side of it. On each table a game of dominoes was in progress. The middle-aged Domino, his color restored to a normal, healthy hue, a small bandage on his head, sat in the chair, playing dominoes with two of his associates simultaneously.

"These bones," he said, "are doing exactly what I want them to do today." He turned from one table to the other, picking up the oblongs of ivory and manipulating them with ease as he moved first against one and then the other of his associates. The gang members, at best bored by the game, played dutifully. Both of them knew that Domino was cheating, but they also knew better than to complain.

Conversation was limited to the requirements of the game. Occasionally one or another player would

call "Go!" and his opponent would immediately take
up the challenge. Eventually the convalescing man
would cry "Domino!" and that particular game would
end in another victory for him.

He did not mind in the least that his cheating
enabled him to win. Victory for its own sake was his
goal, and his triumphant "Domino!" was the only
talk that mattered.

Eventually Domino grew tired of the game. Taking a thick watch from a waistcoat pocket, he glanced
at it, then turned to his underlings. "I'm expecting a visit," he said, "from a wench who works in one
of our brothels. Send her in to me when she gets
here, please."

The pair exchanged a quick look. "Oh, she's
been here for some time," one of the men replied.
"We've been waiting until we finished playing before
telling you."

Domino lost his temper. "When will you boys
ever learn that time is money?" he demanded. "Send
her out to me right now! And stay around. We'll play
a few more games after I'm finished with her."

The pair exchanged another look as one of them
quickly rose to his feet and hurried off to the main
house. Apparently they had been mistaken in their
assumption of the purpose for which their employer
wanted the prostitute.

The man reappeared shortly, leading across the
lawn a heavily made-up blonde. Her skirt fitted her
so tightly that her hips rolled as she walked, and
every male within eyesight, including several guards

stationed on the premises, watched her with obvious pleasure. "I thought you forgot all about me, honey," she said to Domino, a hint of complaint in her voice.

He shook his head, then growled at her, "I was just now told you were here. Sit down!"

She sat in a chair that one of the men had vacated, and a slit appeared at one side of her skirt to display a svelte leg encased in a black lace stocking.

"You know who I am?" Domino demanded.

"Sure," she replied. "All the girls in the house know that you're the big boss."

"Do you know why you're here?"

She was surprised. "Well, no, not exactly, but I thought—"

"Leave the thinking to me," Domino told her brutally. "You'll stay out of trouble that way. All right, my dear, let's take a look at you."

The woman knew what was expected of her. She rose to her feet, slowly ran her hands down the front of her body, then raised her skirt high above her knees and lowered it again, inch by inch.

"You'll do," Domino said candidly, and waved her back to her chair. "I expect you know how to get a man interested in you."

"I've yet to meet one who will run away," she replied confidently.

Domino liked her. He grinned, and she returned his smile boldly. "I have a job for you," he said, "a very simple job. Do you know a man named Karl Kellerman?"

She shook her head. "No, sir."

"He's tall, and he isn't bad looking, and he thinks he's irresistible to women."

"I know the type," she said, her distaste evident in her voice.

"I want you to snag him, take him to an apartment that I'll have set up for you, and then go to bed with him. That's all there is to it. Some of my boys will show up, and the instant they appear, you're to grab your clothes and get out. That's the end of it."

The blonde was astonished. "That's all you want me to do?"

Domino was maddeningly calm. "That's all," he assured her with a steady smile.

The woman was confused. "But why—"

"No questions, please!" Domino said sharply. "The less you know, the fewer questions you'll have to answer and the safer you'll be. I hope I make myself clear."

There was a long pause in the conversation while the woman pondered his words. "Very clear," she said at last.

He removed several bills from a large wad that he carried in a pocket. "Here's one hundred dollars," he said. "Come back after you've done the job, and there'll be another hundred waiting for you. In the meantime, get it into your head that you've never come near this place, you've never set eyes on me, and you've never held a conversation with me."

The woman took the money, folded it, and raising her skirt, deposited it in the top of her stocking.

"I'm glad to see you at last, honey," she said sweetly. "I've never met you before, but it's a real pleasure."

Domino chuckled appreciatively. "Eddie," he said to one of his underlings, "take her to Charlie. He'll give her the key to the apartment and will fill her in on the details of where she can make contact with Kellerman."

Watching the swivel-hipped woman as she made her way to the main house with his subordinate, Domino nodded his head in pleasant anticipation. His men would trap Kellerman in the apartment and then slowly, brutally put him to death. It was time for Kellerman to suffer the tortures of the damned for what he had done.

Karl Kellerman's streak of good luck seemed unending. That night at his favorite gaming and dining club, he had more than quadrupled his original evening's wager. Knowing nothing of the events aboard the *Diana* earlier in the day, he was looking forward to meeting Captain Robin Kayross later that night for the last time and collecting the balance of the money for the shanghaied recruits, whom he had delivered to the Greek sea captain in the early hours of the morning. In the meantime, he had not only rid himself permanently of Millicent Randall but would be paid a great deal of money for her after she was turned over to the Chinese viceroy in Canton. Now the blonde he had met earlier in the evening, the woman who had brought him good luck by sitting beside him at the gaming table, had invited him back to her apartment with her that evening, an invitation he had accepted with alacrity.

Now, he studied her over the rim of his wineglass. "If you knew me better," he said, "you might have thought twice about that invitation."

The blonde moved closer to him and pressed her leg against him. "Why is that?" she asked demurely.

He smiled faintly. "Although I'm fairly new in town," he said, "I've already acquired a reputation that does a lady's name no good."

"I'm willing to risk it," she replied, flirting with him over the top of her glass.

He drained his wine, picked up the bottle, and refilled both their glasses.

As the blonde raised her glass, returning his silent toast, she reflected that she had never earned the enormous sum of two hundred dollars so easily. It had been a simple matter to meet Kellerman and to arouse his interest in her. Now he had accepted her invitation to accompany her to the apartment, and the rest of the evening would be sure to go according to plan, too. Then she would be paid the second hundred dollars. She had no idea whether Domino merely planned to embarrass Kellerman or whether his intent was more sinister, but she had no intention of finding out. Several of the girls at the brothel had assured her that Domino was the most important gang leader in New Orleans and that his influence was as widespread as his reputation for ruthless behavior. He was treating her fairly, with great generosity, and she wanted to return the favor, to do as good a job as she possibly could for him.

After they finished their light supper, Kellerman hesitated for a moment at the gaming tables.

His companion took his arm. "Don't play again," she murmured. "Your luck has been too good tonight and might change."

He nodded. Her advice made sense.

"Besides," she went on in a still lower, sexy tone, "I think we have things to do that will be far more exciting than gambling."

He thrilled to the promise in her voice and, turning away, accompanied her down the stairs.

Kellerman hired a closed carriage and driver, and he and the blonde sat close together on the plush seat, kissing whenever the carriage moved through a park or down a particularly dark thoroughfare. At last the driver deposited them in front of the building in which the woman allegedly occupied the apartment on the second floor, a suite of rooms that had a large balcony overlooking a parklike area. As she searched in her handbag for the key to the flat, she caught a glimpse of several dark figures loitering behind a clump of bushes growing across the street. Domino's men were already in place, waiting for her signal, which would bring them hurrying to the apartment.

When the couple reached the apartment, which the woman had visited previously, she mixed Kellerman a stiff drink of whiskey before disappearing into the bedroom to change into a negligee and high-heeled slippers. Following her detailed instructions to the letter, she placed her own attire in a neat pile near the door so she could snatch her clothes, change quickly, and leave the place at once when the time came for her to vanish.

Kellerman was reclining on a divan in the living room; he had drained his drink, and his boots were resting on the floor beside him.

The woman refilled his glass, then stood in front of him until he took the hint and swept her into his arms. She allowed her negligee to fall open, and she let him caress her nude body as he pleased. When she was certain that he was aroused, she murmured the suggestion that they adjourn to the bedchamber.

As Kellerman turned away, accepting her invitation, she clutched her robe together and stepped out onto the balcony for a moment, where she yawned and stretched. This was her signal to Domino's accomplices, notifying them that she and their victim were now going to bed and that they could break in.

When she joined him in the bedchamber, she saw that he was still dressed except for his boots and that he was glaring at her suspiciously.

"What the hell was the meaning of that?" he demanded roughly. "What the hell were you doing?"

A sudden fear gripping her, she shrank from him. "I—I don't know what you're talking about."

"When you went out to that balcony just now, you were signaling to somebody, I swear it."

A vice of terror gripped her heart. "I don't know

what you're talking about," she repeated. "You're imagining things."

"Like hell I am," he replied. "I've got a lot of enemies, and the way I confound them is by staying one step ahead of them. Either tell me the truth—fast—or suffer the consequences."

She was so frightened she could say nothing. Kellerman reached out and caught hold of her by one wrist. As he did, he heard the front door of the apartment open cautiously. His suspicions were confirmed!

Not wasting an instant, he reached into his belt, where he carried a double-edged knife, and with no feeling whatever, he slashed the woman's throat with it, cutting her from ear to ear. As she toppled backward onto the bed, he stooped down, picked up his boots with his free hand, and still clutching the knife, raced out onto the balcony.

Knowing he had no choice, he leaped off the balcony into a clump of bushes below. He landed with a jarring jolt that caused him to drop his knife, but he picked it up instantly. Wiping the blood from it onto the ground and putting it back into his belt, he sprinted in his stockinged feet toward the trees that beckoned at the far side of the yard. When he gained the temporary sanctuary, he pulled on his boots, reasoning that the death of the woman in the apartment should give him a brief respite. But he knew that within seconds, the chase would be on.

He beat a hasty, blind retreat across the yard and through alleyways between houses, ignoring the

barking of watchdogs and the cries of people who
were aroused by their pets. Eventually he came to a
busy thoroughfare, and hailing a passing carriage, he
sank into it after first giving the driver the address of
Dugald's Bar, where he was supposed to meet Captain Kayross anyway.

His luck, he decided, was still good. Once again
he had escaped intact, and he had repaid the treach-
erous woman in her own coin. He felt no remorse for
what he had found it necessary to do to her; she had
deserved her fate. He wondered who could have
hired her to set him up. Perhaps he would never
know.

As the carriage entered the streets of the working man's district, Kellerman reflected that what he
had told the blonde was true. He was tough and
resilient, he had plenty of money, and he managed
to stay one step ahead of his enemies.

When they reached Dugald's Bar, Kellerman
paid the driver, tipping him generously. Then he
unlocked the tavern door and entered the building,
which was eerily quiet. The sign in the window said
Closed, and that was how Kellerman wanted it, for
his meeting with Kayross was to be in private.

He didn't have long to wait before the breathless,
nervous-looking Robin Kayross, accompanied by three
of his crew members, showed up. Refusing Kellerman's offer of a drink to calm him down, the Greek
ship's captain launched into an account of all that had
taken place earlier that day on the *Diana*, which he
had learned about when his surviving crew members

joined him in New Orleans. "I think we're done for," the captain said. "I don't dare go back to the ship. We lost nearly the entire crew when those shanghaied men got loose. They're going to be after us, and I'm sure by now the authorities are swarming about my abandoned ship."

Taking out a cigar and lighting it, Kellerman listened quietly, managing to appear calm, though inside he was agitated. Perhaps his luck was turning for the worse after all. With the damned Englishman Edward Blackstone now on the loose again, Kellerman was not going to have an easy time of it. Could it have even been Blackstone who had attempted to waylay him with the blonde in her apartment?

Kellerman at last replied. "Well, now. This certainly calls for a change in plans. I suggest the first thing we do is get out of here before we're found."

Suddenly Kayross heard something. Reaching out, he grasped the other man's arm. "What's that?" he demanded roughly.

Kellerman had heard the same sound. His cigar forgotten in a saucer, he was already on his feet, beckoning sharply. Together, they moved the short distance to the back of the establishment, where Kellerman swiftly and silently opened a window, then climbed through it and dropped to an alleyway outside. Kayross and his men were on his heels.

At the front of the saloon, Edward Blackstone and Wallace Dugald, accompanied by the other men who had been shanghaied, halted while Wallace lighted the gas jets that ordinarily illuminated the bar. Dugald wondered why the sign said Closed and yet the door was unlocked. They searched the empty place quickly as they made their way to the rear.

"Look yonder," Dugald muttered as he waved his pistol at Kellerman's still burning cigar.

Edward saw the open window, raced to it, and peered out into the dark night. The alleyway was empty. "Our bird," he said, "has flown."

Wallace raised a fist, brandished it in the air, and brought it down on the table with a crash. "I swear to you in the name of all that's holy," he cried, "that I'm going to find Karl Kellerman if it's the last thing I do on this earth! And when I get my hands on him, I'm going to repay him in full for the misery he's caused me, so help me God!"

Domino disliked the taste of rice and wasn't fond of boiled chicken either, but the doctor had ordered him to continue eating bland foods, and his discipline was so great that he did precisely what he was told. He discovered that by waiting until late evening, when his resistance was lowered, it was far easier for him to down an unpalatable meal, so he rarely ate supper before midnight.

He sat now in solitary splendor, eating the foods that he disliked so intensely, shoveling them into his mouth, then chewing them rapidly and swallowing them. He was lost in thought, his one purpose that of finishing the unappetizing meal as rapidly as possible.

A bodyguard came into the dining room. "Excuse

me for interrupting," he said, "but some of the boys have come back from the Kellerman job."

Domino brightened immediately, and even the unflavored boiled chicken and rice dish tasted much better to him. "What are you waiting for?" he demanded jovially. "Send them right in!" He sat back in his chair and grinned expectantly.

Two burly young men in their late twenties, both of them heavily armed, entered the room.

"Don't keep me in suspense," Domino said and chuckled. "Tell me you nailed his hide to the wall and slowly tortured him to death."

The pair exchanged a quick glance, and then the shorter of them spoke. "The girl is dead," he said. "Everything went off fine until the very end, and then when we broke into the bedroom, we found that Kellerman had cut her throat from ear to ear."

"She was still bleeding," his companion said, "so it had just happened."

"We ran out to the balcony," the first thug went on, "but by then it was too late. We could tell from the way the bushes down below were squashed that Kellerman had jumped from the balcony, and by the time we got outside, he was gone. We scoured the neighborhood, but it was like looking for a needle in a haystack. We even went to that bar you told us he owns, but the place was empty. It looked like someone had been there earlier, but we couldn't find any sign of Kellerman."

As always, Domino exerted great willpower in an emergency. The color drained from his face, but sitting unmoving, he asked quietly, "How did he discover that we'd set an ambush for him?"

The pair shrugged. "Damned if we know," the taller of the thugs declared. "But whatever it was that happened, it must have been awful sudden. The girl died without putting up a struggle."

"What's happened to her body?" Domino demanded.

"The other boys were going to dispose of it after they got the apartment cleaned up. Everything happened so quietly that the neighbors were left undisturbed, and there's no danger of the constabulary being called in."

"It's a shame we lost the girl," Domino said. "She seemed smarter than most, and we could have used her on all sorts of jobs. Oh, well." He sat in silence for a moment. "What are you doing about trying to locate Kellerman?"

"All the boys have been alerted," the shorter of the pair replied, "and they're searching the whole town for him. Eventually they'll catch up with him."

"And then what?" Domino asked sarcastically. "Are they going to shoot him on sight so that he dies without suffering, without being in agony? That's not the way I want to pay him back. What's more, your little posse is sure to bring the constabulary down on our necks. This is a civilized community, you know, and there's a law here against wanton killing. No. I want strict orders issued to every member of the organization. I am to be notified the moment Karl Kellerman is located, but under no circumstances is any member of the organization to lift a finger against him without getting specific orders from me first. Kellerman is too clever, and he's done us quite enough damage. When we find out where he's staying, I'll have to devote some serious thought to finding a foolproof method of eliminating him once and for all, and doing it so that he feels the pain and agony he caused me to suffer."

After much hesitation and self-doubt, Kale Martin finally concluded that the time was right for her to enter Oregon's state politics. Thus she announced her candidacy for the board of trustees of Oregon State College, a position that required a majority vote throughout the state. Newspapers everywhere printed the story.

That same night, Kale and her husband Rob were entertaining Cindy Holt and Clarissa, whose husband had not yet returned from the assignment that took him to San Francisco. As Rob carved the roast, Kale added vegetables to the plates and passed them around the table.

"You certainly touched a nerve when you decided to run for office, Kale," Clarissa said. "I've never read such an excited stir in all the papers."

Rob grinned at her, feeling enormous pride in his wife. "That's because, as luck would have it, Kale's going up against Frank Colwyn, who's running for reelection as a trustee."

"I read about this Colwyn in the paper," Clarissa

said, "but I don't see anything particularly significant in the fact that Kale's running against him."

"It's very significant, I'm afraid," Kale said. "It's rumored that Colwyn has been pocketing money that has been appropriated for the college's use by the state legislature. If so, he and the people he's paying off will fight like fury to get him reelected and keep the cash flowing into their pockets." Kale noticeably stiffened. "So that gives me all the more reason," she continued, "to try to win the election myself!"

"Good for you," Cindy told her. "It makes me furious when I think of the men who are ready to take advantage of a new state and trade on the political inexperience of that state's people. What's more, a woman has every bit as much right as a man to be elected to a position of trust in Oregon. According to the stories I've heard from my mother—and from my father, too—women contributed as much as men to the founding of this state. They suffered equally on the first wagon train that crossed North America, and they fought just as hard against the elements and savages and all the other dangers of travel in those days. I'll work hard for your election, Kale!"

"So will I," Clarissa said. "What's more, I know at least a dozen women who will gladly go from door to door persuading people to vote for you."

"I don't care what kind of pressure Frank Colwyn uses!" Cindy cried. "You're going to win this election!"

Rob exchanged a quick glance with Kale. Both of them knew the difficulties she faced, but at the same time they also believed that there was at least a chance that Kale would succeed in bringing off the unexpected and winning the election.

Over the next few days, Kale and Cindy worked out the schedules for the women who were volunteering in large numbers to help Kale in the coming election. Clarissa was busily engaged drumming up the support of still more women.

"The response has been marvelous," Kale said. "I've heard from women all over Oregon—hundreds of them. There are more of them who want to help than there are jobs to be done."

"Don't you believe it," Cindy told her. "We face an uphill struggle all the way. The men who have been obtaining graft at the taxpayers' expense aren't going to give up without putting up a tremendous fight, and we'll need all the help we can get!"

There was a tap at the front door, and Kale admitted two well-dressed men of early middle age, who introduced themselves as Jeremiah Bates and Tod Caspar. She politely invited them to come in and sit down and presented them to Cindy.

"I'm glad you're here with Mrs. Martin, Miss Holt," Bates said. "This simplifies our task, so to speak."

"We represent a bipartisan group," Caspar said, "that's been formed to ensure the reelection of Frank Colwyn as a trustee of the college. We're calling on you, Mrs. Martin, in the hope that we can persuade you to withdraw as a candidate for the board."

"We realize, Mrs. Martin," his companion said, "that you regard the election as something of a lark, but we're here to assure you that Mr. Colwyn thinks of his reelection in the most solemn manner and that he's deeply concerned about the issues that the board faces."

A flintlike quality crept into Kale's voice. "What gives you the impression that I regard the election as a lark, gentlemen?" she asked softly.

Bates shrugged and grinned. "Well, you know how it is, Mrs. Martin," he said with a slight laugh. "After all, you're a married woman, and you have a child now. I assume that there'll be others on the way to join it. All of these interests take precedence over the affairs of the college."

"They're personal interests as opposed to business interests," Kale said succinctly, "but I wouldn't say they take precedence. Quite the contrary. As it happens, Miss Holt is an undergraduate at the college, and the education she receives is of very great interest to me. So are the business affairs of the school that she attends."

"As a student at the college," Cindy interjected, "I know that Mrs. Martin has my best interests at heart. Furthermore, my classmates and colleagues feel exactly as I do." Not mentioning the rumor that Kale's opponent was pilfering state funds, Cindy went on, "We have nothing against Frank Colwyn, but we have no idea where he stands on the subject of education, even though he's been a trustee for several years."

There was a moment's pause, and Caspar turned

back to Kale. "You're the daughter-in-law of Dr. Robert Martin, if my information is correct."

"It's correct," Kale said flatly.

The man smiled. "He's practiced medicine here since he arrived as a member of the first wagon train, and he's achieved enormous popularity in the state. We'd hate to think of anyone trading on his standing in order to win the election."

"I make no mention in my campaign of my relationship to Dr. Martin, and I have no intention of bringing it up," Kale said tartly. "I believe in standing on my own feet. What's more, sir, I resent your innuendo that I intend to rely on my father-in-law's name to help me win an election."

Caspar chuckled softly, but Bates, a big man with heavy jowls, bristled and glowered at the young woman. "We know how to take a hint," he said, "and how to deal with those who are stubborn. Frank Colwyn is going to be reelected, and anyone who stands in his path will be trampled. We've gone to some pains to look up your background, Mrs. Martin, and I wonder if the voters of Oregon will approve of your past."

"I'm not ashamed of my background, Mr. Bates," Kale said in a tense voice. "I've traveled a long path in my lifetime, and I've made many mistakes, but I've overcome them, and I haven't repeated them. So you can do your damnedest, sir, and both you and your candidate have my permission to go straight to hell!" She rose to her feet, went to the door, and opened it. "I'll bid you good day, gentlemen. You've outstayed your welcome."

The pair looked at each other, then rose.

"You're making a serious mistake, Mrs. Martin," Caspar said in the doorway. "We don't want to be unpleasant, and we have no desire to drag you through the mud, but if you force our hand, we'll have to act accordingly. We'll just have to see whether the voters of Oregon will elect a retired prostitute as a trustee of their state college!"

Kale continued to face them defiantly, her back straight, her chin outthrust as they climbed into their carriage and drove off. Then suddenly she crumpled. "They weren't making idle talk when they threatened me," she said, her eyes filling with tears. "They meant every word!"

"Don't give in to them, Kale," Cindy said fiercely. "We'll beat them yet! They've declared open war on us, and we're going to fight them with their own weapons!"

Kale usually followed the same routine in her public appearances for her campaign to win a seat on the board of the state college. She accepted all offers of speaking engagements and was always accompanied by Rob, who was present to act as a buffer between her and any in her audience who might cause trouble. Kale had told her husband all about her meeting with Jeremiah Bates and Tod Caspar, and Rob had successfully consoled her, telling her he would let nothing harm her or get in her way as she ran for office.

So Kale went about her business, and in the main, she found that most audiences were sympathetic and friendly. To be sure, some people came to hear her only because they were curious about a woman's running for public office, but it was unusual when anyone was actually hostile.

The crowd that gathered to hear her on Sunday afternoon in a large church located in an as yet unnamed, growing suburb of Portland was bigger than usual. The audience was friendly, applauding her warmly, and the questions they asked were sufficiently sympathetic that she had no trouble in answering them.

The meeting ended at dusk, and as always, Kale's departure was delayed by several members of the audience, who stayed behind to speak to her. Night was falling by the time that she and Rob followed the last of the crowd out to the hitching post in front of the church, where their horses awaited them.

Standing outside the entrance were two men who were handing out leaflets to those who were emerging from the church. They didn't see Kale until she gasped, and then they turned away hurriedly.

Kale caught hold of her husband's arm and clutched it so hard that her nails dug through the fabric of his coat. "Rob," she murmured in alarm, "those two are Bates and Caspar, the pair from Frank Colwyn's headquarters who called on me and threatened me!"

Rob responded instantly. Stepping forward, he called out, "Not so fast, you two. You're handing out some papers there. Let me have one."

Jeremiah Bates reluctantly handed him a single sheet of paper.

Rob glanced at it in the light of the nearest street lamp, and a headline in heavy black type immediately caught his attention: "DO YOU WANT A WHORE IN CHARGE OF YOUR CHILDREN'S EDUCATION?"

Rob instantly crumpled the paper and threw it away, hoping that his wife had not seen it. But Kale's gasp of dismay and anger told him otherwise. She was standing beside him, staring down at the ground, her whole body trembling, and her eyes filled with tears.

Rob saw red, and before he quite realized it, he had drawn his Colt six-shooter and cocked the hammer with his thumb.

"We didn't start anything," Caspar complained in a high, whining voice. "We were just following Frank Colwyn's orders." His partner, too frightened to speak, could only nod his head in vigorous assent.

"Save your breath!" Rob told them, his tone savage. "I don't care to hear your flimsy excuses."

Both of them, staring into the muzzle of the gun, started to speak simultaneously. Rob gestured, and they fell silent.

"I'm only going to say this once," he told them harshly, "so listen carefully. If I ever catch you passing out such filth about my wife again, I'll terminate

your miserable lives instantly by putting bullets into
your hearts. I'm not joking, so I warn you—don't
tempt me! As for your employer, that rotten worm
Colwyn, tell him from me that he'd better keep out
of my sight. If I ever set eyes on him, his wife will
become a widow in a hurry!"

Badly frightened, the pair could only nod.

"My trigger finger is beginning to itch," Rob
went on, "so you'd better get out of my sight fast,
before I relieve it by pulling the trigger. Get moving!"

Bates and Caspar raced to their waiting mounts,
vaulted into their saddles, and spurring the unfortunate beasts, went galloping off down the road at
breakneck speed, both crouched low in the saddle to
avoid being hit if Martin changed his mind and decided to fire at them.

His narrowed eyes cold, Rob watched them as
they raced off. "Scum!" he said, pronouncing final
sentence on them. Then, all at once, his manner
changed. He put his arm around the still-trembling
Kale and said softly, "Put them out of your mind,
honey. I give you my word, this incident won't be
repeated."

"Frank Colwyn and his cronies made good their
threat against me," she said miserably. "Somehow I
thought they were bluffing, that they wouldn't have
the audacity to attack below the belt like this." Suddenly all her self-control snapped, and the tears flowed
freely.

"Colwyn has a rude shock waiting for him," Rob
replied, holding her tightly. "He's going to find that

vicious personal attacks are counterproductive and create sympathy for you."

She looked up at him, shaking her head and starting to protest.

"Hear me out," Rob said, "and heed what I say. I know what I'm talking about. Every dirty trick like this that Colwyn tries to pull creates that many more votes for you. Don't give him another thought. Just keep on running your own campaign in your own way."

Looking into her husband's eyes, Kale felt great reassurance. They had both known that it was going to be difficult for Kale to be the first woman in Oregon to run for a statewide office, but Rob had never waivered in his support of his wife, and Kale was damned if she was going to let him—or herself— down now. She would fight to the bitter end!

Willie Rowe, generally acknowledged as the best newspaper reporter on the Pacific Coast, sat in his shirt-sleeves in the cavernous city room of the *Oregon News*. Stocky, with tousled, dirty-blond hair and an open, friendly face, the newspaperman studied his guest. It was his business to know something about prominent people in the state, so it came as no surprise to him that the young woman opposite him was the daughter of the fabled Whip Holt and the stepdaughter of Major General Leland Blake. What he found completely unexpected was her intensity, which crackled like lightning in a storm, and her remarkably attractive appearance. It seemed to him that her natural beauty would rival that of the actresses from New York who appeared on the stage of the Portland Theater.

"Give me the facts once more, Miss Holt," Willie said. "I want to be sure that I have them straight."

"It's been rumored," Cindy said patiently, "that Frank Colwyn has been stealing state funds intended for the college. I've tried to find out more on the subject, but I can't get a thing on him."

"Why have you come to me?" Willie Rowe asked.

"If anyone can prove that Frank Colwyn is dipping his hand into public funds, you're the fellow who can do it," Cindy said. "Your record has been marvelous, and you've proved you're not afraid of anyone."

"Thanks very much," he said modestly. "It's nice to be appreciated."

"It'll be nicer still to get a headline story on Colwyn," Cindy said.

"Why are you so eager to expose him?" Willie asked, looking at her intently.

"Because I hate to see Kale Martin deliberately smeared with filth. Her background is no secret. She's never tried to hide the fact that she was once a prostitute, but to have Colwyn's supporters threaten to expose her past and to make an issue of it is quite another matter."

His interest was aroused. "Who threatened her?"

"Two men named Jeremiah Bates and Tod Caspar. I was right there and heard them myself. And their threats weren't idle. A few days later they went out and started distributing handbills full of filth about Kale. Her husband, Rob Martin, had a little run-in with Bates and Caspar, but I don't think they're through playing dirty politics."

"This becomes more involved and still more fascinating," Willie said. "Caspar and Bates are fellow trustees at the state college. Apparently they're afraid their own power will diminish if Colwyn loses the election to Mrs. Martin."

"Apparently so."

"You're sure that everything you've said to me is true?"

She met his gaze without flinching. "Dead sure."

"Are you willing to take a risk that'll mean serious trouble for you if you're caught?" he asked.

"I'm willing to do anything that's necessary to expose Frank Colwyn as a crook and to keep him from winning the election," Cindy said.

Willie Rowe snapped the pencil into two parts, threw the broken halves into a wicker wastebasket, and grinned at her. "That's what I like to hear! You have the soul of a true reporter. Have supper with me at a place I know that serves the best salmon in Oregon, and then we'll drop in on Frank Colwyn's office after hours and snoop around until we find something. This promises to be an evening that neither of us is going to forget quickly!"

A few hours later, the young couple finished dinner, arose from the table, and strolled through the Portland business district, pausing occasionally to window shop. They looked like any young man and

woman enjoying a walk on a balmy evening, with
nothing in their manner revealing their mounting
anxiety.

When they came to Frank Colwyn's office
building, they ducked inside, and Willie produced a
ring of skeleton keys. He found one that opened the
inner door, and they quietly made their way up to
the second story, then crept toward the rear, where
Colwyn's office was located.

"Keep away from the windows," Willie warned,
"just in case somebody down below should be looking up. Fortunately, there's enough of a moon tonight that we can see well enough without being
forced to light a lamp." He sighed. "There's only one
way to do this. You take the two filing cases over
yonder, and I'll start going through these two. If you
run across anything that you think might give us a
lead, let me know."

Cindy's heart hammered in her ears, and her
breath was short as she opened the top drawer of the
nearer filing cabinet. She realized she was engaged
in an enterprise that was illegal, and if she should be
apprehended, the fact that she was Whip Holt's
daughter and General Blake's stepdaughter would
not save her from a prison term.

She fully intended to go through the files in an
orderly way, but she couldn't resist the temptation to
glance first through a thick folder marked *Finances,
Oregon State College*.

Within moments, she was utterly absorbed in
what she was reading and forgot her sense of danger.

"Willie," she called softly, "I think I may have found something."

The reporter joined her and looked at some documents still in the folder. "My God!" he said in tense excitement. "You've stumbled onto a gold mine! These are figures for three years ago. Now we have to find similar forms for last year and this year."

They searched frantically, and within a short time, they found what they were seeking.

Willie was satisfied. "We'll just help ourselves to these papers," he said, "which will be enough to convince any judge in the state, and then we'll get out of here. Make certain you leave everything else exactly as you found it."

They hurriedly straightened the file folder before they departed, taking the telltale documents with them.

Once they reached the street, they abandoned their pose of being a young couple out for a stroll, and they hurried back to the offices of the *News*. There, Willie examined the papers with greater care, shaking his head and whistling softly under his breath as he inspected them. As Cindy continued to wait, he hurried up to the desk of his editor in the center of the room and conferred at length with him. He was smiling broadly when he came back to his own desk.

"I have a go-ahead sign," he said. "We're going to explode a bomb under Frank Colwyn in tomorrow's *News*." He sat down and began to scribble rapidly on sheet after sheet of foolscap. As he finished each page, Cindy barely had time to read it before someone whisked it away for editing and delivery to the printer downstairs. She lost all sense of time and was surprised when Willie sat back in his chair and lighted a cigar. "We don't have long to wait," he told her.

As he had predicted, his article soon was in print. For the first time since the *News* had announced the election of U. S. Grant as the President of the United States, a full banner headline ran across all eight columns of the paper. Frank Colwyn and two of his fellow trustees were flatly accused of stealing state funds that had been granted to the college.

Looking at the article again, Cindy was stunned. It was far more authoritative in print than it had been when handwritten, and the columns of figures beside it taken direct from Colwyn's own files told the story themselves. He and his two fellow trustees had stolen many thousands of dollars in state funds. There was no doubt in her mind that charges would be filed against Colwyn.

"I'll get you a cup of coffee," Willie told her, "and then I'll ride you out to your brother's ranch for what's left of the night. All I ask in return is that when you wake, you set up an early appointment with Mrs. Kale Martin for me. Our readers will want to know all about her, now that her election as a trustee seems to be assured."

The United States Military Academy cadets spent Saturday morning drilling on the parade ground overlooking the Hudson River at West Point, New York.

Prizes were awarded at the conclusion of the exercise, and as always, the first place in close-order drill was won by the squad commanded by Cadet Sergeant Henry Blake, the adopted son of Eulalia Holt Blake and Major General Leland Blake.

Hank Blake and his subordinates, all of them underclassmen, took no undue pride in their achievements. There was a task to be accomplished, and they performed it to the very best of their joint ability. The squad members took their cue from Hank, who was a perfectionist. Never totally satisfied with what they did, they kept pushing themselves to their limits. It was predicted in the corps of cadets that someday all sixteen members of the squad would wear the stars of generals on their shoulders.

The weekends for cadets normally began at noon on Saturdays, but there was no way Hank could take off any time for pleasurable pursuits. He had to practice sprints with the track team for an hour, and after noon dinner he would be required to put on an exhibition of rifle shooting for parents and other visitors. The rifle team was scheduled to hold a contest with Yale University in midafternoon, and everyone was rooting for Hank, who was just beginning his junior year, to lead the army to another victory. He had never suffered a defeat in two years of contests, and there was no reason he should lose today.

Other cadets would attend a dance on campus that night, but Hank had decided to spend the evening in the West Point library. Not that he was behind in his subjects. Indeed, he consistently won high honors in all of his classes, and there was no need for him to spend a Saturday night at his books. He intended, however, to devote the better part of the evening to the luxury of writing a letter.

Academy rules made it impossible for Cindy Holt and Hank to announce their engagement before his senior year, but that did not prevent them from having a private understanding. After Hank was graduated and had won his commission as a lieutenant, they intended to be married. Separated from Cindy by three thousand miles, Hank preferred sending her a letter to spending an evening with some other girl. He had tried to date other girls, but had found them poor substitutes. If the truth be known—and Hank didn't care who knew it—his love for Cindy was the most important factor in his life.

He walked alone to the mess hall, where relatively few cadets were on hand for Saturday night supper. After finishing his meal, he strolled to the library, passing en route the hall in which the dance was being held. The strains of a Viennese waltz, currently the most popular music with the younger generation, drifted out to him but in no way tempted him. If he could not spend the evening with Cindy, he would devote the time to her in another way.

Reaching the nearly empty library building, he sat down at one of the desks and began his letter to her, first rereading her last communication to him. The coming of the transcontinental railroad had made a significant difference in the delivery time of mail; a letter between the Atlantic and Pacific coasts was now delivered within the remarkable time of ten days. Thus he was able to read all about her recent campaign to elect Kale Martin to public office and how she had joined a young newspaper reporter, invading the offices of the incumbent, with startling results.

The incident was typical of Cindy, Hank reflected. Once again, she had demonstrated courage, unflagging determination, and bulldoglike tenacity in the pursuit of her goal.

Ordinarily shy and somewhat inhibited, Hank poured out his love for Cindy onto paper. He told her he would not be fulfilled or become a whole person until they were married. For her sake, as well as his own, he was working hard, and so far he continued to rank first in his class. He wanted General and Mrs. Blake to be proud of him, and above all, he wanted Cindy to take pride in his accomplishments. General William T. Sherman, the army chief of staff, had indicated to General Blake that if Hank ranked high enough in his class, he would win a special assignment with the cavalry when he became a second lieutenant. He had no idea of the nature of that assignment, but for Cindy's sake, he was determined to win it.

He confessed to her that he was counting the days until the time when they could make their engagement public.

The letter flowed easily, filling page after page, and when he finished it, Hank was tired but satisfied.

He had occupied himself in the next best way to spending the evening with his beloved Cindy.

Despite his inability so far to apprehend either Karl Kellerman or Captain Kayross, Edward was determined to find his missing cousin, and he called on the New Orleans constabulary to perform the painstaking task of checking the registration ledgers of every major hotel and lodging house in the city. At last Edward learned that a woman who called herself Millicent Kellerman was a guest at the Louisiana House.

Edward and Jim went there immediately, accompanied by Tommie and Randy, and discovered that although the rent had been paid in advance until the first of the month, Kellerman had already checked out. Gaining admission to the suite, the quartet discovered that the wardrobe closets were filled with a woman's clothing, but that Kellerman had taken all his belongings. They gathered in the parlor of the suite to discuss the problem.

"It's as though she disappeared from the face of the earth," said Tommie, shaking her head.

"All we know for certain," Jim said, "is that Kellerman has cleared out of this suite. By the same token, we can assume that Millicent is still here, although there's no way of knowing where she may be at the moment."

They were interrupted by the unexpected arrival of Jean-Pierre Gautier. After he introduced himself, he explained, "I must ask you to pardon this intrusion, but I will be blunt with you. I've had the pleasure of meeting Miss Randall several times, and I have fallen head over heels in love with her. I am exerting every possible effort to locate her."

Tommie recognized Jean-Pierre's name and identified him as a member of one of the wealthy, old French families of New Orleans. She went out of her way to welcome him and was so cordial that her male companions were equally pleasant to him. After bringing Jean-Pierre up to date on what little they knew of Millicent's whereabouts, they became involved in a long, complex discussion of the best way to proceed to find her.

While they were weighing various proposals, the front door of the suite slowly opened, and Millicent staggered into the room. Everyone present jumped up and began talking simultaneously.

Jean-Pierre, however, had the presence of mind to put a supporting arm around Millicent and lead her to the divan. Her makeshift dress still covered her body, but her feet were cut, bruised, and bleeding, swollen to almost double their normal size. Giving a deep, tremulous sigh, she collapsed onto the divan.

Edward ordered tea and toast sent up to the suite, and all the men left the room while Tommie removed the woman's filthy garment, helped her bathe, and clothed her in a nightgown and dressing robe. At the same time, Jean-Pierre sent a messenger to his family doctor, asking the physician to come to the hotel at his earliest convenience.

Only then was it possible for Millicent to relate what had happened to her. She told her story between bites of buttered toast and sips of tea, and her listeners were horrified as she recounted her incarceration on the *Diana*, the escape from the Malay woman who had tortured her, and the grueling four-day walk back to New Orleans through the Louisiana bayous, during which time she had repeatedly gotten lost.

"This is all Kellerman's doing," Tommie exclaimed. "He must be mad!"

"I thought this was a matter to be handled privately," Edward said, "and I tried. But all of you know the results. I succeeded only in making matters worse for everyone concerned. I'm going to the constabulary and swear out a warrant for Karl Kellerman's arrest."

Jean-Pierre was equally realistic. "I have no intention of leaving Millicent here, where Kellerman could return at any time and do her harm." Turning to Millicent, he said, "As soon as the doctor has been here, I'm going to have you moved to my parents' house. You'll be safe there."

Millicent tried to protest, but Jean-Pierre refused to listen. "I'm running no risks with your safety," he went on. "I almost lost you once, and I'm not going to take that chance again."

The physician soon arrived and subjected Millicent to a thorough examination. He applied an ointment to her feet and gave her an extra supply in a small tin to be rubbed in twice a day. The bruises on

her backside would soon disappear, he said. She was
in good enough condition to make the move to the
Gautier house as soon as she wanted. After the
physician's departure, Jean-Pierre busied himself arranging Millicent's immediate transfer to his parents'
home, while she hastily dressed and made up her
face.

Before the afternoon ended, she was carried on
a litter to the house in the old French Quarter, and
all of her belongings were moved with her. Her stay
with Karl Kellerman at the Louisiana Hotel became
a memory buried in her past, and as she began to
recover, she was able to look forward with confidence toward her future for the first time since she
had impulsively left Idaho.

VII

Shortly after his arrival in San Francisco, Toby had received an invitation to dine at the home of Chet and Clara Lou Harris. He accepted with pleasure, and when he arrived at the big granite mansion on Nob Hill, he was delighted to find Wong Ke and his wife, Mei-lo, also present.

After Toby told them about his earlier meeting with Kung Lee, the Chinese couple expressed their deep gratitude to him for trying to help. "All the same," the diminutive, black-haired Mei-lo said, "I'm worried for you, Toby. The tong is vicious and cruel toward anyone it considers an enemy, and I'm afraid they have you on the list now."

"That's good," Toby replied, "because I've become their enemy, and I don't care who knows it."

Ke shook his head. "I urge you to tread softly, Toby," he said. "My wife is right when she talks about the viciousness of these people. There's literally no controlling them, and they're always out for blood. Please watch your step."

Chet grinned. "I don't think we need to worry overly much about Toby," he said. "He's Whip Holt's son, so you can be sure he can take care of himself."

"I've heard countless stories of your father's exploits," Clara Lou said, "just as I've heard nothing but good about you in more recent years. All the same, Toby, be careful!"

They dined on clam chowder, sauteed abalone, and the steamed hard-shelled crabs that were a San Francisco delicacy. The talk flowed freely, and not until they were enjoying an after-dinner drink in the library of the Harris mansion did Toby become aware of the time. "I'd better get back to my hotel," he said, "before I overstay my welcome."

Wong Ke and Mei-lo left when he did, and the weather was so balmy and the view from the crest of Nob Hill was so spectacular in the moonlight that Toby decided to walk back to the hotel, first escorting the Chinese couple to their own house a short distance down Nob Hill.

"Remember—take care, Toby," Mei-lo said as they parted.

He assured her that he would, and after they had gone into the house, he stood for a time looking down at the waters of San Francisco Bay and at the islands in the water. The view, he thought, was unparalleled in any American city.

Suddenly he froze. Turning the corner less than a block away and coming toward him in single file

were six men, all of them wearing the black cos-
tumes of the Chinese tong. In the lead was a squat,
ferocious-looking man carrying a throwing knife in
each hand. It was Ho Tai.

Toby realized at once that having seen them
clearly in the moonlight meant that they had been
able to see him, too. It was obvious that they had
been waiting for him outside the Harris house and
had followed him to the Wong house. The tong
proposed to even the score with Toby Holt.

Toby thought for a moment of asking Wong Ke
and his wife to give him refuge, but he discarded the
thought as soon as it crossed his mind. They had
been made to suffer enough, and he did not want to
involve them with the murderous tong again.

Walking briskly, but not allowing himself to break
into a run, Toby turned the next corner and resolutely headed back toward the peak of Nob Hill. The
area was made up of private homes, many of them
surrounded by brick walls, and no one else was
abroad at this hour. In fact, he saw no lights burning
anywhere.

He went no farther than a half-block, when he
halted and stepped into the deep shadows cast by a
large shade tree. From this vantage point, he saw his
pursuers clearly, when they, too, rounded the corner.
Ho Tai was still in the lead, gripping his knives as he
moved swiftly up the steep incline. The expression
in his dark eyes was grim and in spite of Toby's
courage, it sent chills up his spine.

As Ho Tai and his companions drew nearer,

Toby glanced over his shoulder and saw a brick wall about five feet high that stood at the edge of the sidewalk, marking the boundaries of the property on the far side of the wall.

Giving himself no opportunity to weigh the consequences, he suddenly leaped up onto the crest of the wall and dropped down into the garden within. He was just in time. As he landed, he distinctly heard the soft patter of rushing footsteps on the far side of the wall as Ho Tai and his companions continued their pursuit.

But Toby was not yet out of danger. He felt rather than saw a dark shape materialize nearby and heard a low, deep, menacing growl.

His eyes adjusting to the darkness, he soon made out a large dog—obviously a watchdog—cautiously approaching him. Fortunately it had not yet started barking.

Toby had no intention of doing anything that would cause the animal to attack him or to bark. Standing very still, he waited for a time until the footsteps outside the wall began to fade. Then he started to speak soothingly to the dog, keeping his voice pitched very low. For what felt like an eternity, the dog continued to growl softly, but eventually the stranger's lack of hostility caused the animal to stop. It continued to hold its head cocked to one side, however, with its ears erect.

Toby knew he couldn't delay indefinitely, that one false move and the dog would attack as it had been trained to do. Continuing to address the animal quietly, the young man measured his distance from the wall and, gathering himself together, suddenly leaped toward it and managed to scramble to the top.

The dog, its fangs bared, hurled itself at the retreating target. However, it succeeded only in crashing into the wall, leaving the man unscathed.

From the relative safety of the parapet, Toby saw that Ho Tai and his associates had vanished. He dropped down into the street and started downhill at full speed, running as he had never before raced.

On the far side of the thick wall, the dog began to bark, but its quarry was gone.

Slowing his pace momentarily at every street intersection to see if Ho Tai and the other tong members were anywhere within sight, Toby ran on, heading downhill for two blocks, then crossing over a side street and heading upward again for a block before crossing another side street and resuming his downward journey. Even though he was in superb physical condition, he soon was gasping for breath, and his legs felt like lead.

Finally he found a coach for hire, and hailing the driver, he climbed into the backseat and fell onto the seat in exhaustion. But he did not feel truly safe until he reached his hotel room and bolted the door behind him.

Looking back on the encounter as he relaxed, Toby had no reason to take any pride in the evening's incident. At the very least, the hatchet man for the tong had forced him to flee for his life, and he knew this had been an inauspicious beginning for a venture that required boldness as well as courage.

For the next few days, Toby spent most of his time in his hotel, thinking about the situation with the tong. He realized he was no closer now to the achievement of his goal than he had been when he accepted the assignment of breaking up the tong.

After piecing together everything he had learned about the tong, Toby concluded that the key figure was not Kung Lee, the executive, but Ho Tai, his bodyguard and strongman. Ho Tai was the symbol of the brute strength that characterized the tong, of the terror that the organization generated in the hearts and minds of the residents of San Francisco's Chinatown and other cities. It was Ho Tai's wanton cruelty that enabled the tong to flourish and to flout the law as it chose. Those who were persecuted and intimidated by the tong were afraid to bring legal charges against the organization and, instead, preferred to suffer in silence. Immigrants from China were so frightened they bowed to the will of the tong, as did those who had been in the United States for as long as two or three generations.

Kung Lee might be the brains of the tong, but few American Chinese would recognize his name or his portrait. Ho Tai, however, would be immediately familiar to them. The ruthless strongman, who carried out the will of his superiors, was the symbol of tong rule in America.

It occurred to Toby that if he bested Kung Lee

legally, few Chinese would hear of his victory and fewer still would applaud. His triumph in that respect would be met with indifference. But if he scored a victory over Ho Tai, it would be celebrated wildly in every Chinatown in the United States. Since the tong's hatchet man was regarded as the embodiment of evil, his defeat would be an achievement that no one would forget. The tongs would lose stature, ordinary men would be heartened and would rebel against them, and the power of the secret societies would be vastly reduced.

Therefore, Toby reasoned, the best way to attack the tongs would be to launch an assault on Ho Tai, no matter how great the risks.

Realizing that he would be exposing himself to grave dangers, he told none of his friends in San Francisco about his specific plans. Visiting innumerable restaurants, curio shops, silk stores, and other retail establishments in Chinatown, he carefully spread disparaging remarks about Ho Tai, declaring that he was dishonorable and a coward and deserved to be whipped out of the community.

Some of those to whom Toby spoke pretended not to hear him, but others listened avidly, and a number of them made notes of his remarks, so he was fairly certain that word of his insults was getting back to Ho Tai.

Three or four days after Toby launched his campaign, a stranger approached him in the hotel dining room while he was eating his noon dinner. The man came up to his table, asked his identity, and after learning that he was indeed Toby Holt, thrust a small scroll into his hand.

The message was crudely printed in English and bore no signature. It said: *Meet me at three hours past midnight tonight at the offices of the tong. Then we will see who has courage.*

Convinced that the Chinese bodyguard had taken the bait, Toby was satisfied. In the confrontation that was certain to take place, Toby had certain natural advantages, and he intended to exploit them to the fullest. As his father before him, he was endowed with extraordinary eyesight and hearing, qualities that would stand him in good stead in a middle-of-the-night battle with a wily foe. He also knew he was second to none as a marksman, a fact that had been highly publicized. Equally expert with throwing knives, Toby would carry a full set of those weapons with him, too.

Early that evening, Toby ate a light meal, then forced himself to go to bed, where he dropped off to sleep for several hours of necessary rest before he faced the challenge of his life.

Awakening after midnight, he dressed carefully in black boots and trousers, a dark shirt, and a dark, broad-brimmed western hat. As he strapped on his repeating pistols and placed his throwing knives in his belt, he vividly remembered advice that his father had given him years earlier: "Whenever you're involved in a close fight, where the outcome is in doubt, never lose sight of the fact that your most important asset is your attitude. If you're convinced that you're going to win, you will win. Doubt your own abilities, and the outcome of the fight will be in doubt."

It was easy to understand why Whip Holt had never lost a battle, Toby thought and smiled. All he had to remember was that he was Whip's son, and everything would fall into place.

Feeling the need for physical exercise, he walked to Chinatown, stretching his legs and pumping his arms in order to limber them.

When he reached the tong headquarters, he stood in the shadows of the doorway across the street and examined the building with care. The curio shop that occupied the better part of the ground floor was dark, and the second story, where the headquarters of the tong was located, seemed equally deserted, with no lights burning anywhere in the building.

Looking at his pocket watch, Toby saw that he was only five minutes early for his appointment. Rather than wait for the short time to elapse, he would act immediately.

Deliberately crossing the street some distance up the block where he knew he could not be seen from the tong headquarters, he retraced his steps until he reached the front door. The latch responded instantly to his touch, and the door opened silently. Toby quickly stepped inside and found himself in a narrow hallway adjacent to the curio shop. Directly ahead the staircase to the upper story loomed in the dark, and as he approached it, he stopped and smiled ironically.

Directly in front of the bottom stair stood two tin buckets, each of them with several metal kitchen utensils protruding from their tops. Clearly, Ho Tai had placed the crude obstacle in his path as a means of warning that Toby was approaching.

Toby made a detour around the pails and silently began to mount the stairs, one hand on the hilt of a throwing knife. Common sense told him that the knives were preferable to pistols as weapons because the latter would reveal his whereabouts with· a flash when ever one of them was fired.

Another obstacle had been set as a trap for him just before he reached the top of the stairs. The top of one step below the landing had been removed, which meant that someone unwary would trip, stumble, or fall into the hole. But Toby's excellent vision came to his rescue for the second time, and he carefully avoided the hole in the step as he moved up to the landing.

Cautioning himself to take his time, he moved slowly down the corridor toward the offices of the tong. He had succeeded in avoiding two crude traps that had been set, and he was inclined to believe that still others awaited him.

The entrance to the tong's suite of offices was wide open, and Toby stopped short, peering hard at the open doorway. At first he saw nothing, but at last he thought that he caught sight of a thin string that was stretched across the opening at waist level. He moved closer to it and saw that it was indeed a trap. One end was tacked to the wall, and the other was attached to the open door itself. Against the door, a number of tin cans had been placed so that a mere touch of the string would cause the door to move and make the cans rattle, alerting someone hiding in the offices beyond the door.

Exerting still greater caution, Toby bent almost double as he advanced under the trap without setting it off.

Taking care to station himself near a wall rather than be exposed by standing completely in the open, he peered hard around the office in which he found himself.

Dividing the room into rough segments, he studied each section separately as he searched for Ho Tai. But his efforts were in vain. He finally had to satisfy himself that his foe had chosen to await his coming somewhere else.

Toby was forced to advance still farther into the suite. Again he came to an open doorway that separated two offices, and he hesitated before he stepped over the threshold. He saw no semblance of any obstacle, no hint of any trick, yet he was convinced that Ho Tai would not miss this opportunity to try to get rid of him.

Then he looked down at the carpet, and for an instant he froze.

Something was inching toward him on the floor. On close examination, it proved to be a snake about a half-inch in diameter and two feet in length. It was impossible to distinguish any of the snake's markings in the dark, but Toby assumed that it was poisonous.

The snake raised its head to strike. Toby was ready for it. Grasping a throwing knife by the hilt, he threw it at the serpent. The snake's head was severed from its body, which thrashed violently on the floor and then continued to writhe feebly.

Knowing he had been spared another time, Toby retrieved his knife and crossed the threshold, where he scrutinized the room with infinite care. As his eyes adjusted further to the light, he saw that the richly furnished room was much as he remembered it. The thick Oriental rug had been changed, but the porcelain jars and the magnificent wall hangings were the same, as was the delicate tea service of porcelain that graced a low table.

On the far side of the room, beyond the tea set, a dark shadow loomed.

Making no move, scarcely daring to breathe, Toby studied the shape intently and finally made out that it was indeed a person. Ho Tai was crouching on the floor, poised for action, ready to attack the moment Toby drew nearer.

Toby realized luck was with him. Ho Tai hadn't counted on his foe's extraordinary eyesight and no doubt believed he remained undetected in his hiding place. Slowly drawing one of his throwing knives, hoping the darkness concealed what he was doing, Toby raised his arm inch by inch until it was in position to release the blade. He had only one chance to hit his target before Ho Tai would launch his own attack.

All at once, Toby realized with chagrin that Ho

Tai had indeed detected his foe's movements and was about to throw his own knife at the newcomer. There was only one way Toby could protect himself. He realized he had to unleash his throwing knife before his foe could let fly with his own knife. If his aim was less than perfect, he might be unable to avoid Ho Tai's blade and would be killed.

Reacting instinctively, Toby threw his knife. The blade was a dark blur as it sped across the room. All the years of Toby's rigorous training proved effective: The blade found its target, and Ho Tai grunted as the steel sank into his flesh, killing him before he had an opportunity to release his own knife.

Toby strode across the room and stood above his fallen foe. Ho Tai stared with sightless eyes at the ceiling, his knife wound spewing blood on the precious Oriental rug.

Rather than retrieve his blade, Toby preferred to let it continue to protrude from Ho Tai's body, where it would serve as a warning to the leaders of the tong. Realizing that the tong could say that Ho Tai was sent back to China to perform some duty, and then replace him with another hatchet man who would continue the tong's reign of terror, Toby carried an Oriental armchair to the busiest street in Chinatown. Then he went back for the body of Ho Tai, which he dragged through the streets, then sat upright on the chair, the blade still protruding from his heart. Toby assumed that in the morning when people started on their daily rounds, everybody in Chinatown would get the message.

Toby promptly took his leave and went to the nearest police station, where he reported on the incident in full.

"You're one in a million, Mr. Holt," the sergeant in charge of the night shift said. "You have no idea how many men have sought vengeance against Ho Tai and how many of them have died for their pains. I don't know what will happen next: Either the tong will send a whole squad of assassins after you now, or they'll decide to leave you alone."

"I have an idea," Toby replied, "that Kung Lee's reign of terror will come to an end now that his henchman has been killed and disgraced. But if I'm wrong, he'll find out soon enough that I have more knives and that I haven't lost the knack of throwing them!"

Jean-Pierre Gautier held the chair for his mother, Helene, as she seated herself at the table in the opulently furnished dining room. Then the handsome, brown-haired young man seated himself and bowed his head as his father, Josef, said grace. According to family tradition, conversation was permitted only after grace was said, but Josef Gautier waited until the serving maid had brought steaming dishes of large, delicately flavored Gulf shrimp to the table and retreated to the kitchen.

"I think it's only fair to tell you, Jean-Pierre," he said, "that I'm investigating your upstairs guest."

His son registered alarm. "What do you mean, Papa?" he demanded.

Helene Gautier intervened smoothly. "You brought this young woman to us when she was too ill to walk," she said. "We've given her our hospitality freely, and we've had our own physician taking care of her. It seems to your father and me that the least we can ask in return is some information on the girl's background and standing."

Jean-Pierre bristled. "Isn't it enough," he demanded, "that I've fallen in love with her?"

"To be sure," his father replied, "if you should marry her, that will more than suffice for everyone in town whom we know. A Gautier writes his own rules in New Orleans society. All the same, your mother and I have a right to want something substantial in the way of the girl's background."

"You sound," Jean-Pierre said accusingly, "as though you're dubious about Millicent."

His parents exchanged a quick glance. "To tell you the truth," Josef said, "we do have a number of questions about her."

"I'll grant you that she was exhausted and helpless when you brought her here," Helene said, "but, nevertheless, you must admit her face was plastered with far heavier makeup than any New Orleans lady has ever worn, and her dress was extraordinary, to say the least."

"She was lucky to escape with her life and to be able to make her way back to the city from the bayous," Jean-Pierre said indignantly. "When she dressed and made herself up before coming here with me, I doubt if she was giving much thought to her appearance."

"We aren't necessarily being critical," his mother assured him. "On the other hand, if you're as serious about her as you appear to be, I think we have a right to inquire into her background."

"Regardless of what your investigation may disclose," Jean-Pierre said, "I intend to do my very best to persuade Millicent to marry me."

His parents sighed, and his mother deliberately changed the subject. She knew from long experience that Jean-Pierre was stubborn, single-minded, and utterly determined to have his way once he was sure of his course.

Helene talked about the New Orleans Symphony Orchestra, of which she was a patron, then father and son, being in business together, talked briefly about various contractual matters that were pending at the office. Conversation flagged somewhat as they ate their roast, and they paid no attention when they heard the doorbell ring. A few minutes later one of the maids came into the dining room with a yellow envelope resting on a silver tray.

"Pardon me," the maid said, "but this telegram has just arrived for monsieur."

Josef excused himself, opened the envelope, and took quite a long time reading and digesting the message that had been sent to him.

"This," he said, "is a telegram from the banker in Baltimore from whom I made inquiries about Millicent Randall. He begins by assuring me there's no need for him to hire Mr. Pinkerton's agency to look into the young lady's background. He assures me that her social and financial standings are impeccable and that she comes from one of the oldest families in Baltimore. In addition, she has acquired a considerable reputation as a flutist, and she has also composed music for the flute at the Baltimore Conservatory."

Helene stared down at her plate in silence, then raised her head and looked at her son. "We owe you an apology for doubting your taste and your judgment, Jean-Pierre," she said, "and we owe an apology to Millicent as well."

"She's suffered quite enough," Jean-Pierre replied. "If you don't mind, Maman, I much prefer that you make no mention of having doubted her."

"Of course," Helene said. "Rest assured that she'll be accorded every courtesy."

After supper Jean-Pierre went up to the room that Millicent was occupying and found her in bed eating a small portion of chicken cooked in wine on a bed of mushrooms and rice. "How do you feel this evening?" he asked her.

"I'm much better," she replied, sighing contentedly. "The ointment the doctor prescribed for my feet is doing wonders for them, and they should be fine in another day or two."

"What about the rest of you?" he asked.

Millicent smiled. "I haven't felt this free of care and worry for a long time. I'll soon be back to normal, too."

"That's good news," he declared.

"Now it's my turn to ask the questions," she said. "Whose bedroom am I using? From the way it's furnished, it looks like it's a young girl's room."

"So it is," Jean-Pierre said. "This was the room of my little sister, Marie. She died of the plague that broke out in the city during the last year of the war, and my parents were so heartbroken they've left her room exactly as it was when she was still alive."

"I didn't know," she murmured. "I'm sorry."

"This will interest you," he said, and standing, he went to a bookcase, where he picked up an oblong case. He brought it to the bed and handed it to her.

Millicent opened the case and was delighted when she saw a flute resting on a bed of satin. Removing the flute from the case, she fingered it experimentally. "This appears to be a very good instrument," she said.

"I'm sure my parents bought Marie the best that's made," Jean-Pierre told her. "She had a great deal of promise as a flutist, and the music world suffered a loss when she died."

Millicent put the flute into its case, which she placed on the bedside table beside her. "I've got to hurry my convalescence," she said. "I'm afraid I'm taking unfair advantage of you and your family."

"You're not imposing on my parents or on me," Jean-Pierre said flatly. "The least we can do is to take care of you after all that you've suffered."

"I have no right to expect such kindness from strangers," she said.

He looked at her, common sense warning him not to press too hard or too fast. He needed to become better acquainted with her before he revealed his true feelings, and he didn't want to frighten her after her terrifying experience with Karl Kellerman.

"We look forward to a relationship where we'll no longer be regarded as strangers," he said, and felt himself growing red in the face.

Millicent instantly understood what he was trying to say, and he was so ill at ease that she became embarrassed, too. The atmosphere changed suddenly, and they had such difficulty in communicating that Jean-Pierre finally was compelled to cut short his visit. He took his leave, promising that he would see her in the morning after breakfast, before he went off to his office.

Alone now, Millicent thought about him at length. Jean-Pierre was a member of her own class, and she understood him completely, just as he appeared to understand her. She recognized his thoughtfulness and generosity, and she knew that there was no way she could measure his kindness to her.

She doubted if she loved Jean-Pierre and could not pretend otherwise to herself. After her recent experience with Kellerman, she was incapable of loving any man. But the potential for a deeper relationship with Jean-Pierre certainly existed, and she was content at the moment just to wait and see what happened. She felt peaceful and serene in his

presence, and she suspected that given sufficient
time, love would grow.

Millicent glanced at the flute lying in its case,
and gradually a yearning to play the instrument crept
over her. She had not really thought about the flute
since her days in Idaho, but now the need to express
herself through music grew in her until it became an
overwhelming force.

Scarcely realizing what she was doing, she lifted
the flute to her lips and found herself playing a
sonata by Handel, the music soon filling the house.

Every note was clear in the private sitting room
located at the far end of the second floor. Josef
Gautier put down the commodities report that he
was reading and listened intently, his eyes staring off
into space. Helene, who was knitting an antimacassar
for the back of a chair, stopped her efforts, her
needles poised in midair. "Listen, Josef!" she whispered fiercely.

"I am listening," he replied in a barely audible
voice.

By now tears were streaming down Helene's
face, and she took a handkerchief from her pocket
and wiped her eyes. "I can't explain it," she said,
"but I know now that our Marie has been restored to
us! In a way that defies all reason and logic!"

Josef was weeping openly, too. He removed his
spectacles and carefully wiped his eyes. "Our Marie
has come to life again in the person of Millicent
Randall," he said. "No one else has ever played the
flute in that loving, special way."

*   *   *

Edward Blackstone and Jim Randall decided to stay in New Orleans until they finished the business that had brought them there. Millicent had been found and was safe, but there was still the matter of bringing Karl Kellerman and Captain Kayross to justice. For his part, Wallace Dugald, who had reopened the bar bearing his name, had not let up in his desire to repay Kellerman for the abuses he had made the Scotsman suffer. Patrons of his bar were invariably treated to one of Wallace's tirades about his need for revenge, and the fact was, business at Dugald's fell off greatly, no one wanting to go there and be lectured to. As for the other men who had been shanghaied, having no personal knowledge of their abductors, they were now glad just to have the nightmare over with, to be able to resume their normal daily lives.

Meanwhile, Edward and Tommie, certain they were meant for each other, wrote to Tommie's father, announcing their desire to be married. Captain Harding wired back, giving them his blessing and saying that he would join his daughter and her fiancé in New Orleans so they could plan to be married there.

Randy Savage, Jim Randall's foreman, returned home to Boise in Idaho. Jim had asked Randy to take a letter to his wife, Pamela, at their ranch. He wrote to say that Millicent was safe at last, and although she had made no specific plans as yet, he suspected that before long, she would agree to marry Jean-Pierre Gautier. In addition, Edward and Tommie were also intending to be wed, and Jim told his wife to be prepared to come to New Orleans in order to attend the weddings.

As Millicent convalesced, Josef and Helene Gautier used their considerable influence on the young woman's behalf, and, as a result, every door in New Orleans opened magically to her. She met the conductor of the New Orleans Symphony Orchestra at a dinner party they gave at their house, and she and the orchestra leader discovered they had a number of friends in common in the musical world. After supper, Millicent entertained the guests by playing several pieces on her flute, with the orchestra leader accompanying her on the piano, and the result was an invitation to appear as a soloist the following month with the orchestra. Excited by the challenge, she gladly accepted.

Millicent was thrown into frenzied activity that allowed her no time to brood on the mistakes she had made and on the suffering she had undergone. She spent several hours each day practicing the flute, and for the two weeks prior to the concert, she rehearsed daily with the orchestra.

Dressing and making up—and, above all, thinking and acting—as a lady, Millicent experienced a transformation that was so gradual she had no idea it was even taking place. Totally absorbed in her music, which meant everything to her, she became what she once had been—a lady—and the reversal was permanent.

She was busy, too, with fittings for the new

gown that Josef and Helene Gautier were having made for her to wear to the concert, and there were parties given in her honor almost every night by leaders of New Orleans society. Millicent had returned to her own milieu, the world she knew best, and she flourished happily there.

Jean-Pierre was her constant companion, escorting her to social events, taking her to and from rehearsals in his carriage, and appearing constantly at her side. It was assumed by everyone in New Orleans society that she and the young widower had arrived at an understanding, but the truth of the matter was that Jean-Pierre had carefully refrained from mentioning marriage to her.

"I love her, and I want to marry her," he told his parents when they questioned him, "but I don't want to rush her. She's had some dreadful experiences that would have ruined a lesser person, and I want to give her the time to regain her bearings and stand on her own feet again."

Helene Gautier was both amused and somewhat nettled by her son's attitude. "When do you intend to propose to her?"

Jean-Pierre shrugged. "I can't say for certain, Maman," he replied, "but I'll know when the time is right, and I'll act accordingly."

His mother sighed, shook her head, and kept her own counsel. She thought it ironic that there had been a time when she had been afraid her son would ask Millicent Randall to marry him, and now that Millicent had proved more than socially acceptable,

Helene Gautier was afraid that he would propose too late or otherwise bungle matters.

While Millicent was leading a life of activity and excitement, Karl Kellerman was forced to lead a far different existence. By making discreet inquiries of various small-time underworld figures, he had learned that Domino was still alive and that the powerful gang leader sought vengeance against him. It was Domino's men, no doubt, who had tried to waylay him in the blonde's apartment, he thought. Kellerman knew, too, that Wallace Dugald would not rest until he evened the score with his former partner, and he also realized that Edward Blackstone and Jim Randall were on his trail and would not relax until they obtained justice for his misdeeds in his relationship with Millicent.

So Kellerman was in hiding. He grew a beard and a long, drooping mustache, which he dyed brown along with his hair, and he took up permanent residence in the slum quarters of the city. He took care to avoid saloons, restaurants, and gaming houses where he might be recognized, and he avoided the company of the beautiful women he had made a practice of squiring around town. Buying his food from local greengrocers, he was even reduced to cooking his own meals. He became something of a recluse and spent hours each day railing against fate and building up his hatred for Millicent, whom he regarded as responsible for all his troubles. And the longer he remained mired in the depths to which he had descended, the greater his anger became.

He had no one to whom he could turn for assistance. Captain Robin Kayross, his natural ally, was also in hiding, his ship having been impounded by the New Orleans authorities. There was obviously no reason for Kayross to pay Kellerman the money for the two shanghaied men who had gotten loose and set the others free, and so at the moment, at least, there was nothing that he and Kellerman wanted from each other.

Common sense told Kellerman to get out of New Orleans, but he knew that if he left the city behind him, admitting defeat, he would find it exceptionally difficult to start anew somewhere else. Word of success or failure spread as rapidly in the underworld as it did in the realm of legitimate enterprise, and he would be disgraced for all time if he fled from New Orleans now.

The greatest irony of all—and the thing that caused Kellerman the most dismay—was that he was wealthy beyond his wildest dreams, having in his possession the money from the robbery of the gaming house, the profits from Dugald's Bar, and the sum he had earned shanghaiing the first four men for Kayross. But as financially well-off as he was, he could do nothing about it and was forced to live as if he were in dire poverty.

With time hanging heavily on his hands, Kellerman determined to learn all he could about Millicent's life and movements. On two occasions he saw photo-

graphs of her printed in local newspapers. He read
with interest that she was escorted everywhere by
Jean-Pierre Gautier, and he devoured the news that
she would appear as a guest soloist at a special performance of the New Orleans Symphony Orchestra.

On several occasions Kellerman concealed himself in the underbrush outside the Gautier mansion
and observed Millicent's comings and goings. Her
appearance was no less striking than it had been at
the height of her affair with him, but it was far more
subtle now. Her cosmetics enhanced her natural
beauty rather than called attention to their use. Her
new gowns emphasized her superb figure but were
also discreet, those of a lady.

The realization slowly dawned on Kellerman that
Millicent bore only a slight resemblance to the woman
with whom he had lived. When he had first met her,
she had been under the influence of Luis de Cordova,
and he himself had seen to it that she continued to
dress and act like a trollop. Now she was reverting to
her normal, well-bred state, and he found that she
was even more attractive to him than she had ever
been.

The more he wanted her, however, the more he
sought revenge against her, and his waking hours
were filled with mental pictures of destroying her.
He decided that her forthcoming concert would give
him the opportunity for which he yearned.

The concert would be held in a large auditorium
that he had visited on other occasions with his various lady friends, even Millicent. They had always

had seats in one of the boxes high up on each side of the auditorium, and it was the boxes that captured Kellerman's imagination. Each of these upper boxes had two seats, and the sight lines to the stage were excellent. He knew he would have no trouble in shooting at his target when she appeared on the podium at center stage, next to the grand piano.

Best of all, there was an exit adjacent to each box. By moving only a few steps, he would be able to reach the exit and descend stairs that would deposit him on the street outside the theater.

Now that his plan was gelling, Kellerman proceeded with care. First, he insured himself of privacy by buying both seats in the box for the concert. Next, he enhanced his disguise by buying a pair of spectacles with plain glass in them, and he also purchased a dark, inconspicuous suit and cloak for the occasion. Paying special attention to the weapon he would use, he cleaned and oiled his pistol. He would keep the pistol concealed beneath his cloak and would fire it at Millicent at an appropriate moment.

Rehearsing the scene repeatedly in his mind, Kellerman could find no fault with it. He would be able to obtain his revenge and to get away afterward without any problems.

On the day of the concert, Millicent slept late and ate a breakfast in her bedchamber, Helene Gautier thoughtfully sending the meal to her room. She dressed quickly, then settled down to an hour of practicing scales and doing fingering exercises on the flute. This accomplished, she firmly put the instrument aside and refused to allow herself to dwell on the coming concert.

It was now early afternoon. Jean-Pierre appeared, and when he suggested a carriage drive, Millicent eagerly accepted. She was in the mood for such a drive.

The couple went driving in a phaeton, an open carriage that was pulled by a team of matched grays. Jean-Pierre handled the reins himself. He drove north of the city on a plantation-lined road that followed the Mississippi River. Traffic was light, and he and Millicent engaged only in desultory conversation.

Jean-Pierre let Millicent take the lead, and when she said nothing, he, too, remained silent. Eventually he pulled off the road onto a little spur that led toward the river, and they sat for a time watching the waters of the Mississippi swirling and racing toward the sea.

"I've given great thought to the subject I'm now bringing up," Jean-Pierre said. "I'll be frank with you because I feel that I must." He paused and looked out across the water. "When my late wife passed away, I thought my life would come to an end, too, and for many months, I felt dead inside. Then I saw you, and even before we met, I fell deeply in love with you. From that time until the present, my love has grown with each passing day, until now it has become the core of my very being. I've chosen this particular time deliberately. The concert tonight represents a big event in your life, and I want to share it with you. I want you as my wife."

Millicent was not surprised by his proposal of marriage. In recent days he had approached the subject on numerous occasions, only to hesitate and then back off again. She had thought about their relationship at length, and she knew fairly well where she stood. His kindness to her had been overwhelming, he was generous and gentle as well, and she had grown very attached to him.

Although she had spent countless hours on the subject, she had pondered in vain and was no closer now than she had been at any time to answering the question of whether or not she loved him. If love included the wild, pulsating sense of excitement that Luis de Cordova had generated, that she had felt so strongly for Karl Kellerman, then to her infinite sorrow, she did not love Jean-Pierre Gautier. That animallike feeling was not present in their relationship.

She suspected, however, that such a desire might not be good for her. Certainly, it had brought her nothing but grief whenever she had felt it. Thus she was prepared to accept Jean-Pierre's marriage proposal. He offered her fidelity, and she would give him fidelity in return. He offered her loyalty, and she would be loyal to him beyond all else.

She was encumbered by no lingering shreds of affection for Karl Kellerman or for the late Luis de Cordova. They were a part of her past, a past that she viewed with shame. The woman who had associated with them was far different from the Millicent

Randall who sat now in the phaeton with Jean-Pierre Gautier looking out at the rapidly moving waters of the Mississippi River.

Millicent folded her white-gloved hands in her lap and peered at him from beneath the broad brim of her black straw hat. "I won't abide by the rules of the courting game and pretend I'm surprised, Jean-Pierre," she said. "I've known for some time that you were going to propose, and I've thought a great deal about it."

"I hope your thoughts have been favorable," he said with a slight smile.

"What bothers me is that there are periods in my past about which you know nothing."

He shook his head. "I don't care to know about them," he said.

She reached out gently and placed a hand on his arm. "Say what you will. I've done things that have caused me great mortification and shame. I can't excuse myself for having behaved as I did, and I'm afraid that my past conduct will haunt me for the rest of my days."

"Forget the past," Jean-Pierre told her. "We live in the present, and I love you for what you are. Your past means nothing to me, and I want to know nothing about it. All that interests me is your future, and I demand the right to look after you from this time forward, as long as we both live."

Millicent extended a hand to him and said timidly, "With your help, I'll do my very best to live only in the present—for the future. Our future. Together."

"You won't regret this," he told her huskily.

She removed her hat and lifted her face for his kiss. Their lips met, and Millicent pressed closer to Jean-Pierre.

Something stirred deep within her, and Millicent was first astonished, then elated as she recognized the familiar signs of physical arousal. She had been mistaken; there was a physical aspect to her relationship with Jean-Pierre after all. The future was even brighter and more promising than she had imagined it could be.

Their kiss grew more passionate, and when they moved apart, they looked long and hard at each other. Jean-Pierre reached into the pocket of his cutaway coat and brought out a small box, which he opened. Millicent saw a large, perfect diamond gleaming in the sunlight. She removed her glove from her left hand, he placed the ring on her third finger, and they kissed once again.

Later, when they parted, Jean-Pierre laughed shakily. "I guess there won't be any need to announce our betrothal," he said. "That ring will blind everyone in the audience when you're playing the flute tonight."

She joined rather tremulously in the laugh. "I think," she said, "my finger work with my left hand is going to be busier tonight than it's ever been before!"

The auditorium was filling rapidly a half-hour before the concert began, and a large crowd was gathered outside the stage door to await the arrival of the soloist.

Millicent did not disappoint her many admirers. She appeared wearing a bare-shouldered black evening gown trimmed with white feathers, and over her long, thick brown hair she had thrown a Spanish scarf as a protection from the rain that had been threatening to fall the past few hours.

The audience was in a festive mood. Word of Millicent's betrothal had leaked out that evening, and when Jean-Pierre appeared and joined his parents and Millicent's cousins, Edward Blackstone and Jim Randall, as well as Tommie Harding, in the front lower box on the right side of the theater, the audience warmly applauded him. The embarrassed young man became flustered, and his face turned crimson as he acknowledged the applause.

Millicent's performance followed the intermission. When she accompanied the conductor to the podium, the applause of the audience was tumultuous. She curtsied deeply, then gave a special smile to Jean-Pierre.

The audience became silent as she took her stance and began her first piece, Bach's Suite in B Minor, in which the flute was accompanied by the string section of the orchestra. The audience was enchanted by her spirited playing, and the applause that greeted her at the end of the piece echoed and reechoed throughout the auditorium.

Sitting alone in the box at the rear of the tier at the right, Karl Kellerman was bathed in perspiration.

A cape lay folded in his lap and concealed the loaded pistol that he held there, ready to fire at the opportune moment. His disguise was better than he had expected it to be: Certainly no one who knew him would recognize the bearded, bespectacled man with a scholarly air. He had tried the exit door adjacent to his box when he first entered the theater and to his relief found the door unlocked. Everything was working in his favor. He had seen no one he knew, no one who might recognize him. After he shot and killed Millicent, he could escape easily and the police would have a difficult time identifying her killer.

She looked lovelier than he had ever seen her, and he stared at her openmouthed as she began to play. It was difficult to imagine that this austere, talented woman and the abandoned creature who had been his mistress were the same person.

Her black dress fitted her snugly and reminded him that her figure was magnificent, far better than those of the women with whom he had associated since he had abandoned Millicent. Her cosmetics had been utilized with such subtlety that they brought out her rare beauty.

Above all, she carried herself with a confident air, a sense of sureness of who she was and of what she was doing. She gave no sign of the hesitation, the almost apologetic air that had marked her whole approach to other people. She seemed to be saying that she was a professional flutist who played with great skill. The audience recognized this quality in her and responded in kind to it.

What astonished Kellerman beyond all else as he sat in the dark of the box fingering his pistol beneath the cape was the effect that Millicent's music-making was having on him.

Crude, unprincipled, and totally lacking in morality, Kellerman was motivated by his self-interest and never, he thought, by his feelings. But that was not the case at the moment. He was aware that Millicent was casting a deep spell on her audience and over him. Every note played on his emotions.

He was totally ignorant about classical music and consequently had no idea what she was playing. All he realized was that her second number was so sad, so melancholy that it threatened the very roots of his being. He felt a deep, shattering loneliness, a sense of despair that brought tears to his eyes. He had no idea why he was weeping, but he realized that his vision was being affected: He could no longer see Millicent clearly enough to aim his pistol at her accurately.

When she finished playing the piece, it was so deathly quiet in the auditorium that the sound of rain falling on the roof and on the street outside could be heard. Then the audience reacted with a storm of applause that shook the inside of the theater.

Millicent consented to play an encore, and Kellerman was greatly relieved. He hoped he could use the respite to calm down. But to his astonishment, he found that his hands were trembling violently. He realized that he would never be able to hit a target with a pistol until the tremors ceased.

Millicent's playing continued to affect him, however, making it impossible for him to regain his equilibrium. She submerged him in the depths of melancholy, making it impossible for him to react, and he sat very still, transfixed by the sounds of her flute, unable to move a muscle.

Her solo ended. Again the theater rocked with applause, and Millicent graciously consented to play one more encore. She changed her whole approach, and this time she launched into a lively piece that lifted the spirits of the entire audience. People smiled broadly, their feet tapping in time to the music, and Kellerman told himself, "Now! I've got to shoot her now!"

In spite of his urgent desire to right the wrongs for which he imagined Millicent to be responsible, he could not move. He felt as though his wrist were being held in a giant vise, and he could neither raise it nor wrench free long enough to aim at the slender woman in the black dress standing on the stage.

The music ended, and Millicent curtsied low, acknowledging the enthusiastic applause of the audience.

Kellerman realized he had only seconds in which to carry out his plan, but he still could not move. Try as he might, something restrained him and made it impossible for him to aim his pistol and squeeze the trigger. Rivulets of sweat poured down his face and soaked his collar.

Millicent curtsied again, then left the stage with the conductor. The lights were lowered, and the

concert was over. As the members of the orchestra
filed off the stage, the audience rose and began to
leave the theater.

Kellerman had lost his chance. A feeling of great
weariness crept over him as he dropped the pistol
into his pocket, threw his cape over his shoulders,
and slowly followed the crowd out of the theater. He
felt very dispirited, very tired. He had fought the
hardest of battles within himself and, in his own
opinion at least, had lost it. All he wanted to do now
was to return to his quarters, fall into bed, and sleep.

The rain had stopped, leaving puddles on the
sidewalk and on the cobblestone road beyond it.
The air was fresh and clear, and the audience, invig-
orated by Millicent's performance, chatted happily.
Then the crowd parted, and Millicent herself, holding the arm of Jean-Pierre Gautier, moved from the
theater entrance to the curb, where a carriage awaited
them.

Tugging his hat lower over his eyes, Kellerman
huddled beneath his cloak as he stood almost within
reach of Millicent. She had come to life since the
days they had been together, and he had never seen
her more animated or lovelier. He studied her as
Jean-Pierre handed her into the carriage, and somehow he knew that he had suffered an irrevocable
loss. The woman could have been his for all time had
he treated her honorably and with love, but he had
abused her trust and instead had turned her against
him. No matter how many beautiful women to whom

he might pay court in the future, none could be like Millicent. She was unique.

As the carriage pulled away from the curb, the wheels rolled through a puddle and splashed mud on Kellerman's trousers and shoes. But Millicent, unaware of his proximity, leaned back in the carriage and exchanged a look of pure love with Jean-Pierre. "This," she told him, "is the happiest night of my life."

VIII

Kung Lee had been badly disturbed since the morning when Ho Tai's body had been found sitting in an armchair on the busiest street in Chinatown. He knew his luck had changed when his path had crossed that of Toby Holt, and now the recent news from New Orleans was the latest blow. He had received word from a tong member in that city that one of the oceangoing ships owned by the American tong had recently been impounded, the authorities charging that the vessel had been used illegally to smuggle Chinese aliens into the United States. What was more, the captain of the *Diana*, Robin Kayross, was accused along with a man named Karl Kellerman of shanghaiing several men and even abducting a young woman, a prominent socialite named Millicent Randall. The ship's captain and the man named Kellerman had seemingly disappeared from New Orleans, but there were warrants out for their arrest, and the police were determined to find them.

Kellerman, Kung Lee learned, was also wanted by members of the organized crime unit headed by the gang leader Domino.

So Kung Lee found himself in an extremely unpleasant situation, and he pondered on his next course of action. Deciding to kill two birds with one stone, Kung wired tong members in New Orleans, telling them he was coming to that city and that they should spread the word that Kung wanted to see Robin Kayross.

Traveling with a bodyguard, Kung took a train from San Francisco to St. Louis and then transferred to a Mississippi River steamer that brought him to New Orleans within the time that he had specified. He took quarters in a private dwelling that the tong had long owned, a place where a full domestic staff was already on duty. He was no sooner ensconced in the house than a trembling, nervous Robin Kayross was brought to him.

Kung Lee immediately put the Greek ship's master at his ease, serving him tea and smiling benevolently at him. The fact was, Kung had no rancor for Kayross and did not blame him for the loss of the *Diana*. Those things happened, and now the ship's captain could be of use to him again.

Kung read the copy of the court order confiscating the ship, which one of his underlings handed him, then he looked up at Kayross and said gently, "We'll forget all about matters with regard to the ship. We'll make no effort to recover possession of her."

Kayross was surprised. "Why is that?"

The tong leader shook his head. "The reason should be fairly obvious. If I were to step forward and claim ownership of the vessel on behalf of the tong, the federal government would order my arrest. I'd be charged with the illegal importation of Chinese immigrants, and in addition, they'd bring a civil suit against me for the importation of opium. The lack of such charges appears to be an oversight on the part of the federal authorities, but I'm sure it isn't. It's a deliberate trap, and they're waiting for me to step into it. Frankly, I prefer to suffer the loss of the ship rather than run the risk of being sent to a federal penitentiary. We owe ourselves a more modern ship, although I hate to undergo the expense of purchasing one. I don't suppose you happen to know anyone who might be interested in sharing the cost with us?"

Kayross was lost in thought for some moments and then grinned wryly. "There's one possibility," he said. "Karl Kellerman."

"Ah, yes—Kellerman. I learned about him in San Francisco. Is he still hiding from Domino?"

"Indeed he is," the Greek ship's master replied. "As if it's not enough that he has to hide from the police, he also has to worry about being seen by Domino or some of his people."

"Kellerman must be exceptionally foolish," Kung said, "to incur the enmity of a man like Domino."

"In my judgment," the Greek said, "he is not as

foolish as he is impetuous. He often acts without thinking of all the consequences."

"Be that as it may," Kung replied thoughtfully, "he might be useful to us, and he might welcome the opportunity to travel to far places on board a comfortable, safe ship. Invite Kellerman here to dine at your earliest opportunity, and let me look him over."

Karl Kellerman, who was bored almost senseless by his life in hiding, accepted Captain Kayross's invitation to dinner with alacrity. He was somewhat surprised when he was taken to a private home in New Orleans and was introduced to Kung Lee, but he soon learned that the cultured Chinese gentleman was the employer of Robin Kayross and owner of any number of cargo ships. Knowing he had been invited for business rather than social reasons, Kellerman bided his time, spoke only in generalities, and waited for his host to reveal the reason for the invitation.

Kung Lee was a gracious host and talked about sights of interest in both San Francisco and New Orleans as they ate a dinner of dishes that were completely strange to Kellerman. Not until they had finished their soup, the last course served to them, did Kung reveal his hand.

"I have learned from Robin Kayross," he said, "that your movements are somewhat circumscribed these days, Mr. Kellerman. Therefore, the thought has crossed my mind that you might be interested in a deal that would offer you constant changes of scene."

"I might be very much interested," was the

cautious reply. "It depends on the nature of the deal."

"My associates and I," the tong leader said, "are planning to invest in a new ship to replace the *Diana*, which we inadvertently lost. We intend to engage in the Pacific trade with China."

"Will this be the same type of trade in which you had the *Diana* engaged in?" Kellerman asked politely.

Kung smiled and nodded. "There's a steady demand here—a demand that pays very high prices—for merchandise from China, and we would be negligent if we failed to take advantage of that natural phenomenon. So you might say that we plan to be in the same business that we were in previously."

"May I ask what this has to do with me?" Kellerman demanded bluntly.

Kung studied him for a moment and then was equally blunt. "Those who find themselves in special circumstances," he said, "often make unorthodox investments."

"So they do," Kellerman replied politely, "provided they're not too exorbitant."

"What is exorbitant?" Kung asked rhetorically. "That which John Jacob Aster finds to be a reasonable price well might be regarded as exorbitant by one who is poverty-stricken."

Kellerman knew he could not engage in a battle of words with such a man. "Quite so," he murmured.

"My associates and I," Kung said, "are searching for someone who will invest perhaps one-third of the sum necessary to purchase a new trading vessel, a ship that burns wood or coal and that does not take months to cross the Pacific."

"What are you thinking of spending for such a ship?"

"Somewhere in the neighborhood of one hundred thousand dollars," Kung said. "Your share would amount to approximately thirty-five thousand."

"I'm not sure I could afford that much," Kellerman replied.

Kung lifted an eyebrow. "You took away almost that amount on the night that Domino was injured," he said, "and you much more than made up the difference with your profits from Dugald's Bar. Even allowing for all the money you spent on women, you should have more than thirty-five thousand left."

Kellerman looked at him in anger and astonishment. "It seems to me," he said, "that you know one hell of a lot about my business."

"To be sure," Kung said pleasantly. "My associates and I make it a standard practice to learn everything useful there is to know about those with whom we do business. But your private life, I assure you, is quite safe with me. I have no intention of revealing your finances to anyone, and certainly I'm not going to tell Domino your whereabouts. I'm not in business with him, and my associates and I mind our own affairs; just as we expect him and his associates to mind their own and to stay out of our business."

Kellerman was somewhat mollified. "I see," he said in a more normal tone of voice.

"As one of the owners of the vessel," Kung continued, sweetening the pot still more, "you'd be free to conduct such negotiations as you wished in China and elsewhere in the Orient. You would represent all the owners in a sense, and therefore, you would speak for all of us whenever you felt inclined to do so."

"How soon will this voyage take place?" Kellerman asked, and in his voice was the longing of one for the liberty he was currently being denied.

The tong chieftain continued to spread the bait. "You'll depart very soon," he said, "as soon as we purchase the ship and Captain Kayross makes her ready for sea and finishes hiring his crew." He refrained from adding that such activities could take many months, although he, too, preferred to see Kayross depart on his voyage as soon as possible.

He was pleasantly surprised, therefore, when Kayross reported the next day that he had found their ship. It was the *Neptune*, an all-metal cargo steamship with screw propellers, which had been built in New England yards at the end of the Civil War; for all practical purposes, the *Neptune* was virtually a new vessel. Her overly ambitious owners were on the verge of bankruptcy and eagerly accepted Kung Lee's offer of cash for the freighter, so the tong acquired the ship it needed at a bargain price, and Kayross immediately went to work hiring a full crew.

Kellerman was forced to pay the full price to which he had agreed in return for a one-third inter-

est in the freighter. He knew he had no choice, so he
made no complaint. He was quietly determined,
however, to take over the vessel whenever the opportunity presented itself and to leave the tong with
nothing. That desire was sharpened by the knowledge that Kung Lee fully intended to squeeze him
out of his partial proprietorship whenever he had the
chance. When dealing with persons whose motives
were highly questionable, Kellerman knew it was
always wise to strike first and to strike hard, and he
was confident of his own ability to get in the first
blow.

His investment provided him with certain short-
range benefits, and he lost no time taking full advantage of them. Primary among these was the offer of a
guest cabin on the *Neptune*, which was preferable
to the squalid apartment in which he was living near
the waterfront. Giving up his apartment, he moved
to the *Neptune*, and there he felt fairly safe. Certainly it would be difficult for any of his pursuers to
surprise him and to capture him while he was on
board.

In the meantime, on the Pacific Coast, a new
foe, far more dangerous than all the others, was
about to be added to those who were already searching for Karl Kellerman.

Toby Holt, following his battle to the death with
Ho Tai, went to the tong headquarters to request a
meeting with Kung Lee and demand that the tong
cease once and for all their criminal activities in

America. With the death of Ho Tai, the tong had lost
much prestige and power and had no choice but to
desist. When Toby found out that the tong leader
was out of the city, however, he repaired at once to
the offices of his business counselors, Chet Harris
and Wong Ke. Ke immediately launched his own
investigation, and in a surprisingly short time, he
reported back to Toby.

"I've learned," he said, "that Kung Lee has
gone to New Orleans on urgent tong business. It
must be urgent because he almost never leaves San
Francisco."

Thus matters were left at a standstill. At least,
Toby reasoned, Ho Tai was out of the picture, and
the tong would never be able to operate in the same
way again.

Wasting no more time, Toby immediately returned to his ranch on the Columbia River in Oregon.
He was glad to be home at last, and all he truly
wanted to do now was settle down and be with his
family and continue building his ranch the way he—
and his father before him—had dreamed. But there
was one more duty to perform, and before even
seeing his wife and son—who were out riding—he
quickly crossed the river in order to confer at Fort
Vancouver in Washington with his stepfather, Major
General Leland Blake. The general had been back at
Fort Vancouver only a few days after his tour of army
bases, and he was going to have to leave once again
the next morning, having been called East to meet

with President Grant, about a matter that was still unknown to him.

The generals words came as a shock. "Are you free to follow Kung to New Orleans, Toby?" he asked at once. "If so, I'll give you a warrant for his arrest, together with some blank warrants for any associates you might pick up as well. You see, we now have a crime we can pin specifically on him—namely, the shanghaiing of crew members onto a ship registered in his name."

Toby was stunned. He had thought he was coming back to start a new life at home with his family and instead found he was being sent far away. But he felt he was in no position to refuse the request. "I'm at your service, sir," he replied crisply.

"Thank you," the general said. "I know we keep talking about your desire to stay on the ranch and run it the way your father would have wanted, but this is a job that only you can perform well. I'll telegraph the army garrison at New Orleans and request them to cooperate with you in every possible way. I'll also activate your commission as a major, so you'll be on duty and will be authorized to act with the full force of the army behind you. I realize you've been deputized by the Portland authorities, but the justice department believes that only the army has the strength and the manpower to capture a criminal of Kung's stature. Kung has a start of only a few days, so if you move quickly, you should reach New Orleans soon after he gets there. I'll have the navy meet you with a motor launch in St. Louis to take you down the Mississippi quickly."

The words came at Toby like a torrent. For a moment he wished there was someone else who could do the job, someone who didn't have a home and a family he loved. But he would not shirk his duty, and he replied simply, "I'll be ready to leave first thing tomorrow morning."

At the ranch that evening, when Toby broke the news to his wife, Clarissa showed her own courage and understanding. "I've known from the start that this trip of yours to San Francisco was only the beginning," she said with a sigh. "The fact that you were called away for only a few weeks was too good to be true."

"I have no choice but to make this trip," Toby said. "My country needs me."

"I know," she replied. "Still, these separations become harder for me as time goes on."

"There's no reason for you to worry," Toby told her. "You know I can look after myself."

"Yes," she said. "All the same, the law of averages is bound to come into play sooner or later, and your luck will give out. You've had more near escapes than I care to remember or count, and what makes me afraid is the realization that one of these days you're going to face a situation in which even your talents won't help you."

"I see no point in anticipating trouble," Toby told her. "Besides, this is a clear-cut case. I'm going to New Orleans to locate Kung Lee, place him under arrest, and with the aid of the entire U.S. Army garrison there if need be, haul him back to face a trial."

Clarissa merely nodded and made no reply. It would serve no purpose to tell him her premonition that he was going to be in the greatest danger he had ever faced and that she was worried he might not survive it.

The U.S. Navy cutter that awaited Toby in St. Louis was a vessel about thirty-five feet in length, the main portion of its single deck being occupied by the boiler used to provide steam, along with the pile of coal that was fed into it at regular intervals. The crew consisted of a boatswain and two mates. The noncommissioned officer acted as the little ship's captain and pilot, and his two crew members' principal duty was keeping the boiler fed.

Toby had literally nothing to do except sit on deck and watch the passing scenery. As the vessel moved swiftly down the Mississippi, he had time to think. It was unfair, he once again reflected, that he should be summoned so frequently to serve his government, when others could follow their normal civilian pursuits. He was required to make constant sacrifices, to place his life in jeopardy, and to be separated for long periods from his wife and son.

His mood did not improve as the cutter continued its southward journey. Each night the vessel halted, and the passenger and crew went ashore at some town for overnight accommodations. The boat-

swain and his men were not communicative, and
Toby was left to his own devices for the better part of
each day and night.

As the cutter moved down the Mississippi River
from Memphis, the scars of Civil War fighting became more evident. They passed many buildings
that had been shelled but had not been repaired.
There were graveyards everywhere filled with both
Union and Confederate dead.

The war had come to an end for the people of
these communities, however, and the three sailors
and Toby were greeted warmly everywhere. Nowhere was this friendly attitude more evident than it
was in Magnolia, Mississippi, a tiny river town of
several hundred inhabitants located on a slight bend
in the great river. Leaving their cutter tied up at the
dock, the quartet rented rooms in a boardinghouse.
There they were served a sumptuous southern meal
by their hosts, the McAdams. Early the next morning as they were eating a breakfast of eggs, hominy
grits, bacon, and biscuits with butter and honey,
they were interrupted by Bud McAdam, the teenage
son of the proprietor.

"I—I don't rightly know how to tell you this," the
boy stammered, "but your boat sure is an almighty
mess!"

The quartet raced down to the waterfront, where
they stared in astonishment at the boat. Axes had
been taken to the hull of the cutter, and not only was
the boiler damaged, but the railing and deck had
been severely gashed.

The boatswain hastily inspected the damage, then ran a hand helplessly through his thinning hair. "This is a pretty kettle of fish," he roared. "We gotta get Major Holt to New Orleans fast, but this here cutter ain't fit to be rowed down the river!"

Trying in vain to mollify him, several people in the crowd that had gathered said that Mr. Legett had been notified and was on his way into Magnolia at this very moment. It seemed that Mr. Legett was the wealthiest and most prominent citizen in the community, a plantation owner whose mansion could be seen on the hill behind the town.

Fortunately for the blood pressure of the boatswain, the plantation owner soon arrived and made a careful inspection of the vessel. Then he hurried ashore and approached the three sailors and Toby.

"Gentlemen," he said in a thick southern drawl, "I can't begin to tell you how sorry I am, not only for the damage to government property but also to the good name of Magnolia. There are a couple of stupid gangs hereabouts who won't admit the war is over, and they're probably responsible for this outrage."

At his shoulder stood a slender, almost painfully thin girl in her early teens, with masses of black hair and enormous dark eyes that seemed to take in every detail of what was happening around her.

"We'll delay your voyage no longer than is absolutely necessary," Legett continued, "but you must give us the opportunity to make amends."

He turned to the crowd and began to give rapid-fire orders, pointing a bony forefinger first at one onlooker and then another. To Toby's astonishment, everyone in Magnolia appeared to be a carpenter or a metal worker.

Legett turned suddenly to the girl, his daughter. "You've got some work ahead of you, too, honey," he said. "You get your friends together, and as soon as the boys are finished fixing the decks, you scrub them clean. Get them so clean they shine!"

The girl hitched up her voluminous skirts and raced off.

"It won't do you much good to loiter here at the docks," Legett told Toby and the trio from the navy. "There's no place for you to rest your feet, and that sun gets mighty hot as it climbs up in the sky. I suggest you all come up to my house with me, where you can be comfortable." Without further ado, he led them up a hill.

The house proved to be magnificently furnished, and their host and his wife insisted that the visitors sit on a shaded porch, where they were served tall glasses of iced tea. They remained at the house as the guests of the Legetts until afternoon, and they were given a superb dinner at noon. The soup, which was called a gumbo, was unique in Toby's experience, and the smoked ham was one of the best-tasting delicacies he had ever eaten.

After the meal, the party returned to the porch, where the visitors were regaled with stories about Legett's ancestors, who had owned this same property for almost a century and a half. While he was finishing a story, his daughter approached, considerably the worse for wear. Her gown, which had been prim and pristine, was bedraggled. Wisps of her dark hair straggled down her face, and one cheek was badly smudged with dirt. But her expressive eyes were shining.

"We're through, Papa," she said. "Fact is, everybody's done work, and I swear, the new deck is so clean you could eat off it!"

Legett led the little procession downhill to the dock, and Toby marveled when he saw the refurbished cutter. The boiler looked new, and the deck and railing were as sturdy as they were spotless.

The boatswain tried to stammer his thanks, but Legett held up a hand, silencing him. "Those idiots damaged United States property," he said, "and tried to make it impossible for you to carry out your mission. Well, Magnolia is pleased and proud to have been of service. We don't rightly know why it's important that Major Holt get to New Orleans quickly, and we have no need to know. All that matters is that it's important to the government that he get there fast, and that's good enough for us. In spite of the damage that was done to your boat, we're all Americans in this town, and we share in the future of this country. If there's one thing we learned in the war, it's the fact that we're all Americans. We all have the same goal, and we're heading toward it together."

Thanking his host and the people of Magnolia, Toby went on board, and a short time later, the cutter was again under way, heading down the river at a rapid clip, making up for the time that had been lost.

Standing on deck and leaning against the rail, Toby looked out at the flat, green land on both sides of the Mississippi. The incident in Magnolia had taught him a lesson he would never forget, and the enthusiasm of the volunteers who had repaired the cutter would remain fresh in his mind as long as he lived.

He no longer felt he was being singled out to make sacrifices for his country. As his host in Magnolia had put it so succinctly, all Americans were marching in step together toward the same goal. If he had talents that could aid the United States, it was only right that he should be summoned and that he should give freely and unstintingly.

Straightening his shoulders, Toby looked out across the land at the distant horizon. This was America, his country, and he was pleased and proud that he had the opportunity to serve her and her citizens.

Edward Blackstone, Tommie Harding, and Jim Randall had just sat down to supper in their hotel when they were electrified by the sight of Toby Holt crossing the dining room to their table. Warm greetings were exchanged, and Toby was introduced to Tommie. Everyone talked at once, and some minutes elapsed before a semblance of order was created. Then, after Toby sat down with his friends and ordered his meal, Edward brought him up to date.

"If you're going to be here for the next couple of weeks, Toby," he said, "you're just in time for Millicent's wedding. She's marrying a local man, son of one of New Orleans's best families, and I've never seen her so happy."

"You well might have come to New Orleans in time for our wedding, too," Tommie said. "We haven't set a date, as yet. We can't until we find out exactly when my father is going to arrive, but we're expecting him any day. We've been in touch with him by telegram, and he has rearranged the schedule of his ship, the *Big Muddy*, so he can return in the near future. He is as anxious to be here as we are eager to have him—and the sooner the better."

"I don't know of anything that will give me greater pleasure than to see Edward married," Toby replied. "Unfortunately, my time isn't completely my own. The length of my stay here depends on how soon I'm able to establish contact with a Chinese man named Kung Lee."

His listeners' faces were blank; it was plain that none of them had ever heard of the head of the tong. So Toby told them about his encounters in San Francisco with Kung and his bodyguard Ho Tai and how it was that he had followed the Chinese tong leader to New Orleans. "Tomorrow," he said, "I'll go to the army garrison here in New Orleans and seek the cooperation of the new commandant."

Now his friends explained to him the dramatic events in their lives since they had come to the city.

"It appears to me that this fellow Kellerman is a bad apple," Toby commented.

"He's as bad as they come," Jim agreed.

"We've been staying in Louisiana for two reasons," Edward added. "One is that we're going to attend Millicent's wedding. The other is that we hope to nail Kellerman—or at least Wallace Dugald, Kellerman's one-time partner, intends to nail him. He forced us to promise him that once we find Kellerman, we'll let him confront the man face to face. I'm sure that will take care of the problem."

"If I should learn anything about him in my own investigations," Toby said, "I'll let you know at once."

While they were still at the table, a note in a flowery, feminine handwriting was delivered to Toby by their waiter. It read: *Meet me in the lobby of the hotel after supper to discuss a matter of mutual interest.* The communication had no salutation and no signature.

It was possible, Toby thought, that he was being led into a trap of some kind, but there was only one way to find out. Telling his companions only that the message invited him to meet with someone who might shed some light on his quest, he dropped the folded paper into a pocket and went on with his meal.

After supper the others retired to their rooms while Toby went to the hotel lobby. There he sat on a brown sofa in a corner of the room.

He did not have long to wait. Within a few minutes, a striking green-eyed redhead, with hair streaming down her back, her snug-fitting dress emphasizing her curvaceous figure, came into the lobby, looked around, and headed straight for Toby. A score of eyes watched her hip-wiggling walk as she approached him.

"Mr. Holt?" she asked politely in a musical voice, extending a gloved hand to him, and then continued without waiting for an answer. "I'd know you anywhere from the pictures I've seen of you."

References to his fame invariably embarrassed him. "Won't you sit down?" he asked her, aware of the fact that she had not introduced herself.

"This is too public a place for a confidential talk," she told him with a laugh. "Besides, I'm just a messenger."

Not waiting for a reply, she took his arm and led him out of the lobby. At the entrance to the hotel, a large, enclosed carriage pulled by a matched team of horses, with a driver in livery on the box, was waiting for her. The driver tipped his hat, jumped down, and opened the door.

The woman preceded Toby into the carriage, the scent of musk that she wore filling the compartment. The thought occurred to Toby that if Kung Lee was setting a trap for him, he was going to a great deal of trouble. Also, as far as he could see, the woman carried no pistol or other weapons.

The driver shut the door, mounted the box, and the team of horses started off.

The woman appeared to know that Toby was a stranger to New Orleans, for as they rode, she calmly pointed out sights of interest to him. He responded in the same vein, seemingly relaxed while carefully concealing any wariness.

At last the carriage pulled into the driveway of what seemed to be a solid, middle-class home and rolled to a stop under the porte cochere. Not taking any chances, Toby removed one of his pistols from his belt and held it in his hand.

A burly man appeared in the entranceway to the house, saw the pistol in Toby's hand as he alighted, and grew taut.

"Mr. Holt may keep his firearms," the woman said as she took Toby's hand and stepped to the ground. "He has the boss's permission."

Her reference to "the boss" increased Toby's sense of alertness. Kung Lee must have indeed been behind this meeting all along. Well, he was on his guard.

The woman took Toby's arm and guided him through a room filled with plants into a pleasantly furnished parlor. Sitting in an easy chair at the far end of the room, reading a leather-covered book by the light of an oil lamp, was a mild-looking, middle-aged man with gray hair. His face looked thin and somewhat drawn, as though he had been ill, but when Toby came into the room, the man smiled, rose easily to his feet, and extended a hand. "Welcome, Mr. Holt," he said. "I am Domino." His handshake was surprisingly firm.

Now the man turned and called over Toby's shoulder, "That's all right, boys, you can leave."

Toby turned and saw two heavily armed men in the entrance. One of them gestured in annoyance. "He's carrying a loaded gun in his hand, boss, and he has another in his belt."

"That's Mr. Holt's privilege, I believe. I'll let you know when I want something. You're excused, too, Martha," he said to the woman.

She flashed a brilliant smile at Toby, then, still smiling, turned to the older man. "He's my type, Domino."

"We shall see, Martha," he said patiently. "We shall see. Right now I want to have a little private chat with Mr. Holt, if you don't mind."

The woman withdrew reluctantly.

"Sit down, Mr. Holt." Domino was scrupulously polite. "Please accept my apologies for bringing you here under mysterious circumstances. I hope you'll accept something to drink or eat."

"I've eaten, thank you," Toby replied, using an equally polite tone.

"As I say, I am known as Domino," the gray-haired man said. "I am engaged in business locally—I own a number of establishments, including several gaming houses and a number of brothels. I'm also involved in various other enterprises in New Orleans. It's to my advantage to know everything that takes place in the city, which is how I happen to be acquainted with you and your mission. I know why you're here, who sent you, and under whose jurisdiction you're functioning."

Toby's reply was deliberately noncommittal. "That's interesting."

"You and I," Domino went on, "happen to be in positions where we can benefit each other by working together and pooling our resources. I believe we can do each other a great deal of good." He paused and waited for a response.

"I'm listening," Toby said.

"You're seeking a San Francisco tong leader named Kung Lee," Domino said.

Toby stiffened. "Go on."

Domino smiled. "Kung made a very unfortunate error when he first came here. Ordinarily a man in his position would get in touch with me at once, as soon as he entered my territory, and would let me know that he had no intention of interfering in the affairs of my organization. Kung neglected to contact me and to give me such assurances, which I consider a serious lapse in good manners. I've had a discreet watch kept on him, and I believe I'm in a position to tell you what the army commandant and the New Orleans police cannot reveal because they don't know it. Namely, the present whereabouts of Kung Lee."

"That would be very useful," Toby admitted, then added, "What would you expect of me in return for this favor?"

Domino smiled broadly. "Ah, we understand each other, Mr. Holt. It's a pleasure to be doing business with someone as sharp as you. You may have heard of a criminal here by the name of Karl Kellerman."

"I learned a great deal about Kellerman at supper this evening," Toby told him.

A hard edge crept into Domino's voice. "Kellerman not only broke his word to me—something that no man ever does—but he stole a large sum of money and almost succeeded in murdering me. I have a score to settle with him."

"Am I correct in assuming that you want my help in tracking down Kellerman?" Toby asked.

The older man nodded. "Yes, but hear me out first. Kellerman knows I'm looking for him and that I'm not the only one. So are the police, and so are a number of individuals whom he's wronged and who have become his worst foes. He's gone into hiding, and I'm fairly certain he's wearing a disguise. But you're new to the community, and as far as Kellerman knows, you have no connection with me, with the police, or with anyone else. You stand a far better chance than any of the rest of us in locating him. If you'll agree to conduct an active search for him, I'm sure I can help you locate Kung Lee."

Toby pondered the situation in which he found himself, the strangest he had ever been in. For years his name had been synonymous with obedience to the law, yet here he was being offered a deal, a partnership, by a man who lived and earned his living outside the law.

But in spite of the fact that Domino was the head of a large and powerful New Orleans criminal gang, his offer in no way obstructed justice. On the contrary, Toby realized the cause of justice would be served admirably if he entered into such an agreement. He had everything to gain and nothing to lose. Furthermore, his honor, which was sacred to him, would be untarnished.

Domino handed him a drink.

"Here's to a very odd partnership," Toby said, and raised his glass.

Domino, who was endowed with a keen sense of humor, chuckled appreciatively and raised his own glass in return. "Long may this partnership flourish!" he declared.

They raised their glasses, sipped, and put the drinks down.

"There's a large modern freighter, built at the end of the Civil War, that's currently tied up at the New Orleans docks," Domino said. "Her name is the *Neptune*, and her captain is a penny-pinching Greek named Robin Kayross. She was purchased just recently for utilization in the Orient trade. She'll carry legitimate cargo to China and will return to the United States loaded to the gunwales with illegal Chinese immigrants—who will be overworked and taken advantage of in every possible way by the tong—and with opium. Her owner is Kung Lee, and he has spent time on board her every day since he's come to New Orleans. He usually arrives there early in the afternoon and stays until dark. The ship is still taking on cargo, so if he keeps to his regular schedule, you should be able to find him on board tomorrow afternoon."

Toby thanked him, and they shook hands. Their business, for the moment, was concluded.

"I'll pay the *Neptune* a visit tomorrow," Toby said, "and I'll be in touch with you as soon as I have a lead for you on where to locate Kellerman." They sat back in their chairs, both of them satisfied with the deal they had struck, and as they finished their drinks, Domino said, "If you have nothing to keep you occupied until tomorrow afternoon, you might want to consider spending at least a part of that time with Martha, the girl who brought you here. You'll find her amenable to any activity you might have in mind."

Toby shook his head and smiled. "Thanks all the same," he said firmly, "but I have a wife, and I happen to be a one-woman man."

At breakfast the following morning, Toby told Edward and Jim, "I've tracked Kung Lee to a ship that's anchored at the river docks here, and I'm going to pay him a surprise visit this afternoon."

Both were astonished, and Jim asked, "How did you manage to get a line on his whereabouts so fast? Did it have something to do with that message sent to you at supper last night?"

Toby felt it was necessary to protect the privacy of his agreement with Domino, so he merely nodded but added nothing else.

The cousins, realizing he was reluctant to pursue the subject, did not press him for an answer. After breakfast, Toby excused himself, and a short

time later, he was closeted with the commandant of the New Orleans army garrison, to whom he explained his mission and said that he was going to pay a surprise visit to Kung Lee that afternoon on board the *Neptune*.

"I suppose," the commandant replied, "that you will want about a dozen army troops on hand, ready to accompany you on board."

"I think not," Toby said. "I've given the matter considerable thought, and I'm afraid that their mere presence would virtually guarantee a nasty fight. I don't want anyone killed or injured."

The commandant was alarmed. "I realize you've acquired a formidable reputation for yourself, Major Holt," he said, "but surely you don't intend to tackle Kung Lee by yourself! You'd be walking alone into the dragon's mouth!"

"I prefer to try alone in order to prevent bloodshed," Toby said. "But if that isn't effective, I have no desire to be a dead hero. What I have in mind is this: I intend to go on board the freighter alone and to confront Kung Lee. I think—at least, I hope—that he'll be reasonable when he sees that I have a warrant for his arrest. If he does, he'll come ashore with me peaceably, and that will end the crisis. If not—in the event that he tries to kick up a fuss—then I'll need help. So here's what I propose: I'll present myself on the freighter at two o'clock exactly. I'll let your troops show up precisely one hour later, at three o'clock. If I don't appear and come ashore with Kung Lee as my prisoner by half-past three, then I suggest that they force their way on board and conduct a thorough search for me, though I hope that won't be necessary."

"The stories I've read about you in newspapers and magazines haven't exaggerated your courage," the commandant said in admiration, shaking his head. "Obviously you're well aware of the risks that you're taking."

Toby shrugged. "Yes, and quite frankly, I don't think they're very great. You're forgetting that Kung Lee is a civilized man who is anxious to stay on good terms with the United States government. If he behaves in a threatening manner toward me when I serve him with the subpoena, he's going to destroy the façade that he's spent many years creating. I'm not anticipating any trouble, you understand."

"You well might be mistaken."

"I grant you that," Toby said, "and for that reason, your troops will be most welcome. But I believe everything should work out for the best. For all concerned."

Toby ate lightly that noon, then set out for the waterfront, armed with his two repeating pistols and with a knife protruding from his belt. He located the *Neptune* without difficulty and studied her with interest, observing that she was one of the few vessels he had ever seen that was flying the flag of the empire of China. As Domino had indicated, she looked new. She had been freshly painted, and her decks were loaded with boxes and crates of merchandise that, presumably, would be transferred to one of her holds before she set sail for the Orient. A guard, armed with a short, leather-covered club, stood on the dock near the gangway, and another, similarly armed, was wandering about on the deck near the cartons and crates, disappearing and then reappearing again as he made his way between them. Above, on the open bridge of the ship, a man with the tarnished braid of a captain on his uniform was engaged in earnest conversation with someone much taller and huskier. Toby guessed that the officer was Robin Kayross, but he had no idea of the identity of the other man, who was brown-haired, wore spectacles, and had a large, drooping mustache and a beard. Kung Lee was nowhere to be seen.

The pair on deck became conscious of his scrutiny, and the taller man promptly disappeared from sight into the interior of the vessel.

Glancing at his watch and seeing that two o'clock had come, Toby moved swiftly to the gangway and went on board. The guard who had been moving aimlessly on the deck hurriedly approached him.

"I'm here to see Kung Lee," Toby announced in a clear voice.

The man hesitated for a moment. Then, his gaze shifting rapidly, he announced, "I never heard of him." It was plain that he was lying.

Toby had anticipated such a response and had planned on how to deal with it. "In that case," he said, "I must speak with Captain Kayross. Tell him that Major Holt of the U.S. Army is here."

He held his ground as the guard stared at him

for a moment. Then the man bolted and ran up to the bridge. He quickly returned and pointed toward the bridge. "He's up there," he said. "Don't loiter on the way."

Taking his time, Toby sauntered to the short flight of stairs that led up to the bridge, where he could see Captain Kayross waiting for him, obviously ill at ease.

Mounting the stairs, Toby refrained from drawing either of his pistols. This was not yet the time to demonstrate strength. "I am Major Toby Holt, U.S. Army," Toby said as he approached the captain. "I've come to see the proprietor of this ship, Kung Lee."

Beads of sweat appeared on Kayross's forehead. "I'm afraid that Mr. Kung isn't available at present, Major Holt." It was plain that he not only recognized Toby's name, which he spoke with a measure of awe, but that he was very much worried.

"Perhaps you'll be good enough to tell me what time he's expected on board," Toby suggested politely.

Kayross took his time replying. Moistening his lips, he suggested they adjourn to his cabin in order to discuss the matter. Toby was amenable but was very much on his guard.

Kayross headed toward the rear of the bridge's interior, where he opened a door into a combined sitting room/bedroom, simply furnished. He turned to face Toby and spread his hands out in front of him. "To be truthful with you, Major Holt," he said, "I don't know what you're talking about."

Toby remained patient. "You'll admit," he said, "that Kung Lee is the principal owner of this ship."

The words were no sooner out of his mouth than the door behind him opened and five seamen came into the room. Toby whirled around and drew his pistol, but he was too late. Two of the seamen grabbed Toby's arms, and another two held his legs. Meanwhile, the fifth man looped a rawhide noose over his neck and attached the other end of the strand to his arms and wrists, which were bound together. Then his legs and ankles were bound with a separate strand of rawhide, which was also looped around his neck and attached to it. This meant that any violent moves that Toby might make with either his arms or his legs would result in tightening the noose and cutting off his breath. If he was overly active, he could easily choke to death.

The fifth man now took Toby's pistols and removed the knife from his belt.

"Thanks very much, Kellerman," Kayross said. "Major Holt was becoming too damned inquisitive."

Toby turned his head slightly and, in spite of his extreme danger, he carefully scrutinized Karl Kellerman. The man was tall and brawny, and his hair obviously had been dyed, as had his beard and mustache. In addition, he had a pair of spectacles perched on his nose. In all, his appearance, Toby guessed, was very much changed.

Then Kung Lee entered the room. He was very calm, very much in command. "You're wasting time," he announced. "See what documents he's carrying."

Kellerman was the first to obey. Reaching into Toby's inner jacket pocket, he took out a sheet of parchment, which he unfolded. "This is an order signed by Major General Leland Blake, commander of the U.S. Army of the West," he said. "It authorizes Major Toby Holt to apprehend and arrest one Kung Lee for crimes committed against the people of the United States and contrary to that nation's laws."

Kung Lee smiled lazily. "Well, Holt," he said, "it seems that we've turned the tide just in time."

Careful not to move his arms and legs, Toby said, "Kung, no matter what you may do to me, you'll never get away with this. You've broken the laws of the United States for years, but those days are ended. The government has become aware of your crimes and will put you in prison because of them."

"All that you say may be true, Holt," Kung replied gently, "but you won't be alive to see me arrested and to attend my trial. I hope your ghost enjoys the spectacle, because you won't be here." He turned to Kellerman and Kayross. "Captain," he said, "cast off immediately and take this ship out to sea. We're sailing for the Orient immediately."

Kayross was stunned by the sudden, unexpected order. "We're not yet ready to sail, Mr. Kung," he said. "I don't have enough food supplies and water to sail from here to China."

The tong leader gestured impatiently. "We can put into any one of a half-dozen ports as we sail around South America, and we can get any supplies we need at all of them. Do as you're told! Holt isn't stupid, so he certainly didn't come here alone to seek me out. The dock will soon be crawling with U.S. Army troops. I want to be at sea by then."

"Aye, aye, sir." Kayross hurried out to the bridge and began to bark commands into his speaking tube.

"As the junior partner in this venture," Kung said to Kellerman, "you have certain responsibilities for our safety. As soon as we leave the Mississippi River behind us and reach the open waters of the Gulf of Mexico, I want you to dispose of Toby Holt."

"Do you want him shot?" Kellerman asked.

Kung laughed and shook his head. "Certainly not! Use your imagination, Karl! Throw him into the water the way you have him tied right now. If he tries to swim, he'll choke to death, and if he doesn't, he'll surely drown. I'll leave him to contemplate his fate while I go out and enjoy watching us putting out to sea. Join me on deck, Karl, and we'll breathe the fresh air of freedom together." Chuckling quietly, he left the cabin.

Kellerman hooked his thumbs in his broad belt and looked down at Toby, who lay, carefully unmoving, on the floor. "You may be the most famous law-enforcement official in the United States, Holt," he said, "but you really are a damned fool. You should have known better than to have come after Kung Lee single-handed. By the time your helpers arrive at the docks, we'll be well on our way out to sea, and you'll be several leagues below the waves." As he spoke, the *Neptune*'s engine began to rumble and the big vessel trembled as she slowly started to edge away from her dock. Ordinarily her master would have allowed more time for the boilers to build up a larger head of steam, but Captain Kayross was in too much of a hurry to put distance between himself and the land before Toby's reinforcements, whoever they might be, arrived at the waterfront. It was a good thing, Kayross reflected, that he had given orders earlier in the day to fire up the boilers.

Kellerman glanced out the porthole. "Good," he said. "We're under way. I'll leave you to contemplate your fate, Holt, until we reach the Gulf of Mexico." He sauntered out, closing the cabin door behind him.

As soon as Toby was alone, he went into action. He had not forgotten the Cherokee trick that Stalking Horse had taught him many years earlier, and while his bonds were being tied, he had deliberately tightened the muscles in his arms and legs, causing them to swell. By relaxing completely now, they became loose, and he had an opportunity to move without drawing the nooses around his neck tighter.

Wriggling and working his wrists systematically, Toby managed to loosen the bonds sufficiently to free his hands. Gingerly removing the noose from his neck, he untied the rawhide thong that bound his ankles and legs together, and then he slipped that noose over his head, too. He was free.

His mind had been working busily while he had undergone the taunts of Kung Lee and Karl Kellerman, and he knew precisely what needed to be done. Not wasting a single, precious moment, he hurried to the door, opened it cautiously, and when he saw the passage outside was empty, he slipped into it and went to the next cabin. It, too, was unlocked. He looked inside, and on a small desk in the corner he saw a small black notebook. He hurriedly thumbed through it. Several pages were written in Chinese, which he could not decipher, but then he came to a large section of charts with neatly printed words and phrases in English on them. He knew that this notebook was Kung Lee's private property and that he was looking at the entire system for the distribution of illegal immigrants and opium in the United States.

Armed with this evidence, the U.S. government would have no trouble in sending Kung Lee to prison for years or deporting him, whichever course of action the Justice Department chose to follow.

Toby's exceptionally acute hearing, as sensitive as his father's, stood him in good stead. Suddenly he made out the sound of the faint patter of footsteps outside on the deck. Shoving the notebook into his pocket, he stepped behind the cabin door.

One of Robin Kayross's Greek seamen thought he had heard someone in Kung Lee's cabin, and wanting to make sure that his imagination was not playing tricks on him, he had come to investigate. Taking his only weapon, a double-edged knife, from its sheath, he grasped it in one hand and opening the cabin door with the other, stepped inside.

As the door quietly closed, Toby struck, aiming

a blow with the edge of his hand at the back of the seaman's neck. The sailor's peripheral vision was sufficiently good that he caught a glimpse of Toby and turned his head just in time to absorb a portion of the blow on the side of the neck, rather than the back. Therefore, instead of being knocked unconscious, he was merely rendered groggy as he sank to the floor.

Toby well knew that his own life was in mortal danger, and he remembered the advice that his father had always given him: "When the chips are down, forget you're a gentleman. Use any and every means at your disposal in order to win. Just make sure when you get into a fight that you come out of it a winner." Thus, stifling his natural tendency to abide by the rules of fair play, Toby launched a vicious kick that caught the seaman under the chin. His head snapped back hard, striking the floor and knocking him unconscious.

Toby quickly bound the sailor's ankles and wrists, then picked up the knife. At least he was not totally helpless now.

Opening a wardrobe closet, Toby rummaged inside briefly and found what he was seeking—an oilskin coat that Kung Lee undoubtedly had brought with him to wear when the weather was foul. Using the knife, Toby cut a long strip from the hem of the coat up to the armholes about twelve inches wide. Then, after securing the knife in his belt, he wrapped the precious notebook in the strip of oilskin, which

he doubled and made sure was tightly closed before
he placed it, too, beneath his belt.

Casting a last glance at the unconscious Greek
seaman, Toby stepped out of the cabin into the open.
The throbbing of the ship's engine was louder here,
the trembling sensation more pronounced.

Looking out beyond the starboard rail Toby saw
that the *Neptune* was moving slowly down the Mississippi River toward the open sea. The docks had
already disappeared behind a bend in the river, and
the increasing sparsity of buildings was an indication
that New Orleans was being left behind.

Never having visited the area previously, Toby
had no idea whether the freighter would reach the
open Gulf of Mexico in minutes or hours, but he was
taking no chances. After assuring himself that no one
was on deck, he began to work his way aft, crouching
low among boxes, barrels, and crates of cargo that
filled the open deck. He took care to stay behind the
bridge, which was one deck higher, so that neither
the captain nor any of his officers there could see
him on the crowded deck below. Cautioning himself
not to rush with freedom already close at hand, Toby
made his way forward with extreme caution, making
certain that the area directly in front of him and on
both sides was unoccupied before doubling over and
running to hide in the shadows of another box or
crate.

At last, after playing a deadly game of hide-and-
seek, he arrived at the aft rail, and as he looked
down at the Mississippi below, a new problem pre-

sented itself. The *Neptune* was sailing slowly but
steadily downstream, and Toby realized that if he
were to jump overboard into the river, he might
injure himself on the sharp metal blades of the
Neptune's propeller. Instead, he moved about ten
feet toward the port side of the ship.

Toby was aware that when he jumped into the
river below, he would be plainly visible to men on
the bridge if they happened to turn and look in his
direction. If they should see him, it would be a
simple matter for them to halt the *Neptune* and
either lower a boat to retrieve him from the water or
to use him as a target. Either way, he would be
killed. But he had no choice. He had to take his
chances.

He estimated that the distance from the *Neptune*
to the shore on the port side of the ship was about a
half mile in all, and he had no doubt of his ability to
swim to land. He was far more at home near the
mountains and on wilderness trails than in the water,
but he had grown up near the lakes and rivers of
Oregon, and swimming presented him with few
challenges.

Climbing the port rail, Toby looked swiftly up at
the ship's bridge and saw that the three men standing there were looking ahead, down the river, and
that none were aware of his presence behind them.

Making sure that Kung Lee's oilskin-wrapped
notebook was secure beneath his belt, Toby took a
deep breath, then dived out as far as he could into
the waters of the Mississippi River.

The force of his dive plunged him deeply beneath the surface, and when he rose to the top again, swimming rapidly, he saw that the *Neptune* was now far ahead of him and that every passing second increased his distance from the ship.

His relief mounting as he swam, he felt the cool air clearing his mind. It was premature to celebrate, but he appeared to have outwitted the most powerful tong leader in the United States.

"There's somebody swimming in the river!" a woman's voice called suddenly. "It's a man, and he's fully dressed! Maybe he fell off the big ship!"

The startled Toby looked up and saw a strange craft bearing down on him. It was a type of raft, made of logs lashed together, and standing amidships was a crude little structure that served as a cabin. A woman wearing a bulky black sweater and men's trousers rested on one knee in the prow of the raft. Even her bulky sweater could not hide her voluptuous figure. With her waist-length, jet black hair, enormous eyes, and scarlet lips, she was very exotic-looking.

"Louis! Charles! Pole more to your left! That's it, get ready to throw him a line, Etienne!"

The raft slowly drew closer to the swimming Toby as it was poled by two burly young men, while the third began to twirl a length of rope. The rope landed within Toby's reach, and he grasped it with both hands.

"All right, Adele, I've hooked him!" the man named Etienne called. "Now what?"

"We'll take him on board, naturally!" she replied, and began to haul in the line, hand over hand.

Etienne did the same, and Toby was pulled to the raft. He managed to scramble aboard without any assistance. Rising to his feet and breathing hard, he found all three of the young giants and the attractive woman staring at him. "Thanks," he said. "I appreciate this."

"I am called Adele," the woman replied, "and these are the Raymond brothers, Louis, Charles, Etienne." Each of the young men nodded as his name was mentioned.

"Did you fall off the freighter?" Louis, the largest of the brothers, asked. "If so, we have a flare in the cabin that we can fire, and I'm sure the ship will stop."

"The last thing that I want on this earth is to halt that ship," Toby said. "I was a prisoner on board, and I'm lucky I escaped with my life."

The woman suddenly became concerned. "You're shivering!" she said. "Etienne! You're smaller than your brothers, so your clothes will be the most likely to fit him. Get him some pants and a shirt, please." She turned back to Toby. "You can go in the cabin and change," she told him, then directed her attention to the pair who were poling the craft. "Pull ashore and start to build a fire," she ordered. "I'm going to make our visitor a good hot meal."

Before Toby went into the cabin to change his clothes, he saw a gleam of jealousy in Louis Raymond's dark eyes.

The interior of the little cabin was as crude as the exterior. Items of clothing were hanging from a number of hooks, and the only signs that a young woman was on board were the presence of a broken mirror, a small jar of lip rouge, and a hairbrush, all of them bunched together on a small, homemade table.

"Here you are, mister," Etienne said, and handed Toby a dry shirt and a pair of trousers.

Toby peeled off his wet attire, changed into the dry clothes, and taking no risks, put the oilskin-wrapped notebook into a hip pocket and then slid the knife he had taken from the unconscious Greek seaman into his belt. When he returned to the deck of the raft, he saw that it had been run aground near a copse of trees and that hanging off the aft end of the ungainly craft were several large nets filled with fish, which moved about helplessly in the shallow waters.

"We've spent a couple of days near the mouth of the river fishing like we always do," the woman said as she led Toby ashore. "The fish run heavy and good there. Then we were taking our catch back to sell in New Orleans when we saw you in the water behind that big freighter. Tell us what happened to you."

Her companions, who were gathering wood and building a fire with it, stopped their activities to listen.

"My name is Toby Holt," Toby said, "and I went on board the *Neptune* to arrest an international criminal. His men overpowered me, but I was fortunate enough to escape."

The woman blinked at him in surprise and admiration. "You're really the famous Toby Holt?" she asked, clasping her hands together.

It was obvious that Louis Raymond was jealous. "Like hell he's Toby Holt!" he said. "If he's the great Holt, I'm General Andy Jackson." He laughed raucously at his own humor. Toby made no comment. Suddenly Louis, who towered above Toby by at least half a head, drew a knife. "If you're Toby Holt," he said, "let's have us a little duel. I see you have a knife, and I got one, too, so we'll have us a fight and may the best man win."

Toby shook his head. "You and your companions rescued me just a little while ago, Mr. Raymond," he said. "I'd be repaying you rather poorly if I fought you now. I urge you to forget the whole thing."

Louis sneered at him and addressed his brothers, although he was actually speaking for Adele's benefit. "I knew it! The Toby Holt we've read about ain't afraid of nobody or nothing." Then he turned to Toby. "But you got a yellow streak up your back a mile wide, mister. What do I have to do to get you to fight?"

Toby smiled. "If you go about your business quietly," he said, "you'll live a long, happy life down here in Cajun country."

The big man looked disgusted. "Put up or shut up," he growled, and spitting on the ground at Toby's feet, he waved his knife in front of the other man's face. "You hear me? Put up or shut up!"

Toby sighed, then moved with lightninglike speed. Using a trick he had learned several years earlier from the Shoshone Indians of Idaho, he struck swiftly, one hand cracking down onto Louis Raymond's wrist and hand. As Louis dropped his knife into the dust, Toby drew his own knife and held it poised a fraction of an inch from Louis's throat. "I tried to warn you, Raymond, but you refused to listen to me. I hate to repay your kindness by carving you to ribbons, but you're not giving me any choice. Now hear me. I'm tired after a busy and exhausting day. I'm hungry, and I'm looking forward to a night's sleep. I don't want any interference with my dinner or with my night's rest. You'll either behave yourself, or your brothers will be forced to carry you home, and it'll be a long time—a very long time—before you're able to go fishing again. What do you say?"

There was a long moment of silence, and Louis said, "I'm awful sorry, Mr. Holt. I guess I kind of mixed things up when I failed to recognize you. It won't happen again."

The woman laughed and clapped her hands together. "Only Toby Holt could make you back down and apologize, Louis. I never thought I'd live to see the day!" She turned to Toby and put a hand on his shoulder. "You must really be Toby Holt," she said admiringly. "Nobody else on earth could make Louis crawl."

Toby lowered his knife and extended his hand. "No hard feelings, Louis," he said.

"Thanks, Mr. Holt," the big man replied. "From now on we're on the same side."

By now the cooking fire was burning brightly. Adele, who was in charge of preparing the meal, wrapped some sweet potatoes in large, moist green leaves and put them in the coals. Then she went to the nets at the rear of the barge, and from them she took a number of fish, which she proceeded to clean, then to fry, sprinkling them with a pepper sauce that was peculiar to the Cajun country.

While the fish sizzled in two large frying pans, Toby learned more about these backwoods people from Adele. The young woman lived in her parents' house in the bayou country near that of the Raymonds and sometimes went with them on their fishing expeditions. Living in the remote countryside made her restless, and it was her dream to move to the city. Louis, who was eager to marry her, had promised her a home in New Orleans if she would wed him, but she had not yet accepted his offer.

"I've never known anybody," Adele told Toby, "who leads a life as exciting as you do. Will this man you were after be arrested now?"

"Yes," Toby told her, "as soon as he and his companions set foot again on American soil." When that would be Toby did not know, but right then he didn't want to think about it. He was exhausted, and all he wanted to do was eat his meal and get some sleep.

Night had fallen by the time they finished supper. The Raymonds went to check their nets, while Adele went into the cabin on the boat and came out with a blanket and a mosquito net, which she gave to Toby. He spread the blanket on the ground, and when he retired, he put the net over him in order to ward off mosquitoes, flies, and other insects in the humid climate.

Tired after his extraordinary day's exertions, Toby soon drifted off to sleep. When he had been in his early twenties, he would have remained fresh and strong after spending such a day, but now that he was nearing thirty, he found he grew tired and needed his rest. His last thoughts before he fell asleep were of Clarissa, whom he missed desperately.

Later that night—he had no idea of the time—he dreamed that he and Clarissa were making passionate love. He awakened to find himself kissing Adele violently. Their bodies were tightly intertwined, and she had managed to insert a hand beneath his attire and was fondling him.

He was stunned, and his mind almost refused to function, but he knew, nevertheless, that he could not tolerate such a situation. Unless he did something quickly, he would be guilty of infidelity to his wife.

Toby caught the woman by the shoulders and forcibly moved her away. Then he sat up, climbed to his feet, and pulled her upright. Saying nothing for fear of awakening the sleeping Raymond brothers, he walked her to the nearby riverfront and sat her down on a bank overlooking the Mississippi. "You don't want to be doing this with me, Adele," he said. "You're probably only interested in me because you think I'm an exciting, romantic figure."

Adele sat hugging her knees and staring out at the dark, silvery ribbon of the broad Mississippi. She was hurt now and had withdrawn within herself, so she made no reply.

"Let me tell you," Toby said softly, "about Clarissa."

"Who is Clarissa?" she asked in a small voice.

"My wife," he replied. "The woman I love more than I love life itself. She is also the mother, teacher, and nursemaid for our very young son. As for me, I like nothing better than being home with my family, tending to the affairs of my ranch, looking after my horses and my other livestock. You see, Adele, I'm just an ordinary man, married to a woman I love. You should not be interested in me."

Adele was silent for a time. "I'm sorry, Toby," she said at last in a barely audible voice. "I'm truly sorry."

He patted her shoulder. "That's all right," he said. "Everybody makes mistakes, and there's no harm done. You have a good man in Louis. Marry him and live happily ever after, and be glad you have a husband who loves you as much as he does."

IX

The group of officials gathered in the commandant's office of the New Orleans army garrison passed Kung Lee's precious notebook from one to the other. The New Orleans police commissioner, who had also been called in, shook his head, and the director of immigration of Louisiana registered astonishment.

"Major Holt, the detailed information on Kung Lee's illegal immigration network will send him to prison for the rest of his life," the commandant said. "And I'm sure that the data on his dissemination of opium will move the United States Congress to pass laws making the transportation illegal."

"What's more," the police commissioner said, "we have enough evidence about the illegal activities of Karl Kellerman and Robin Kayross to put them behind bars for a good long time—assuming they ever show up here again."

"As in the past, Major Holt," the army commandant said, "you've done the American people great service at considerable risk to your own life."

"When this information is made public," the director of immigration added, "you'll get the recognition you well deserve."

Toby shook his head. "If you please, gentlemen," he said emphatically, "I want no publicity in this matter. I'd appreciate it if not one word appears in print regarding what I've done."

"Aren't you carrying modesty a bit far?" the police commissioner asked.

"This has nothing to do with modesty," Toby replied. "General Blake will want nothing made public until Kung Lee returns to the United States and is placed under arrest. If he's warned, we'll be giving him another opportunity to evade the law."

Each of the officials promptly swore that he would regard the news as confidential.

"I hope, Mr. Holt," the commissioner said, "that you'll stay in New Orleans long enough for us to take you out to supper."

"Thank you," Toby replied, "but I don't think I'll be able to. I have some personal business to attend to, and then I'm going to head back to the West. I promised my wife I'd return home as soon as possible." He deliberately refrained from mentioning that he had made a deal with Domino and that he intended to abide by his end of the agreement. The officials would be shocked to learn that Toby would be going to see the notorious gang leader later that very night. But he had found Kung Lee only with

Domino's help, and now he was obligated to return the favor.

The meeting broke up, and Toby went back to his hotel. Before he had met with the authorities at the army garrison, he had told Edward and Jim about his experiences aboard the *Neptune*, and the Englishman realized that the man who had done him such harm was now out of his reach, on the high seas sailing to the Orient.

"I guess he's in your capable hands now, Toby," Edward said. "Your hands and the government's. But I pity poor Wallace Dugald. When I tell him Kellerman got away from him, he's going to go into a raging fit."

Now at the hotel, Toby found Edward and Tommie awaiting him in great excitement. "We've just had a further telegram from Tommie's father," Edward told him. "He'll arrive in New Orleans day after tomorrow. We've scheduled the wedding for noon that day, and we hope that you'll attend."

Toby knew that Clarissa would understand when he wired her that he had been delayed in his return home because he had agreed to go to Edward's wedding. Saying he would be delighted to attend, he wished the couple the best of everything in the world, and then he went on to supper with Jim, Millicent, and Jean-Pierre Gautier, whom he had not met previously and was eager to know.

Meanwhile, Tommie was totally calm about her upcoming wedding. "My wedding dress is sitting in my clothes closet waiting to be worn," she said, "and

Millicent, as my maid of honor, has her dress. Jim is going to be your best man, so that leaves just one thing still to be settled."

"What's that?" Edward asked.

"We'll have to see the minister tomorrow morning," she replied. "Don't you remember? He said he wanted to have a talk with us on the day before the wedding, and you invited him to the hotel."

"I haven't forgotten the appointment with the minister," Edward told her, "but there's one other thing that's very important."

Tommie stared at him anxiously.

"Fortunately," he said with a reassuring grin, "I remembered it just in time this afternoon, which is why I left you for a while. I went to a restaurant in the French Quarter and made a supper reservation for us for this evening."

She laughed in relief. "Now you're being silly, but thank goodness that's all it is! I thought we'd forgotten something really important."

Her fiancé joined in her laugh but made no reply. If Tommie had been looking at him, she might have realized that he was indeed talking about something important, but her thoughts were elsewhere, and she dropped the subject. She went off to change her clothes for the evening, and soon thereafter they strolled from their hotel to the restaurant.

Edward had gone to great pains to make the evening memorable. When they arrived at their table, a lovely corsage of flowers awaited Tommie, and a bottle of imported French champagne was cooling in a silver ice bucket.

Edward had ordered their meal in advance, and as always, his taste was impeccable. The fresh shrimp from the Gulf of Mexico were large and firm; their gumbo was light but not bland; and their main course, fried chicken, was cooked to perfection. Vegetables, roasted potatoes, and a salad of fresh, chilled greens were served with the chicken. When they were finished, Tommie sighed. "I don't think I could eat another thing," she said.

A few moments later, their waiter brought them a steaming deep dish pie, its crust a golden brown.

"A pie!" Tommie exclaimed. "I couldn't eat a bite!"

"This dessert was ordered for you," Edward told her. "Why don't you break the crust to let the steam out and taste a little of it? Then if you can't eat it, you can just leave it."

She glanced at him dubiously, broke the crust on the top of the dish with her fork, and then blinked in surprise. In the center of the dish, beneath the crust, rested a small velvet box.

Tommie stared at it uncomprehendingly. "This is very odd," she murmured.

"Why don't you try opening the box?" Edward suggested. "It shouldn't be too hot to handle."

She removed the royal blue box from the dish, opened it, and gasped. There, nestling in a bed of creamy satin, glistened a huge, square-cut emerald ring, its rich green hues sparkling and shimmering in the candlelight.

"Oh, Edward," she whispered.

"I've been remiss in giving you an engagement ring," he said. "I've had several jewelers looking, but I wasn't satisfied until they came up with exactly the right gem."

"I've never seen anything so beautiful," Tommie murmured. "It's far too good to wear every day."

Edward picked up the box, took the ring from it, and slipped it on the third finger of her left hand. "There," he said. "You'll take it off only once, so that your wedding ring will go under it. Aside from that, I hope you'll wear it every day, as long as you live."

"As long as I live," she assured him solemnly, and unmindful of the other patrons in the restaurant, she raised her face to his. Their kiss was a promise of lifelong love and fidelity.

Tommie was so deeply affected she seemed to have lost her voice. She sat for a long time holding her hand up to the candlelight, moving it closer, then farther, twisting and turning her fingers and admiring the emerald in every possible light and position. "Thanks to you, Edward," she whispered, "this is the happiest day of my life."

"This is just the beginning of our life together," he said, smiling. "Soon we'll have to decide where we're going to live and what enterprises I'm going to get involved in."

She pressed her hands to her temples. "I can't think straight right now," she told him. "My mind is

whirling, and this emerald is so bright that it's dazzling me. Give me a little time, and then we can
start talking about the future."

He agreed, and they kissed again, then sat back
in their chairs and sedately sipped their coffee like a
couple who had been married for years.

Neither of them knew it, but the whole scene
had been observed closely by two hard-faced men
sitting several tables away from them in the restaurant.
The pair took special interest in the emerald and
exchanged quick, knowing glances, although they
said very little to each other. They hurried through
their meal, then paid their bill, but nevertheless
dawdled over coffee until Edward and Tommie were
finished and rose from their table. Then the men
departed, too, deliberately staying a half-block behind the happy couple.

Walking arm in arm, Edward and Tommie felt
as though they were floating through the air. They
took their time, sauntering along, looking up at the
moon casting silvery beams through leafy trees that
lined the street. They were passing through a neighborhood of large, private homes set back from the
road, with high shrubs and iron fences protecting
them from the public. It was quiet, and they were so
wrapped up in each other that they failed to realize
that they seemed to be the only pedestrians abroad
at the moment.

Suddenly they were confronted by two men,
both of them masked, the taller carrying a cocked
pistol, which he pointed straight at Edward.

"If you'll do what you're told without making a fuss," he said, "nobody will get hurt. But if you disobey our instructions, we can't be responsible for your safety."

Edward looked into the muzzle of the pistol and smiled calmly. "What is it you want us to do?" he asked.

"The girl is to stand still right where she is," the robber directed. "As for you, mister, you can back off about fifty feet or so." He turned to his companion. "Go with him and make sure he does what he's told."

Edward smiled at Tommie reassuringly. "Don't you worry, honey," he said, "everything is going to be all right." Making no objections, he accompanied the smaller of the pair until they had moved about fifty feet down the street. He noted that unlike his companion, this robber was armed only with a knife.

They halted, and the man reached out, helping himself to Edward's pistol. Then the man rejoined his companion, who stood near Tommie.

"And as for you, ma'am," the taller of the pair said to her, "you're too young and too pretty to be burdened through life carrying that green stone on your finger, so I'll just take it right now."

Having removed Edward from the immediate scene and relieved him of his pistol, the robbers conveniently forgot his existence for the moment. But Edward was not lacking in resources. At no time did he leave his quarters without carrying ample means of self-protection, and that evening was no exception. He had replaced the weapons that were taken from him when he was abducted, and now as he shook his arm, the derringer he always carried concealed in a special harness up his sleeve fell into his hand. As his fingers closed over the trigger, he felt much more confident.

Tommie was staring in disbelief at the robber. "You would take my new engagement ring from me? I think not, mister! There's only one way you'll get it, and that's over my dead body!"

"Don't make any mistakes about us, lady," the man told her, his eyes narrowing. "We'll get that ring any way that we have to, and if it's necessary to kill you, that's what we're going to do!"

Edward pulled the trigger, and his aim was true. The bullet penetrated the robber's jugular vein, and he crumpled to the ground, dying instantly. Edward continued to brandish his pistol.

"I have another shot left," he called. "Take my pistol from the rogue, Tommie! And while you're at it, help yourself to his knife, too!"

She complied with his instructions, and then he said, "Now move toward me. No rush, one step at a time. That's it."

Little by little she moved toward safety.

"Now then, you scum," he called. "Unless you want to join your friend in a pool of your own blood, I'd advise you to leave and to put as much distance as possible between yourself and us. This is a special evening in my life, so I'm in a particularly benevolent mood. I'll let you off free, provided you make yourself scarce in an awful hurry."

The robber took off, running down the street and disappearing around a corner in record time.

"I'm afraid," Edward said, sliding an arm around Tommie's shoulders, "that we're going to be slightly delayed in getting back to our hotel. We'll have to stop in at the nearest police headquarters and report the unfortunate death of an extremely luckless robber."

She moved closer to him and shuddered. "I was frightened half to death. I was afraid he was going to kill both of us in order to get my engagement ring."

Edward kissed her earlobe as they started off down the street, walking far more rapidly than they had before the incident. "I told you not to be worried, and I meant it," he said. "I waited far too long to get you exactly the right ring, and I was damned if you were going to lose it to a pair of cheap crooks. When you agreed to marry me, I accepted permanent responsibility for your safety and welfare, and I don't intend to let you down, now or ever."

They were still holding each other tightly when they entered the police station moments later to report the incident.

As Toby Holt went down the walk leading to the entranceway of the large house that was surrounded by trees and bushes, two burly men, both of them carrying rifles, appeared out of the dark. One of the men raised a kerosene lantern and held it so it cast light on Toby's face. "It's Holt, all right," he said. "I'd know him anywhere."

"I reckon we'd better let him in, then," the second guard said. "You know how the boss gets when his orders aren't obeyed."

Instead of replying, the first man bowed slightly to Toby and then led the way into the house. "We'll let the boss know that you're here," he said when they were in the hallway, and the two men both promptly disappeared.

Toby was alone for only a few moments. Martha soon appeared in the doorway, her red hair cascading down her shoulders, her voluptuous figure encased in a skin-tight dress that left little to the imagination. She teetered slightly on stiltlike heels, but her hip-swaying walk was nevertheless seductive. She looked at Toby and didn't seem at all surprised that he was on the property.

"Well, hello," she said, a strong hint of intimacy in her warm, welcoming smile.

"Hello, Martha," Toby replied calmly, and the thought occurred to him that the woman apparently had a highly privileged place in the household.

"The last that I heard," she said, "you were going off on a dangerous mission—for us as well as for yourself."

"I've gone, I've attended to several matters, and now I'm back," he said.

"Domino never takes long to listen to reports, especially at this time of night," Martha said, and putting her hands on her hips, she cocked her head to one side. "Perhaps you and I might have a drink together after you're through talking with him. I have the run of the place here, and I have access to some wonderful liquors and rare wines."

"Thank you for asking me," he said politely. "However, I'm not very keen on wines and liquor."

A deep, resonant chuckle sounded farther down the hall. "No doubt Mr. Holt wants to consume nothing that would adversely affect his miraculous prowess," Domino said, appearing from behind some plants. There was no telling how long he had been in the hallway. "Run along now, Martha," he said patiently. "If Mr. Holt is interested, you may see him later."

Annoyed by his tone, Martha flounced off.

Domino approached a large wicker settee. "Once I learned you were here, I took the liberty of ordering us a light supper, Mr. Holt. I hope you don't mind."

"Not at all," Toby replied politely, figuring he had a good appetite and could always eat another meal. "That's very kind of you."

"I heard that you returned unexpectedly to New Orleans this morning on board a fishing barge and that you then held a conference with a number of officials at the office of the army garrison commandant. Obviously you had something of a rough experience, and equally obviously you had some important news to impart."

"Yes, I did," Toby said, and nodded.

"I hope you'll see fit to relate your experience to me."

"Naturally," Toby replied. "It was only through you that I learned of Kung Lee's whereabouts, and I struck a bargain with you. I fully intend to keep my word."

"It's kind of you to honor our agreement, Mr. Holt," Domino said. "After all, we two operate on opposite sides of the law, and it would be easy enough for you to find a simple excuse for breaking your word to me."

"I learned my approach to life from my father, Domino," Toby said. "I never give my word lightly. I always mean it, and I've never yet broken it. I'm in your debt—and I intend to pay off that debt right now. What's more, I hope to work closely with you until both of us accomplish our ends in this nasty business that we're engaged in."

Struck by his sincerity, Domino extended his hand. Toby shook hands with him without the slightest hesitation, and they sealed an unspoken agreement. They had formed a strange partnership that would last until the world was rid of both Kung Lee and Karl Kellerman.

Toby slowly told the story of his experience on board the freighter, *Neptune*, omitting no details. He hurriedly related his subsequent encounter with the Raymond brothers and Adele because that meeting had no real bearing on his visit to Domino.

When he was finished, the gang leader said, "One moment. I want to be sure I have the facts straight. You say that Kellerman is on board the freighter and is bound for the Orient at this moment?"

"Correct," Toby said. "From what I learned on board the ship, he and Kung are traveling to Canton and Hong Kong in order to pick up a shipload of illegal Chinese immigrants and as much opium as they can carry."

"I don't believe in kidnapping or in killing people with drugs," Domino said. "Kellerman is going to return from the Orient on board the *Neptune*?"

"To the best of my knowledge, he is," Toby replied. "He has no reason to stay in China, and I gather that his interests are in this country."

"I appoint myself as chairman of a reception committee to greet him when he returns," Domino said, "and no matter in what port he may land, I'll be notified, and I'll act accordingly. I thank you, far more than I can ever tell you, for this information."

"Kung Lee, of course, will be nabbed by government authorities the moment he sets foot back in America," Toby said. "As for Kellerman, the New Orleans authorities are on the lookout for him, too, but if you get to him first, you can probably dispose of him without any help. However, in the event that you need some assistance, don't hesitate to call on me. He appears to be an expert at slipping away once you believe you have him cornered. I'll write out my address for you at my ranch in Oregon, and you can always reach me there."

"You're going home soon?"

"Yes, I'm leaving the day after tomorrow, as

soon as I've attended the wedding of a good friend. I'm going by train all the way, first from here to St. Louis and then to Oregon. I'm anxious to rejoin my wife as soon as I can."

Domino smiled broadly. "Do I gather that you have no intention of spending any time with Martha before you head home?"

"I'm grateful for her offers of hospitality," Toby said carefully, "but I'm afraid I won't be able to avail myself of them. I'm one of those strange critters, a one-woman man who happens to be very much in love with his wife."

Domino looked at him curiously. "I've never known a man who would willingly reject the charms of a woman as attractive as Martha," he said. "Now that we've finished our business, I hope you'd have no objection if I invited her to join us for a bite of supper."

Toby shrugged. "By all means, invite her," he said.

Domino tugged at a bell rope and then exchanged some words in private with the man who answered his summons.

A short time later, when he and Toby adjourned to the dining room, they found Martha awaiting them. She had applied fresh makeup to her lovely face, and she looked even more attractive than before.

She devoted her full attention to Toby as they ate, and Domino, casting himself in the role of an observer, sat back in his chair and watched.

Toby seemed to be completely at ease as he

dealt with Martha, answering her questions politely. He suffered her blatant attempts to flirt with him without feeling undue strain, and he initiated as well as responded to her conversation. When the meal ended, he said good-bye to her, then shook hands with Domino and gave the gang leader the address of his ranch in Oregon. He appeared completely unruffled as he took his leave.

"That Toby Holt," Martha said slowly, "is the most incredible man I've ever met."

"Certainly he's the first man I've ever encountered," Domino said, "who failed to respond to you. Holt isn't human—he's superhuman!"

"You've made a mistake," Martha said. "Toby was very much aware of me, as conscious as any man I've ever known."

Domino's interest was piqued. "Really?"

"Absolutely," she replied. "He was so much aware of me, in fact, that he deliberately erected a wall between us, and he hid on his side of it. I had the definite feeling that if he had allowed even a section of his wall to crumble or to fall, he'd have given in to his impulses and would have totally forgotten his principles."

Grinning broadly, Domino murmured, "That's fascinating," and he was silent for a long time, lost in thought.

"I believe I can analyze accurately the way any man responds to me," Martha said. "Toby Holt uses great self-control—greater control than I've ever seen.

That's because he's afraid we'll have an explosive relationship if he doesn't protect himself."

"Do you suppose you can break through that wall of reserve that he's erected?"

"I honestly don't know," Martha said candidly. "I know my own strengths, and I believe I'm capable of breaking down the resistance of most men, but Toby Holt isn't like anyone else I've ever met. I have no idea which of us would win a contest of wills, but I'd love to find out."

"So would I," Domino said, and laughed again.

"Are you planning to set him up?" she asked innocently.

The gang leader smiled slyly. "Holt has done me the greatest of favors, and I'd never harm him or double-cross him in any way. He was loyal to me at the risk of his life, and it's impossible to buy that kind of loyalty. I want to reward him. However, in so doing, I may be able to have a little fun at the same time."

"I hope that I'll be involved in your attempts to 'reward' him, as you call it."

"You shall be, my dear Martha," he replied emphatically. "You most assuredly shall be."

Tommie and Edward received the minister who would marry them the following day and were closeted with him for a long time in Edward's suite. Even Robin Hood, the little monkey who had made himself the couple's inseparable companion, seemed to sense that this was a solemn occasion, and he sat quietly, perched on Edward's shoulder throughout the interview.

"Yours will be no ordinary marriage," Reverend Giddings told Tommie and Edward. "You've already got financial security, and that's a great blessing. On the other hand, you'll find that your separate backgrounds require a greater degree of tolerance and understanding than is required of most newlyweds. You grew up in the genteel Old World surroundings of England, Edward, while you, Tommie, were born and raised on the rivers of the American frontier. That makes quite a difference, and you're going to need a great deal of patience and understanding to compensate for the differences."

"You'll be interested to learn, Reverend Giddings, that I'm intending to apply for American citizenship in the immediate future," Edward said. "I'm also intending to go into the coastal trade. Tommie already knows ships, of course, and I'm convinced there's a great future in it."

Tommie nodded in agreement.

"I wish that every couple I counsel prior to their marriage had prospects equal to yours," the minister said, sighing. "You truly have everything in your favor."

After the meeting came to an end, Tommie and Edward escorted the minister through the hotel lobby, then stood with him for several moments in the entrance to the hotel as they concluded their conversation. They were interrupted when an elegant-looking carriage pulled to a halt in the street in front of the hotel. The coach was pulled by a pair of matching bays, a driver in livery sat on the box, and in the backseat was a gray-haired woman, expensively gowned. Next to her was a little girl, apparently her grandchild.

The lady in the carriage bowed. "Good morning, Reverend Giddings," she called.

The minister brightened. "Ah, good morning, Mrs. Soames." He proceeded to present Tommie and Edward to the woman.

All of them were startled when Robin Hood jumped to the ground, bounded forward, and made a desperate leap that landed him in the carriage.

"Look, Grandma!" The little girl was ecstatic. "Bella has found a new friend!"

The adults were surprised to see a little monkey, smaller than Robin Hood, wearing an ankle-length dress. The creature was seated on the cushioned seat beside the child and was exchanging rapid-fire chatter with Robin Hood.

"Bella found a gentleman friend!" the little girl announced.

"Bella," Tommie said formally, "permit me to present Mr. Robin Hood."

The two monkeys, paying no attention to their human companions, chattered excitedly.

"Can we keep him, Grandma? Please! Can we?" The little girl was so anxious she was on the point of tears.

Mrs. Soames was mildly shocked. "How can you

ask such a thing, Dorothy?" she demanded. "This monkey belongs to Mr. Blackstone."

Edward exchanged a long, significant look with Tommie, and they communicated silently. "If you permit me, Mrs. Soames," Edward said, "my fiancée and I would very much like to make a gift of Robin Hood to Dorothy."

The little girl's joy was unbounded. "Did you hear that, Bella? Did you hear it, Robin? We're going to be together for always! Thank you, ma'am! Thank you, sir!"

"This is too much," her grandmother said firmly. "I simply can't permit—"

"Really, Mrs. Soames," Tommie interjected. "We insist. We want to share our own happiness, and we're sure that Robin Hood will be more than happy with your granddaughter."

"I'll take good care of him," the little girl said earnestly. "I promise!"

Her grandmother wavered. "Well . . ."

"If you please, Mrs. Soames," Edward said gravely. "My fiancée and I will regard your approval as one of the better wedding presents that we've received."

"I cannot refuse a plea of that kind, sir," she said, inclining her head to him. "Dorothy, you and Bella have a new companion. You may keep Robin Hood."

The little girl squealed, the two monkeys chattered more loudly, and the lady ordered her driver to proceed.

"That was a wonderfully kind gesture," Reverend Giddings said as they watched the carriage move off down the street. "You can be sure that your little pet will get excellent care. Mrs. Soames is one of the most upstanding of my parishioners."

"We wouldn't have agreed to part with Robin," Tommie said, "unless we felt certain that he'd have a good home."

"I'm sure," Edward said, "that he's going to be happy living with a little girl who makes an incessant fuss over him and with a fellow monkey who speaks his own language. You may have noticed he was so engrossed that he didn't even look up when they drove off."

Tommie joined in Edward's happy laugh. Looking at them, Reverend Giddings again marveled at how right they were for each other. This, he reflected, was truly a marriage that had been made in heaven.

"Come on, Kale," Cindy Holt urged exuberantly. "Put on your hat, your coat, and your biggest victory smile. Willie Rowe has invited us to get the election results at the newspaper office, where they'll come in first."

Kale Martin demurred. "I don't want to leave Rob just sitting here," she said, "and I haven't made arrangements for anybody to spend the evening watching over little Cathy."

Cindy appealed to her friend's husband. "You can talk her into it, Rob," she said.

Rob smiled at his wife. "Cindy is right, honey,"

he said. "This is a big day for you, and a big day for
every woman in Oregon. You'll be in the history
books as the first woman to be elected as a trustee of
the state college, the first woman to hold a statewide
position in Oregon!"

"*If* I'm elected," Kale replied.

"I'm not much of a gambler," Cindy said, "but
I'm willing to bet you any amount you'd like to
wager that you're going to come in far ahead of
Frank Colwyn. After the articles that Willie Rowe
wrote exposing him as a crook, he couldn't be elected
to dogcatcher or garbage collector in this state. You're
an absolute cinch to win!"

"Cindy may have a tendency to paint larger-
than-life portraits, but in this instance, she happens
to be right, honey," Rob said. "As I've been telling
you day after day, I've made it my business to find
out how people are voting, and I'm predicting a
landslide for you. You're going to win by the widest
margin of any officeholder in the state."

"If that's true," Kale said uncertainly, "I'd love
to go with Cindy."

"Then get out of here," Rob said, grinning. "Cathy
is sleeping, and I'm perfectly capable of looking after
her in the event that she wakes up. You deserve to
hear the news first, so get along with you and good
luck."

Rob almost pushed his wife out the door. Kale,
laughing now, allowed herself to be persuaded and,
accompanied by Cindy, went off to the newspaper
office.

Several large blackboards had been set up in the newsroom and were manned by reporters who changed figures on them as a steady flow of telegrams came in from polling places all over Oregon. Willie Rowe took Kale and Cindy to the board where he himself was chalking up figures. "This," he said, "is the central board. You can tell at a glance how you're doing. As a matter of fact, you're already far ahead of Colwyn. Let's see. You have over one thousand votes to less than two hundred for him."

Cindy cheered, but Kale was embarrassed. "How could it possibly be such a large majority?" she asked. "There must be a mistake."

"There's no mistake," the reporter told her. "People don't want to vote for a crook, and you're the honest alternative."

"Then I have you and Cindy to thank in the event that I'm elected," she replied.

Rowe shook his head. "You have your own efforts to thank. Pure and simple," he said. "The time is right for women to take an active role in politics and to run for public office, and you were smart enough to sense that fact and to act accordingly. You're setting a precedent—not only here, but for women all over the West, and that's why I invited you to watch the returns here. I want to get a victory statement from you that will reflect your feelings on the significance of today's vote, not only in Oregon, but elsewhere."

Kale and Cindy settled down to watch the figures change on the blackboards. Willie provided them with cups of coffee, and as time went on they were fascinated to see the totals mount.

They were particularly impressed by the margin of victory in Kale's favor; at no time was her election in doubt. The state's voters, disgusted with the revelations of Frank Colwyn's wrongdoing, turned away from him in vast numbers, and the vote in Kale's favor was overwhelming. Thus she was not only the first woman ever elected to a statewide post in Oregon, but she was also elected by the greatest majority of any candidate who had ever run for a similar office.

Rowe asked her to write out a victory statement for publication the following morning, and this Kale did. She not only thanked the voters for their confidence in her and for giving her the opportunity to serve them, but she also called attention to the fact that voters in Wyoming and Utah, as well as in Oregon, had already established records by electing women to public office. Kale made the bold prediction that the day would come when women would not only run for such offices as governor, U.S. senator, and member of the U.S. House of Representatives, but actually would be elected to such offices. This hitherto had been a dream that seemed impossible to fulfill.

Returning home, Kale was greeted at the door by a smiling Rob. "Well?" he demanded.

She handed him a slip of paper on which she had written the election returns.

Rob glanced at the returns, then enveloped his

wife in a hug and kissed her tenderly. "You did it, honey!" he exulted. "I'm so glad for you!"

"I'm glad for us," she said, her arms still entwined around his neck. "I'm especially glad for you."

"I wasn't running for office," he replied, somewhat mystified. "The voters went to the polls and cast their ballots for you. The fact that you're married to me was irrelevant. They were expressing confidence in your ability to represent them."

"I know all that," Kale replied, "but there was far more at stake than my election to the board. My past was printed out for everyone to see, and a lot of decent people regarded me as a notorious, fallen woman."

"Which you are not," her husband told her emphatically.

"But which I very definitely was," she replied. "That's all behind me now. It's one of the wonderful things about being an American. As long as one is sincere in one's beliefs and approach, the public will always accept repentance. I'm no longer a pariah. I'm accepted now as a citizen in good standing, and I've been given a position of trust."

She looked at Rob with shining eyes. "I intend to live up to that trust," she said. "I'll be the best trustee on the college board!"

"Just as you're already the best wife and the best mother in the entire Pacific Northwest," he replied.

She threw her arms around him and hugged him again. "This is the happiest day of my life," she said. "Thanks to you and our neighbors and everybody else in the state, I've been rejuvenated, and I'm a new woman!"

It was late when Cindy Holt rode up to the barn behind her brother's ranch house, where she was staying while her mother and stepfather were off again visiting the East, meeting with President Grant. Removing her horse's saddle, Cindy then went to the house itself. She was glad to find her sister-in-law, Clarissa, still awake, and as she put her rifle in the rack that Toby had built for that purpose in the kitchen, Cindy related the election figures.

"I'm so glad for Kale," Clarissa said, "and I'm sure Toby will be, too. In the morning I'll have to send him a telegram in New Orleans and tell him the results before he goes off to Edward's wedding. He'll be anxious to send Kale a wire of congratulations." Cindy nodded but said very little as she wandered aimlessly around in the kitchen.

Her sister-in-law thought she was unusually restless but kept her opinion to herself. "Would you like a cup of hot chocolate, Cindy?"

"Don't bother on my account."

"I won't, but I was making some for myself, and it's just as easy to make two cups as one."

"In that case, I guess I will. Thanks very much." She went to the cupboard and brought out two cups and two saucers, which she gave to her sister-in-law.

While Clarissa poured the hot chocolate, Cindy seated herself at the kitchen table and sighed deeply.

Clarissa stared at her. "Whatever is wrong with you, Cindy?" she asked. "I would have thought you'd be as delighted as I am that Kale won the election."

"Oh, I am," the girl replied. "I couldn't be happier about it."

"But something is wrong," her sister-in-law said.

Cindy stared down at the steaming cup that Clarissa placed in front of her. "Now that you mention it," she said, "I guess there is something wrong."

"If you care to tell me about it, I'll be glad to listen."

"I've been counting the months and weeks and even the days," Cindy said, "until Hank is graduated from the military academy and is awarded his commission as a lieutenant. Until now, I've wanted nothing more than to be his wife, and I can't tell you how much I've been dreaming about the day when we'll be married."

"I know how eager you and Hank have been to be married," Clarissa said, "and I can't blame either of you. It wasn't so awfully long ago, you know, that Toby and I were engaged, and although we got married shortly after that, it felt like we had to wait ages."

"I've always been ambitious, too ambitious for my own good, I suppose," Cindy said, "but that's been one of the penalties of being Whip Holt's daughter. I've always had daydreams about becoming one of the first women lawyers or doctors—or whatever—in America. But once I marry Hank and become Mrs. Henry Blake, pursuing a career of my

own will be out of the question. I realize that one
career—Hank's—in the family will be enough. Oh, I
know enough about the army and army living to be a
first-rate officer's wife, and I'm sure I can be a great
help to Hank in furthering his career—"

"There's no question of that," Clarissa said.

"But," Cindy continued in a voice of doom, "I'm
not sure that will be enough for me. I want to do
what Kale has done, make a mark for myself as a
woman, as a person who has something to offer her
country and her community."

"Has Hank indicated in any way that you have
to be a one-career family?" Clarissa asked.

"Not yet, but he will," Cindy replied gloomily.
"He's a man, and all men expect their wives to stay
at home and raise a family and be nurturing to them."

"Then you don't know men very well," Clarissa
replied, "at least not men like Hank and your brother
Toby." Clarissa put her hands on the younger woman's
shoulders. "Now listen to me," she declared forcibly,
"and hear every word that I say. Like Kale, you are a
woman whose inner needs demand that she find
fulfillment through a career. I happen to be completely fulfilled as a wife and a mother. I admire
Kale, and I respect her for what she's doing, just as
I'm elated over her victory, but I don't envy her, and
I have no desire to change places with her. I'd be
unhappy if I were elected to a post as trustee for the
college, and consequently I'd do a miserable job. I
gain my greatest satisfaction in life," Clarissa went
on, "by doing the very best I can as a wife and as a

mother, and I assure you that doing those jobs is not easy."

Cindy smiled appreciatively.

"My husband knows," Clarissa continued, "that I'm completely devoted to him and to our child, but I can promise you that if I wished to be elected to the United States House of Representatives, he wouldn't love me any less than he does or think I had let him down. He'd give me his full support in whatever I needed to do to fulfill myself as a person, as a woman, as a wife."

"I think I'm beginning to see what you mean," Cindy said.

"Hank will be the same way," Clarissa told her. "Oh, when you're first married, you'll float on a cloud, and nothing will seem important but each other. But then, little by little, the realities of life will begin to seep in, and you'll both realize that you need more to be fulfilled. You and Hank are a new generation, Cindy, and your ways will be different from Toby's and mine. You're both going to need careers that fulfill you, and only in that way will your marriage have stability and peace."

"I can see," Cindy said, "that Hank and I will be carrying a heavy responsibility."

"So you shall," her sister-in-law replied, "but your greatest responsibility will be to yourself. Will you be satisfied—will you find contentment—with life as a wife and as a mother? If you will, you'll make your husband happy, and he'll be equally contented, but if you're bored and restless, he'll become bored and restless, and your marriage will be in trouble. It's up to you. You must not only bolster him in his struggle to make his own career, but he'll have to bolster you as you find just what it is you want for yourself in order to create a good marriage. Wives— women who are just plain, ordinary housewives— have been taken for granted since time immemorial. Well, I say that every last one of us deserves a medal, and I'm sure that a great many husbands will agree. But ambitious women like you and Kale deserve medals, too, and from what I know of Hank, he'll certainly agree." She couldn't help laughing.

The last of Cindy's gloom lifted, and she laughed, too. "You make it all sound so simple, Clarissa," she said.

The older woman shook her head. "Simple, you say! Nothing is simple. It will take work, understanding, patience on both your parts. Just be glad you've got someone to spend your whole life with as loving and as considerate as Hank Blake!"

"Oh, I am. I am!" Cindy said fervently. "That's all that really matters in the whole world."

The corps of cadets of the United States Military Academy at West Point finished their noon dinner in the mess hall and marched off to various afternoon assignments. Some went to classes, while others engaged in intramural athletics. Still others were going to their rooms to study.

Cadet Henry Blake was a member of the group that was bound for their dormitory rooms. He had attended his last class for the day, and since he was a member of several varsity teams, he took no part in intramural sports. He had reading to do, his usual heavy load of reading, which was necessary if he was going to maintain his position as class leader in academic activities as well as in military activities and sports.

A short time after he was at his desk, absorbed in a history textbook, there was a knock on the door. Hank opened it, and he was handed an envelope by a regular army corporal.

Hank tore open the envelope, and his heart sank as he read the message inside. He was wanted immediately at the home of Brigadier General Cavanaugh, the commandant of the corps of cadets. Marcus Aurelius Cavanaugh was a martinet, a taskmaster without equal, and every cadet at the academy was afraid of him. An Indian fighter and scout, he had established an enduring reputation for himself as an infantry leader in the Army of the West during the Civil War, and since that time, he had been making the lives of one class after another of West Pointers miserable.

Leaving his books on the desk, Hank hurriedly left the dormitory and quickly crossed the campus to the commandant's home. He had no idea how he had erred or what he had done wrong, but he would learn all too soon, and he prepared himself for severe punishment. General Cavanaugh was known for treating student leaders far more severely than the academy dullards.

Arriving at the Cavanaugh house, Hank tugged the wrinkles out of his tunic, tucked his garrison cap under his left arm, and standing erect, rang the bell.

A sergeant answered the summons and looked Hank up and down slowly. "You're expected, Mr. Blake," he said quietly. To Hank, that statement had an ominous sound. He expected the general to receive him in the study, which was where infractions or problems were usually dealt with, but the sergeant led him instead to the living room.

As Hank entered the room, a woman, with her thick, dark hair piled high on her head, her violet eyes and trim figure giving her the appearance of someone far younger than her middle years, rose to her feet. At her shoulder stood a distinguished, gray-haired man in uniform who wore the twin stars of a major general on his shoulders.

His heart beating wildly, Hank stood stiffly at attention and saluted. "Cadet Blake at report, sir," he said crisply.

Major General Leland Blake chuckled quietly as he said, "At ease, Blake."

Hank sprang forward and eagerly embraced his stepmother. Until this moment, he had not allowed himself to dwell on how much he missed her.

Eulalia Holt Blake sighed happily. "Every time I see you, Hank," she murmured, "you seem inches taller and pounds heavier. It's remarkable."

Lee extended his hand. "How are you, son?"

"I'm great," Hank replied exuberantly. "I don't think I've ever been better than I am at this moment.

If only Cindy were here with you, my happiness would be absolutely complete."

"Fortunately, for the discipline of the corps," Lee replied, "we had to leave Cindy behind in Oregon. I was called East to a meeting with President Grant, which, as it turned out, was of an informal nature regarding troop dispositions in some of the middle-western states. Now we're on our way back home, but before we head West, we intend to spend the rest of the afternoon and the evening with you."

Hank's face fell. "I'm not sure I can get leave," he said, "even for a few hours."

"You've already been granted leave until breakfast time tomorrow morning," his father said. "General Cavanaugh told me that your record is sufficiently good that you'll lose nothing by being excused for a few hours."

Hank's mind was in a whirl. "I—I see."

"You're coming back to the hotel with us right now," Eulalia said. "And I don't want to hear a word from you about how tough General Cavanaugh is. In my opinion, he's perfectly darling."

Hank had no desire to dispute the point with her or to argue about anything else. The unexpected appearance of his parents made him deliriously happy, and he knew that after their brief visit, he would be much better able to cope with the rigors of academy life. He was learning it was no idle boast that one entered the academy as a boy, and four years later, emerged as a man.

X

Edward Blackstone nervously paced the confines of the living room of the hotel suite. He marched the length of the chamber, wheeled as though on parade, then made his way back to the other end past the oversized couch and the two easy chairs with a lamp between them. When he reached the far wall, he turned without pausing and retraced his steps.

Toby Holt and Edward's cousin, Jim Randall, made no attempt to stop him, but after the one-man parade had gone on for the better part of thirty minutes, Toby decided the time had come to call a halt. "How soon do we leave for the church, Jim?" he asked.

Jim, whose wife Pamela had arrived the day before and was helping Tommie dress, took his time removing his watch from his fob pocket and examining it. "The carriage I ordered will be here in about a quarter of an hour," he said.

"That's plenty of time to relax." Toby's voice became abrupt. "Sit down, Edward!" he commanded.

"I can't," Edward replied. "I'm too nervous."

"Then help yourself to a drink," Jim told him, "or if your hands are shaking too badly, I'll pour it for you."

"No, thank you," Edward replied. "The mere thought of taking as much as a small swallow of liquor makes me ill."

"I suppose we could kill him in cold blood, Jim," Toby said, "but I believe there's a law in Louisiana that prohibits the extinction of bridegrooms one hour prior to their marriage."

"Unfortunately," Jim replied, "that's shortsighted of the lawmakers. My wife is going to be very disappointed in Edward. Pamela has a mental picture of him as being masterful, calm, and always in control of himself and of every situation. I'd hate to let her be disillusioned by seeing him behaving like a gibbering idiot."

Edward halted his march abruptly. "I have not lost control," he said, "and I'm very calm."

"Well, you've succeeded in making us jittery," Toby said. "I don't mind telling you I'm glad I'm leaving by train for home shortly after the wedding. I've been separated from my wife long enough, without extending the time by indulging myself."

Jim nodded understandingly and then turned to his cousin. "Did you hear that, Edward?" he demanded. "Think of the freedom you're losing by voluntarily giving up your bachelor's existence!"

Edward's mental fog wasn't as great as his companions believed. "I don't see either of you giving up married life for the joys of bachelorhood," he said.

They laughed, and Toby pulled out his pocket watch. "It's time to be on our way," he said. "I see you have his ring, Jim. Be sure you don't forget the flower for his lapel. Let's go, Edward. Your misery will soon be ended."

"Those whom God hath joined together let no man put asunder," Reverend Giddings intoned. "Forasmuch as Thomasina and Edward have consented together in holy wedlock, and have witnessed the same before God and his company, and thereto have given and pledged their troth, each to the other, and have declared the same by giving and receiving a ring, and by joining hands, I pronounce that they are man and wife. In the name of the Father, and of the Son, and of the Holy Ghost. Amen."

Edward and Tommie, blissfully unaware of the presence of anyone else, embraced and kissed. Reverend Giddings and Captain Harding grinned at each other, and then the white-haired ship's master kissed his daughter and shook the hand of his son-in-law. It was Millicent's turn next, followed by Jim, and after him came Toby and Jean-Pierre escorting Pamela. The entire wedding party adjourned to waiting carriages, the one carrying the bride and groom decorated with long streamers and with tin cans that rattled on the cobblestones. They returned to Edward's hotel suite, where imported champagne and caviar awaited them, along with huge Gulf shrimp and other delicacies.

The bride and groom were inseparable and stood with an arm around each other's waist as they chattered with relatives and friends. Both were supremely happy. In fact, Toby, looking at them, couldn't help commenting to Pamela and Jim Randall, "I've never seen a bride who looked that radiant."

By now Pamela had had a chance to offer her congratulations to Millicent on her own upcoming wedding. "Jim and I," she said to the other woman, "are happier for you than you can possibly imagine. I wouldn't have missed Edward's wedding for the world, and Jim and I have no intention of missing yours. We're delighted that you set the date for next week."

"Where are you and Jean-Pierre planning to live?" Toby asked.

Millicent smiled broadly. "Jean-Pierre has bought me a new house, or, rather, it's an old house in the French district about two or three blocks from his parents' mansion."

"But it's much smaller and quite modest," Jean-Pierre said hastily. "Millicent and I don't go in much for show."

Toby nodded approvingly and thought that Jean-Pierre was proving to be an excellent stabilizing influence on Millicent. She had grown infinitely calmer since she had been associating with him, and her reckless conduct now belonged to her past. She was once again a modest, unassuming young lady.

There was a subtle difference in her, however.

She had come alive during the preceding months, and her experiences had caused her to develop into a far more well-rounded human being. It was strange, Toby thought, but she had become far more attractive as a woman, too. He would have to ask Clarissa about the phenomenon when he rejoined her. Millicent was not only better looking but was far more confident, far better able to deal with people whom she met.

"I'm afraid I won't be able to stay here until your wedding, but you know that Clarissa and I will be with you in spirit and that we wish you everything good for that day and for the rest of your lives."

They thanked him, then drifted on. Now it was Toby's pleasant duty to offer his own toast to the new bride and groom, Jim Randall having already made his toast. Then Captain Harding drew Toby aside for a private talk.

"My daughter and my new son-in-law have asked me to help them set up a new shipping company in Portland. I'd like your opinion of the idea."

"It's quite feasible," Toby replied. "The mouth of the Columbia River is broad enough and deep enough, as you undoubtedly know, to accommodate oceangoing ships, including freighters that are not only the biggest made but are likely to be the biggest for many years to come. In fact, one of my closest friends is in the business, and I am sure he would underscore the opportunities."

"I'm aware of the physical potentials," Captain

Harding replied, "but I'm wondering about the financial potential."

"I've watched Oregon grow from a wilderness country when I was a small boy into a prosperous, settled, and mature land. I think her financial potential is virtually unlimited. Coastal trade in the Pacific is already extensive and continues to grow rapidly. California has been expanding since the Gold Rush of forty-nine, and not only are towns like Sacramento growing, but new communities, like Los Angeles in the southern part of the state, are mushrooming. The same is true of Seattle, in Washington Territory to our north. Then there's the international trade to be considered. Not four years have passed since Secretary of State Seward bought the Alaska Territory, but the area is already showing signs of promise, and I think there's going to be a considerable trade between the Orient and Alaska. Our trade with Hawaii is also growing, and our business with China and the Spice Islands and India in the Far East is booming, too."

"You're very encouraging, Mr. Holt," Captain Harding said.

Toby smiled. "For whatever my opinion may be worth," he said, "I don't think that Tommie and Edward could have chosen a more promising line of work. I know Edward is already a successful businessman and has money of his own, but I'll gladly invest in their company if they let me, and I can promise them that at least a dozen people whom I know will invest as well."

"It's good to know that my daughter's future is assured," Captain Harding said.

Toby's smile broadened, and he spoke with great sincerity. "Tommie's future," he said, "has never been in doubt from the moment that she agreed to marry Edward Blackstone."

Railroad service between New Orleans and St. Louis was forced to compete for the business of passengers with the great paddle-wheel steamers that plied the Mississippi River, so the trains were more elaborate and luxurious than those found on most American railroad lines. Meals served in the dining car were as delicious and varied as those found in the finest New Orleans restaurants, and the sleeping cars boasted private compartments, which were unknown on the majority of trains.

A private compartment had been engaged by the army for Toby Holt's use, and he also had access to the first-class observation and smoking car at the rear of the train. His train left New Orleans promptly at noon, and he ate a simple but satisfying meal in the dining car and then wandered back to the observation car, where he engaged in amiable, inconsequential conversation with several other passengers. He had left his newspapers and magazines in his own compartment, however, and wanting to read, he wandered back to his own quarters. When he opened the door, he thought for a moment that he had made a mistake and had entered the wrong room. The attendant had made up the bed, and lying on top of the sheets was a ravishingly beautiful young woman with red-gold hair that trailed down across her bare shoulders. She was wearing only a daring, low-cut nightgown of black silk trimmed with lace, and there were slits up to the thigh on both sides. The shades had been drawn over the windows, leaving the room in semidarkness, but Toby nevertheless quickly recognized the young woman. She was Martha, the woman who had led him to Domino.

Reacting instinctively, he hastily closed and bolted the door behind him.

Martha laughed huskily. "Are you surprised to see me?"

"I'm stunned," he admitted.

Martha extended her arms to him and wriggled her fingers, beckoning to him.

"Is this a joke of some sort?" he demanded.

The woman's laughter filled the tiny compartment. "A joke? Hardly! We've missed several opportunities to become better acquainted, and I had the notion—probably false—that you might be avoiding me. So I deliberately chose this train as the best of all places to come to know you. There's no way you can escape from me here, unless you want to jump from the train." She laughed again.

Before Toby could respond, Martha suddenly and unexpectedly reached out, catching hold of his wrists and pulling him closer.

Caught off guard by the unexpected move, Toby lost his balance, and the motion of the train caused him to pitch forward.

Martha immediately gathered him in her arms, nibbled his earlobes, and breathed in his ear. Then, in the same continuing gesture, she pressed one hand against the back of his head, and her lips found his.

Her kiss was passionate, and she pressed close to him, caressing him with her free arm as her parted lips were fastened to his mouth.

Toby struggled to right himself, to regain his balance and to sit upright, but Martha remained in control of the situation and gave him no opportunity. Still kissing him fervently, her tongue flicking in and out, probing, exploring, she guided one of his hands inside her nightgown. Instinctively his fingers closed over the nipple of her bare breast. Martha shuddered with pleasure and continued to take the lead in their lovemaking.

Toby had no chance to think, to weigh the situation, or to do anything that would counteract the waves of erotic satisfaction that he felt. Martha's lush body had taken complete control. She knew precisely what she was doing, how to derive the greatest satisfaction out of every movement. In spite of Toby's reluctance to be trapped in the web that Martha was so insistently and expertly weaving around him, he was caught. He was a young, virile male, endowed with natural, healthy desires, and those feelings took possession and swept reason aside. He could not help responding to her in kind, and he stretched out beside her, his own gestures feverish as he began to caress her.

Their mutual lovemaking was leading them toward an inevitable climax when fate—or perhaps the gods who favored fidelity—intervened. Their railroad car suddenly jounced violently as the wheels passed over some ties that had been badly laid, and at the same moment, the engineer blew a long series of loud blasts on his horn.

The intimacy of the moment was ruined. The jolting and bouncing flung the couple apart, with Martha landing against the wall behind her, while Toby was almost thrown to the floor. Certainly the mood in which they had been enveloped was destroyed.

Martha attempted to recapture the mood by reaching lazily for Toby, but the brief respite had given him what he had needed, a moment to regain his composure, a moment to think of the consequences of infidelity. "We went far enough, thanks," he said, and forced himself to a sitting position.

Martha was not yet willing to admit that she had lost the struggle. She pouted slightly, her expression telling him that all he needed to do to make her his was to reach out and take her. But Toby had the inner strength to turn away from her, the character to resist her.

Martha had the common sense to know when she was defeated, the grace necessary to gloss over a defeat and save both of them from embarrassment. She sighed lightly and, without further ado, reached across him for her clothes, which were piled on a small chair that stood next to the bed.

Toby moved to the foot of the bed and raised

the shade partway. In order to give the woman as much privacy as he could in their cramped surroundings, he resolutely stared out at the passing scene while she dressed.

Then, after she repaired her makeup and made herself more presentable, he summoned the attendant, and they moved out into the corridor while the man made up the bed and reverted the room to its daytime status. Only when the man was finished did they return to the compartment and sit in two small easy chairs facing each other.

"We're stopping shortly before midnight," Martha said. "I'll get off and change to a train that will take me back to New Orleans."

"That will give us ample time," Toby told her, "for me to take you into the dining car and buy you supper."

"Thank you," she murmured, smiling lightly, a pensive expression in her enormous green eyes, and her full lips parted in a half-smile. "Never—not even once—in all my life have I been turned down by a man. I didn't believe it possible. I was so sure of myself that Domino teased me about it."

Toby stared at her. "Are you telling me," he asked incredulously, "that Domino knew you were going to come on board this train and try to seduce me?"

Martha laughed heartily. "He more than knew about it, he planned the whole thing."

"This is unbelievable!"

"It's all much simpler than it sounds," Martha

said. "You see, Domino knew that I—well, that I—I found you attractive, and I was sure you hadn't rejected me the previous times we met because nobody's done anything like that to me in all my life. Well, Domino said I was wrong, and he intended to prove it, so he bought my train ticket and gave me the money to bribe the attendant. You know the rest."

"I'm sorry to disappoint you," Toby said, "but it has nothing at all to do with you. I've never met a woman who's lovelier or more appealing or more desirable than you are. It's just that I'm not available. I love my wife so much that I feel it wouldn't be fair to her or to you if I had an affair with you. I've got to admit, I almost gave in and lost my struggle. I came close to giving in, far too close for comfort or my peace of mind, and I know better than to repeat the experiment."

"You've offered me some consolation," Martha said, then sighed. "Even though I wouldn't bet with Domino, he's unhappy unless there's a wager involved, so he made a bet with himself, so to speak. He gave me a gift to present to you in the event that you rejected me. Well, you did, and here's his present."

She fished around in her handbag and came out with a small package wrapped in tissue paper with a ribbon tied around it.

The surprised Toby hesitated, then took the package and unwrapped it. In his hand was one of the most beautiful pieces of jewelry he had ever seen. It was a bracelet made of large diamonds and matching rubies. He knew it was worth a fortune.

Looking at the bracelet, Martha recognized it at once from descriptions she had read in the newspapers just before she left New Orleans, and she controlled a desire to laugh aloud. The bracelet had been taken from the home of a New Orleans society leader, and the city's constabulary had been unable to recover it. Obviously Domino was behind the theft.

"It's gorgeous," Martha said breathlessly.

"I can't accept this as a gift from Domino," Toby said. He meant every word. It was true enough that he had entered into a partnership of convenience with the gang leader in order to capture Karl Kellerman, a goal that remained to be fulfilled, but it would be unethical, wrong in every way for him to accept a bracelet worth many thousands of dollars.

"Domino said to be sure to tell you that it isn't really a gift for you—it's for your wife. He said that if you had the strength to turn away from me, your wife would deserve this gift, at the very least, because she sure has earned it over the years. I'm not certain I know what he meant—"

"I know exactly what he meant," Toby said, interrupting her, "but even so, I can't accept it for Clarissa either."

Martha shook her head. "I've had my orders," she told him. "Domino made it very plain that no matter what you said or did, I'm not to come back to New Orleans with that bracelet. I'm sure you know how nasty he can be when he's disobeyed, so I have no choice. I've got to do as he says."

This put a different light on the matter, Toby

thought. Even though his conscience would not permit him to keep the expensive bracelet, he could not insist that Martha return it to Domino; he knew the young woman would be made to suffer if she returned to the city with it in her possession. He would deal with the problem later, and in the meantime, he dropped the bracelet into a coat pocket and tried to put it out of his mind.

He took Martha to the observation car, where, as other passengers stared at the beautiful woman, he bought her a predinner drink. Then, as night came, he escorted her to the dining car. All of the tables for two patrons were taken, so the chief steward sat them side by side at a table for four, which they found satisfactory. The other two chairs at their table were unoccupied.

As they were looking at the menu, the chief steward approached the table again and seated a middle-aged man opposite them. The newcomer was stocky and of medium height and had gray hair and a bulldoglike face; he was clad in black and wore a clerical collar.

Introductions were exchanged, and the priest, Father Flaherty, speaking in a rich Irish brogue, revealed that he was en route to Independence, Missouri, to take up a difficult new post. As they ate dinner, he spoke freely about his assignment.

For decades, Independence had been the nation's leading starting point for the wagon trains that traveled west across the Great Plains and the Rocky Mountains to California, Oregon, and Washington.

The coming of the railroads had made the wagon trains obsolete, and in recent years, particularly since the end of the Civil War, Independence had been declining in importance.

Nevertheless, a very large orphanage was being organized there. It was surprising, Father Flaherty said, how many children of lost parents ended their travels in Independence, and it was equally surprising how many youngsters were abandoned there by parents who wanted to go West unencumbered by children.

"There is a crying need for an orphanage," he said, "but there are almost no funds to build and to maintain a proper home. We need money for a school, money for good food, clothing, and shelter for the youngsters. We need funds for a staff physician. The list is almost endless. The director-general of my order convinced me that this job was a great challenge, and so I accepted it. But now that I'm actually on the way to Independence, I'm not so sure. The need for money is overwhelming. The director-general says that if I pray hard enough, my prayers will be answered, but to be truthful with you, I've worn out my knees, and I've yet to see a penny."

Toby fell silent as his mind raced. Martha and the priest continued to converse, but he took no part in their talk until suddenly he reached into his coat pocket and brought out the diamond and ruby bracelet that Martha had given him. "This should help to ease your shortage of funds, Father," he said, and handed him the bracelet.

Father Flaherty peered at the gem-laden bracelet, turning it over and over in the palm of his hand. Then, placing it on the table in front of him, he carefully loaded his pipe and lighted it. "A bauble like this," he said, "was made for a pretty wrist. It would grace your beauty, my dear." He bowed his head to Martha.

She giggled and replied, "I gave it to Toby, Father."

The priest looked slightly confused.

"It was intended as a gift for my wife," Toby explained, "but I'll be as honest with you as I can, Father. She has no use for it and would much prefer that you use it for good works at your orphanage."

Martha picked up the bracelet and pressed it into the clergyman's hand. "Please take it, Father," she said, "and when you sell it, make certain that you have the advice of an honest jeweler. This bracelet is worth a king's ransom."

Father Flaherty was so embarrassed that he puffed hard on his pipe, and his face was half-hidden behind a cloud of smoke. "I thank you," he said huskily. "I thank you for myself and in the names of all the youngsters who are going to benefit from your extraordinary generosity."

Domino's laugh echoed and reechoed through the house.

Martha sat opposite him, her hands still tightly clenched in her lap. She was tense and clearly was worried for fear that he had misunderstood her. "I—I hope you understood what I told you," she said nervously.

"I heard every word," he bellowed, "and I'll remember your story as long as I live. There's nobody in the world like that Toby Holt! Obviously he didn't give a damn that planning and executing the stealing of that bracelet cost me a lot of money. I don't suppose he happened to mention why he was so anxious to get rid of it."

Martha explained what Toby had told her.

"He would be like that!" Domino began to chuckle again. "Toby Holt may have nerves of steel, but he can't fool me. He was scared to death of being indebted to me, so he just couldn't wait to get rid of the bracelet." He wiped tears from his eyes. "I just hope that priest gets plenty when he sells it. That'll make the story perfect." He began to laugh once again, and this time, Martha unfroze and joined in the laughter.

After Martha completed her report to Domino, she had one duty left to perform. She changed into less flamboyant attire, then put on a special necklace. It consisted of two miniature dominoes in ivory on a gold chain. In place of the dots on the dominoes were diamonds, five on one half of each and two on the other. The necklace was prominently displayed on the throat of her high-necked, black gown.

Calling for one of the house carriages, Martha asked the driver to take her to a bar located in a workingman's district, not far from the waterfront.

The burly driver raised an eyebrow. "You got your nerve, goin' to a dump like that," he said.

Martha shook her head, her long red hair swaying from side to side. "It's perfectly all right, Don," she said. "It's one of the places that Domino and I visited last year when we toured most of the bars in town. As a matter of fact, something about this joint caught his fancy, and we went there at least twice. I remember the owner well because he was such a fiercely independent little fellow."

"If you say so, miss," the driver said dubiously.

"You'll be waiting for me outside," she said soothingly, "and you can look in through the windows, if I remember the place accurately. If anything bad happens, you can always dash in and be the hero of the night by saving me."

"Whatever you say, miss," he replied, shutting the carriage door behind her.

They arrived at the bar just as Wallace Dugald was about to close for the night. He was living in a state of perpetual agitation since Kellerman had gotten away from him, and he almost didn't care what was happening around him. Nevertheless he was thrown off balance by the arrival of the lovely young woman.

The only women who came alone to his establishment were prostitutes, but he knew at a glance that this woman was many cuts above the streetwalker level. Her clothes were expensive and tasteful. She wore a minimum of makeup, and she had an air of refinement about her that stamped her as a lady of class. He decided to stay open for a time in order to serve her.

Martha ordered a mild whiskey and water, and when Dugald brought it to the table where she had seated herself, she smiled up at him. "You were away for a time," she ventured.

"Some folks," he muttered, "think I went off on a vacation. Some vacation!"

"I'd never make that mistake," she said. "I have a very good idea of what happened to you, and I offer you my sympathies. You've been through a nasty experience."

"How did you hear about it?" he demanded.

By way of reply, Martha fingered her necklace.

As Dugald stared at the two miniature diamond-set dominoes, recognition gradually dawned. "Excuse me, ma'am, but are you the young lady who was with Domino those times that he came in here? I'm sorry I don't rightly recognize you. I was so flustered when I knew it was Domino himself who was sitting here, big as life, having a drink."

"Yes," she assured him with a quiet smile. "I was with him."

"I've been thinking of going to Domino and asking his help," Dugald said. "From what I hear, that no-good rat, Karl Kellerman, has left town, and I'd be willing to pay Domino to let me know when Kellerman comes back. I've sworn to empty a six-shooter into him, and that's one vow I intend to keep!"

"I know Domino won't accept any money from

you," she said, "and if you go to him, I'm certain
he'll give you the same advice that I'm going to give
you now. Leave Kellerman to him."

"But I've sworn an oath to kill him if it's the last
thing I ever do."

"Domino has sworn a similar oath," Martha said.
"Kellerman not only broke his word to him, but tried
to kill him, and anyone who does things like that to
Domino is lost. His days are numbered."

Dugald could only nod.

"Kellerman has another deadly enemy," Martha
said. "Toby Holt, from the West. He's sworn to help
take care of Kellerman, too."

Dugald whistled softly under his breath. "I'd
sure hate to be in Karl Kellerman's shoes," he said.
"With both Domino and Toby Holt gunning for him,
he doesn't stand the chance of a snowball in hell of
surviving."

Now, looking into the deep green eyes of the
lovely young woman seated at the table before him,
all the venom, all the hatred somehow seemed to go
out of Wallace. He knew his enemy would eventually be taken care of, and for the first time in more
weeks than he cared to remember, the Scotsman felt
peace.

"Ma'am, if you don't mind," Wallace began a bit
shyly, "I'd like to propose a toast." When Martha
smiled in acknowledgment, the Scotsman ran to the
bar and poured himself a drink. Returning to the
table and raising his glass high, Wallace said, "To

you, to Domino, and to the end of Karl Kellerman for all time!"

Martha, still smiling, raised her own glass and sipped from her drink. Then, her eyes connecting with Wallace's, they both began laughing boisterously.

Toby Holt accepted a second helping of the cherry pie that Clarissa had made for his homecoming, sat back in his chair at the dining room table, and sighed. "You have no idea how good it feels to be home again," he said. "I was away for only a few weeks, but it felt like months."

"I know what you mean," Clarissa replied softly, then asked, "Are you going to be home for a while now?"

"To the best of my knowledge. I've done everything that's been asked of me, and my duty is finished. When I wired General Blake from New Orleans, he wired back intimating that President Grant might wish me to go to Washington soon. But he also mentioned that the President might want you present. So I suspect that there may be more involved than meets the eye."

"I just hope," she said, "that he doesn't have some new task that's going to take you away from home again."

"All I can say is that if he does, my mother and General Blake don't know about it because they certainly would have mentioned it to me."

"I realize I'm borrowing trouble," Clarissa said,

"but it occurs to me that every time the United States needs help, the government calls on you."

"I suggest," he said, "that we live in the present. "I'm home now, and to the best of my knowledge and belief, I'm here to stay. Let's make the best of it."

Clarissa went off to the stove in the kitchen for the coffee pot, returned with it, and put it on the dining room table. Then she bent down and kissed Toby before resuming her seat.

"I like that," he said, grinning.

"So do I," she told him.

In the next day or two, he decided he would tell her the story of Martha and of the bracelet that Domino had given him, but such things could wait.

Meanwhile Clarissa tried hard to banish her worries from her mind. Toby was right; it was enough that he had come home, and she would be wise to let her worries fade while she enjoyed their reunion.

As the freighter *Neptune* plowed southward through the waters of the Caribbean Sea, the weather worsened, with rough seas and heavy rains.

In late morning, the weather having cleared, Captain Kayross held the bridge for the current watch, and the ship's first and second officers, Davis and Symes, sat in the officers' wardroom, drinking coffee with Karl Kellerman. Davis rose, took the coffee pot from the adjoining serving table, and refilled their cups.

Kellerman, wearing an open-throated shirt with

the sleeves rolled up, sprawled in an armchair and appeared to be very much at ease. His eyes were alert and bright, however, and he missed nothing that was said.

He had good cause to be awake to possible dangers: Kung Lee, the powerful head of the most prominent tong in all of North America, was also on board the *Neptune*, very much annoyed with him. Kung claimed that Kellerman was solely responsible for Toby Holt's escape. As a result Toby presumably was still alive, able to cause further troubles for the tong and for Kung.

What Kung failed to realize, Kellerman reflected, was that he himself also stood to lose by Toby's escape. Holt had a bulldog quality to him, and Kellerman felt reasonably certain that he would reappear at some time to cause more headaches. Therefore, Kellerman was also highly annoyed with himself for having been negligent and allowing Holt to set himself free, though to give the devil his due, Holt was as slippery as an eel and had the proverbial nine lives of a cat.

Kellerman was not for an instant forgetting that he had invested one-third of the money necessary to take the *Neptune* to China, where her cargo would be exchanged for illegal immigrants and opium to be brought to the United States. It was for the sake of the investment, as well as because of Kung Lee's annoyance with him, that Kellerman was currently courting the two ship's mates.

"Let me show you something, lads," he said,

and removed a roll of paper money from an inner
pocket.

The two ship's officers were very much impressed,
having no idea that Kellerman had prepared the roll
in advance, placing several fifty-dollar bills on the
outside and filling the better part of the interior
with one-dollar bills.

"I'm not ready to make an independent move
yet," he said, "and I won't be until we've been to
China, picked up our cargo there, and are returning
to the United States with it. That's when I'll make
my move. I'll want help—a great deal of help to take
over this ship, and I'm prepared to pay well for it."

Avarice shone in the mates' eyes, but before
they could speak, the door behind Kellerman opened,
and Kung Lee stood in the frame. The two officers
froze.

Kellerman looked back over his shoulder, deliberately sipped his coffee, and said casually, "Morning,
Kung." He felt himself growing taut but would not
show it, no matter what might happen.

Symes hastily muttered an excuse, which Davis
quickly echoed, and the two officers left the wardroom in a hurry, pushing past Kung Lee in their
haste to depart.

Kung Lee took his time, helping himself to a
cup of coffee. As he sat down, a thin smile creased
his face. "The mates," he said, "were in a great hurry
to depart. My experience tells me that I interrupted
a conspiracy of some sort."

"That's a lot of damned nonsense," Kellerman

growled. "You're always imagining some kind of conspiracy or other."

Kung measured a tiny quantity of sugar onto a teaspoon and dropped it into his coffee. "If I wished," he said, "I'd have Captain Kayross clamp you into irons, and then I'd go to work on you myself with a knife. You'd confess your conspiracy soon enough." He paused, looked out at the sea through a porthole, and then went on. "Fortunately for you, I am relaxing on this voyage, so your ugly little secret need not be revealed, at least for the present. But let me tell you something, Kellerman. Even though I accepted you as a partner for this voyage, I still don't trust you."

Kellerman boldly returned the Chinaman's icy glare, his own expression insolent, his manner daring Kung Lee to halt him.

"I will be watching you with great care," Kung said, "and when you step out of bounds—when you overstep the mark by a mere fraction of an inch—I will strike, and you shall suffer the fate from which you so stupidly allowed Toby Holt to escape!"

There was no sound in the office of the superintendent of the new orphanage in Independence except for the scratching of Father Flaherty's quill pen as he wrote to the director-general of his order.

Work has been completed on the new wing, and the population is now one hundred and sixty children, which is our capacity.

We have hired the best cook in the state, and he's filling our larder with provisions of every sort. No one here will ever go hungry.

We have purchased two complete changes of clothing for every child, one to use on school days, and the other for Sundays, holidays, and vacations. I am pleased to report that our faculty is now complete. A full list of teachers and their credentials accompanies this report.

He lighted his pipe, sat back, stared at the ceiling for a time, and then added a final paragraph.

You told me repeatedly that if I prayed hard enough, the Lord would provide. So he has.

Father Flaherty puffed on his pipe, and clouds of fragrant smoke drifted toward the ceiling. He chuckled as he reread his report, and the sound filled the room.

Coming in November 1985 . . .

WAGONS WEST★
VOLUME XVI

LOUISIANA!

by Dana Fuller Ross

Orders from President U. S. Grant send Toby Holt to China with the assignment of breaking the power of the tongs and ending the illicit shipments of opium and coolies to the United States. The trail brings him back to San Francisco and a confrontation with the tong boss in America, then on to New Orleans for more showdowns.

There, Domino, the vice overlord of the area, again proves to be a resourceful ally as they close in on the master criminal, Karl Kellerman. Lovely Millicent Randall Gautier is freed from Kellerman's clutches, and the ravishing redhead Martha, Domino's closest associate, joins him and Toby in the final pursuit of the desperate kidnapper.

The splendor and squalor of China and the drama of the Crescent City of New Orleans come vividly to life in Dana Fuller Ross's sixteenth recounting of the adventures of men and women who were the weavers of the American fabric.

Read LOUISIANA!, on sale November 15, 1985, wherever Bantam paperbacks are sold.

★ WAGONS WEST ★

A series of unforgettable books that trace the lives of a dauntless band of pioneering men, women, and children as they brave the hazards of an untamed land in their trek across America. This legendary caravan of people forge a new link in the wilderness. They are Americans from the North and the South, alongside immigrants, Blacks, and Indians, who wage fierce daily battles for survival on this uncompromising journey—each to their private destinies as they fulfill their greatest dreams.

☐	24408	INDEPENDENCE!	$3.95
☐	24651	NEBRASKA!	$3.95
☐	24229	WYOMING!	$3.95
☐	24088	OREGON!	$3.95
☐	24848	TEXAS!	$3.95
☐	24655	CALIFORNIA!	$3.95
☐	24694	COLORADO!	$3.95
☐	25091	NEVADA!	$3.95
☐	25010	WASHINGTON!	$3.95
☐	22925	MONTANA!	$3.95
☐	23572	DAKOTA!	$3.95
☐	23921	UTAH!	$3.95
☐	24256	IDAHO!	$3.95

Prices and availability subject to change without notice.